D0619810

FROG KISSES

Cañon City Public Library
Cañon City, Colorado

Also by Linda Joffe Hull

The Big Bang
Eternally 21 (A Mrs. Frugalicious Shopping Mystery)
Black Thursday (A Mrs. Frugalicious Shopping Mystery)

Cañon City, Colorado

FROG KISSES

Linda Joffe Hull

Literary Wanderlust LLC | Denver, Colorado

Frog Kisses is a work of fiction. Names, characters, places, and incidents are the products of the author's imagination and were been used fictitiously. Any resemblance to actual events, locales, or persons, living or dead, is entirely coincidental.

Copyright © 2015 by Linda Joffe Hull

All rights reserved.

Published in the United States by Literary Wanderlust LLC, Denver, Colorado.

www.LiteraryWanderlust.com

ISBN 978-1-942856-00-9
ebook ISBN 978-1-942856-01-6

Library of Congress Control Number: 2015941178

Cover design: Ruth M'Gonigle

Printed in the United States of America

Dedication:

For Margie and Bill

Acknowledgements:

First and foremost, I would like to thank the amazing Susan Brooks for finally bringing Sunny into the light.

There've been a lot of people who helped and inspired me in various ways and capacities while I was writing this book including:

Julie Goldsmith, Ellen Haines, Kelly Townsend, Jennee Julius, Amanda Holdsworth, Caryn McClelland, Doug Webster, Sara Singh, Margaret Marr, Ashley Kraas, Dirk McDermott, Tracy Shaffer, Becky and Piper Stevens, Jessica Lourey, Ed and Judy Schenkein, Beth Hooper, Marc Kerman, Nancy Mitchell, Laura Hendrickson, Jenny Springer, Rachel Moskowitz, Bob Moskowitz, Elizabeth Heller, and Dane O'Hara, wherever you are.

Special thanks to the Capitol Hill Gang—especially Monica Poole, Kay Bergstrom, Bob Buettner, and Joel Reiff.

And, as always, my love and thanks to Brandon, Andrew, Evan, and Eliza.

Alan

POSSIBILITY IS A POTENT APHRODISIAC. AT LEAST THAT was my justification for sleeping with Alan the first time I saw his condo.

It was also our first date.

I won't plead *I'm not that kind of girl* because sometimes there's just cause for that sort of thing. Alan had a successful family business, a nice car, and that all-important desire to settle down. While he was maybe a bit more simian than handsome, he wasn't unattractive, and he did have a sweet smile.

After dinner, as we exited the elevator and entered his tenth-floor, Marina Del Rey high-rise, I was overcome with thoughts of forever and, admittedly, an urge to redecorate. As Alan uncorked the wine and gazed deeply into my eyes, all I could think of were the incredibly high ceilings and the odd combination of bachelor Jewish modern and medieval décor. I knew it was my destiny to transform his lonely house into our happy home.

Unfortunately, reality soon disciplined possibility.

Five whirlwind months later, I found myself trapped in our morning embrace. A prong from my new engagement ring and a tuft of Alan's back hair had twisted together, pinning my hand to his shoulder blade. A droplet of sweat rolled from the end of his nose toward my chin.

I closed my eyes and tried to get lost in the moment while his chest hair

1

rubbed against me like the swishy soapy things at the car wash. Finally, I tried to twist the ring off my finger and leave it hanging from his back.

It wouldn't budge.

"Shit, Sunny!" Alan jumped then rolled to his side of the bed. "What are you doing?"

"I'm sorry, honey." I held my hands over my eyes. The sun reflected off the dresser mirror, filling his bedroom with morning light.

"Oww!" He reached for the red spot on his back.

"I thought it would hurt less if I did it fast." I rubbed his arm. "I'm really sorry."

Alan glanced at his watch. "It's almost nine. I'm late for my call to Irma."

"But it's Saturday," I said. I was always long gone before Alan and Irma, his mother and boss, conducted their weekday morning conference calls.

He grabbed a dilapidated robe with *Alan Leonard* embroidered in powder blue across the lapel and opened the bedroom door. "She told me to call."

Over the coffee grinder and Alan mumbling into the phone to his mother, I rolled out of bed. I needed to get somewhere quiet and study. The bar exam loomed and I couldn't *almost* pass again.

I flipped on the recessed lights in the walk-in closet. Alan told me early in our relationship that I should be comfortable and leave things, so I made my own section for the hanging stuff. With my clothing tucked right next to his, I felt almost married. If only there was room left on the "hers" side. The other half of the closet was filled with size one St. John knits. They hung ominously still, waiting for their owner, Irma Fine.

And yes, I thought it was a little unusual for a grown man to share closet space with his mother. When I asked him why she kept so many things in Los Angeles, he simply shook his head.

"Part of my job," he said.

As I grabbed my robe and hurried for coffee, I pictured Irma as a wise-eyed little woman shuffling hangers across the rod in search of the perfect West Coast client ensemble. She'd been too busy to visit since I started seeing Alan, but somehow my robe held a faint trace of her L' Air Du Temps perfume.

I stepped into the kitchen, opened a cabinet and grabbed a mug.

Alan's solid black china was headed to Goodwill immediately after the wedding. Ditto the Old English dining room set, leather reclining sectional, and the myriad framed posters of Miami Beach.

My hand slipped as I closed the cabinet, causing a loud bang, but Alan didn't notice. He lay sprawled on the leather couch with his phone nestled between his ear and the pillow back. A coffee cup rested on his hip, centered on a series of brown rings that formed a Spirograph pattern below the waist of his robe. In his other hand, he held a beer.

I'd never seen him drink before noon.

"Of course I'm not drinking." He took a swig of PBR. "Yes, I'm using a coaster." He put the coffee cup on the edge of the sectional's built-in beverage and remote holder. Coffee sloshed over the edge.

I rushed over with a rag and dabbed at the carpet.

"I told you I'd input the sales report in the morning. I'm about to do it." Alan held the phone away from his ear, leaned back, and closed his eyes.

"What?" He sat straight up as I hung the rag over the faucet, opened the refrigerator, and pretended to look for the milk. A blue vein popped in the center of his forehead.

The last time I'd seen the angry *Y* appear above his brow, he was forcibly removing squatters from his box seats at the Hollywood Bowl.

"Is everything all right?" I mouthed.

"I gotta go, Ma." He hung up the phone and polished off the bottle. Then, he shook his head. "I hate it when she does this."

"Does what?"

He took a deep breath, walked over and kissed me on the lips. "You were dying to meet her, and now you'll get your chance."

"When?"

"Seven."

"Tonight?"

He nodded. "We'll have our engagement dinner."

"We can't..." My stomach flip-flopped. I needed to call Esther. And my Dad. "I don't know if my parents can make it on such short notice."

It took at least a month's warning to get them in the same room.

"This isn't an official event, Sunny. I haven't even told her we're engaged." He walked into the kitchen for his morning granola. "Luckily,

3

she called ahead this time. Usually, she just shows up and lets herself in." He poured cereal and milk into two bowls and smiled. "At least this time I'm the one with the surprise."

My arms and legs began to itch. "She doesn't know we're engaged?"

"Technically, this visit's about business." He dipped his spoon into the bowl and loaded up a heaping bite. "She's convinced we're going to lose our footing in the L.A. market, as it were."

"But you just placed Fine Feet in three new stores."

"Doesn't matter." He shoulders drooped, but then he smiled. "I'll finally get to show you off to Mom."

A sudden wave of prickly perspiration left the robe clinging to my skin. I was going to meet my future mother-in-law in mere hours? "What will I wear?"

"The blue dress I bought you." He tucked a stray piece of hair behind my ear. "It matches your eyes."

The dress also pulled across my butt. I'd relegated it to the back of my closet until I could drop five (give or take) pounds. I watched granola clusters sink to the bottom of the bowl. So much for breakfast.

"Don't worry, Sunny. She's going to love you. You're Jewish and a lawyer." He tipped the beer to his mouth for the last stray drops. "What do you say we take up where we left off while we still have time?"

"I really need to study." Sex was the last thing on my mind. I have to get in the shower and out of here or I'll never be ready to meet your Mom."

"A shower it is, then." He kissed me and pulled me toward the bathroom. On the way, I scraped my leg on a gothic shield attached to the wrought iron floor lamp.

"Alan, after we're married, do you think I could possibly redecorate a little?"

"Talk to Mom about it." He nuzzled my neck. "She designed the place to help me impress the right girl. Now, how about some help scrubbing your back, *right* girl?"

~*~

It took most of the day, but I found a pair of Spanx I could almost breathe in. Still, I held in my stomach as I drove back to the marina and up the drive to the awaiting doorman.

Enrique opened the door to my old Honda as soon as I pulled up in the driveway. "Hello, Miss Sunny." His British accent, honed at the La Brea Shakespeare Academy, was nearly flawless.

"Any promising auditions this week?"

"I got a call back for Caliban in a dinner theater production of *The Tempest.*" He smiled. "And there's talk of a new film version of *Much Ado About Nothing*. I'm a perfect Benedict."

"Good luck." I said. Enrique was seemingly unhindered by the dearth of Shakespearean roles suitable for middle-aged Hispanic valets.

"Will you need your car again tonight, my dear?"

"Yes, I'm going home later." I felt my face redden as I got out and gave him the keys.

"It's so good to see Mr. Fine with a lady friend, again." Enrique smiled.

"Thanks," I said. Alan told me he'd had a serious girlfriend before me. A model.

A Lincoln Town Car pulled up behind us. I glanced casually into the lobby for someone famous.

Alan opened the passenger door from inside. "Sunny, get in. We're late."

"Where's your BMW?" I asked as the thigh fabric of my Spanx met the leather seat and I slid into the center console.

"Mom won't ride in anything foreign, so I rented." He fell silent as we headed toward LAX.

I leaned over the armrest and cuddled him to no response. Finally, I turned on the radio for some companionship.

He flipped the tuner and fussed with the climate controls. "I can't take any music right now."

"Sorry." I checked my makeup in the lighted mirror. I'd had my hair blown out, but my corkscrew curls were already starting to creep back into my coif. Was Alan's quiet distance a sign that he was embarrassed with the way I looked? He hadn't said a word about the dress. "Do I look okay?"

"Huh?" Alan swerved into the left lane. "You look great." He maneuvered the Lincoln into LAX and through the shortcut that let out in front of the United terminal.

Before I could recheck my lipstick, I spotted a tiny blonde surrounded by an enormous real fur coat. Her face, with a surgery-softened twenty-five years, was identical to Alan's.

I took a deep breath and smiled as we pulled up in front of the curb.

This was it—my only chance to make that all important first impression with my future mother-in-law.

Irma was at the driver's side door of the Lincoln with her arms around Alan the moment he stepped out of the car.

I'd never been away from home long enough to warrant an outpouring of love of that magnitude from my Mom Esther. I couldn't imagine my father, Bernie, offering anything more heartfelt than an extra loud air kiss.

Alan, covered in lipstick smudges, followed Irma back to the curb. As he flung her hanging bag into the cavernous trunk, I lowered his window a crack with my controls.

"Careful. The bag is a real Louis V." Her voice was loud and deep, despite her size. "Where are the projections for the new underpants line?"

Alan handed her a manila folder from the trunk.

Irma opened the file and eyed it over the top of her glasses. She snorted a couple of times.

"Sunny's in the car." He swiped at the pink lip marks on his face.

"I see that." She smiled in my direction. She's blond, like a *shiksa*, except for the curly hair. You're sure she's Jewish? Sunny is a funny name and I've never heard of a Jew called St. Clair."

Everything came out as one sentence.

Sweat beaded at the nape of my neck as she grabbed the rear driver's side door handle. St. Clair *was* a funny name for a Jewish family. How was I going to tell her the name was just the tip of my family eccentricity iceberg?

"Hi, I'm Sunny." I smiled as she slid into the back seat. "I meant to get in the back, but I didn't want to interrupt your hello with Alan."

"Alan always drives me around in back when I come into town."

As if on cue, Alan opened the car door and slid into the driver's seat like a professional limo driver.

"The dress looks beautiful." Irma leaned over the seat and stared at my body like a plantation owner examining a slave on the auction block. "I was surprised when Alan said to get an eight. He usually likes them a little more *zaftig*."

Irma bought the dress? I smiled but my cheeks burned. Why hadn't Alan told me it was a gift from his mother? I tried to give him a subtle eye signal, but he was staring glassy-eyed at the neon lights surrounding the restaurant perched in the middle of LAX.

Alan reached into his jacket pocket, pulled out a yellow pill, and popped it into his mouth.

Valium?

"The dress does look beautiful with your eyes." Irma smiled. "Just like Alan said it would."

"Thank you, Irma." Was she offended? I hadn't even written a proper thank you note. "Alan never told me that you..."

She reached for my hand. "Wear it in good health."

I tried to smile. As I extended my hand to meet hers, a ray of light caught the center stone of my ring and lit up the dark interior of the car.

"Oh my God!" Irma flung herself over the front seat, hugged me and started to cry. Tears landed on my shoulder and fur filled my mouth. "I can't believe it!"

"Surprise, Ma," he said.

Irma pulled me into her unusually firm bosom.

"Sunny, Sunny, Sunny. I'm finally going to have a daughter-in-law. What's your real name, honey?"

"It's Sunshine."

"Well Alan, you've finally brought some real sunshine into my life." Irma pinched my cheek.

Alan nodded and smiled.

As we took off down Century Boulevard, I choked back a happy tear or two. The night Alan had asked me to marry him I'd called everyone in my family except for my brother Atlas. Seeing as he is a psychic, and a rather prominent one at that, he'd (of course) already left his congratulations on my answering machine: *Sunny Fine of the fine Fines.* My sister, Luna, said, "What's the rush?" Bernie, my OB/GYN father, said, "I'm not ready for grandchildren." My mother, Esther, who was given to New Age over-emotionalism, wept with

7

the joy of new beginnings.

How was Irma the business maven going to handle Esther the Earth Mother? Would Irma take in stride that Atlas was a radio psychic? Would Luna, who'd likely never outgrown her Goth phase, wear a bridesmaid's dress that wasn't black?

As I tried to think of a way to ease her into my family situation, Alan turned down a side street and veered into the lot of Rapunzel's, an ancient steak house in Westchester. He pulled up to the front steps of the restaurant and stopped the car.

"Park under the lights." Irma pointed to an open space near a street lamp. "Come on, Sunny." Irma popped from the back seat like a well-groomed Pekinese. "It's too chilly not to wait inside."

I got out, carefully patted down the hem of my skirt and followed behind her. Inside, the dim lighting provided ample cover for a multitude of health violations. Bored waiters wandered back and forth from the kitchen. Florescent light, Mexican love songs and curls of smoke rushed out every time a server emerged.

Alan walked through the front door and collapsed into a dilapidated club chair in the lobby.

In general, being out with Alan made me feel like a celebrity. People watched us as we strolled to our table, trying to ID him as some filmmaker or studio exec. We'd dined on the best, at the hippest places. So why, tonight, did he choose Rapunzel's, known for its buxom billboard maiden and fatty prime rib?

Irma grasped my hand and touched the two-carat marquis set in platinum. "Sunny, I'm sure Alan told you this ring belonged to his grandmother." Her breath smelled of too long a flight. "It's very important to us, not just because of its value."

"I'm honored to wear it."

"Not all young women have the proper respect for family heirlooms." She shot Alan a look.

"Sunny's different." Alan said.

Before I had a chance to utter a *different than whom?* Alan rushed over to the hostess in her requisite white off-the-shoulder puffy shirt and floor length, red wraparound skirt.

"Your table is being set up," she said in a voice that was sexy ten thousand cigarettes ago.

"What's the hold up?" Irma asked.

"Mr. Fine requested the corner booth by the window. It'll be just a second. Let me take your jacket in the meantime." The hostess smiled and reached with tar-stained fingers for Irma's coat.

Irma glanced sideways at a waiter of indeterminate nationality as she relinquished her fur.

My legs began to itch.

The hostess plucked three laminated menus from the side of her stand. With a handful of skirt, she rubbed some steak sauce off one and led us to an empty corner of the dining room.

Irma followed us halfway then stopped at a table of ten. "How are the ribs?" she asked the man at the head of the table. "The last time I had them they were fatty and I had to send them back."

I slid into our worn leather booth beside Alan and tried to make myself as invisible as possible while Irma continued her survey.

"Mom wasn't upset about the ring at all." Alan whispered as he rubbed my back lightly.

"No water yet, Al? You know I need to take my medication right away." Irma plopped into her side of the booth. The leather made a ripping sound as she sat. "At least you remembered that I like to watch the car while we eat."

The bus boy magically appeared with three water glasses and placed them on the table.

Alan grasped my hand under the table.

Irma reached into a Gucci bag for a pair of reading glasses and a matching bejeweled pill case shaped like a butterfly. She swallowed a pile of pills with a dramatic gulp. "So, Alan says you need a new car."

"My Honda has seen better days, but it runs great, and it's paid for." I felt my cheeks redden. "With my student loans, I..."

"I was thinking we would get you a new one for an engagement present."

"A new car?" My Dad bought himself a vintage Ford Probe, mostly because he thought it was funny and sold me his old Honda. I smiled at Alan, then Irma, as I pictured myself in a white version of Alan's BMW. "Irma! Thank you."

"Our family trademark color is seashell with white leather," she said. "It's a beautiful opalescent shade with just a hint of pink. Alan's sisters love theirs."

"Ma, maybe she doesn't want a Caddie."

A Cadillac?

Irma ignored him. "When you two move back to Florida, everyone will know you're one of us."

Florida?

"Appetizers or drinks, anyone?" The waiter, whom Irma had watched from the lobby, appeared beside me.

"I'll have a Dewar's, on the rocks," Alan said.

"A Chardonnay please," I said.

"Young man, I'll have a club soda," Irma said. "Please bring the bottle unopened with a glass of ice. We don't want appetizers, and we'll be ready to order when you return."

"I want the artichoke dip," Alan said.

Irma waved off the waiter.

"I'll pay for it myself," Alan said.

"If you want an appetizer, you better believe it'll come out of your pay-check."

He nodded at the waiter. "And make my drink a double."

"You too, Miss?"

A double Chardonnay? "I'm fine, thanks."

I was starting to feel anything but.

"Sunny," Irma said with the waiter's exit. "I guess we could have the wedding here, but I personally think Florida would be better."

I tried to picture my vegan crusader mom and Irma working together on a wedding with the whole twenty-five hundred dollars my father offered, along with the warning, *if you have to get married, elope.*

"It's up to you two," Alan said.

"I don't know if all of my family will be able to make the trip," I managed.

"With Alan's sisters and their families, there'll be so much family to meet, you'll never notice a few missing cousins." Irma smiled as she turned to Alan. "Your sisters love living near their children's grandma."

A waiter headed toward our table with the drinks and the artichoke dip in a giant bread bowl. Alan grabbed the appetizer plate from the waiter. As he tore off a hunk of bread, dip poured over the edge onto the table.

"Alan!" Irma said.

I'd never realized how much Alan looked like a ferret until Irma bared her identical set of teeth.

"Sorry," he said. Bits of artichoke and cheese sprayed back into the dip.

Our waiter reappeared at the table with two other servers hovering behind, as if for back up.

Alan blurted his order through a mouthful of dip-laden bread. "Prime rib, potato, extra sour cream."

Irma nodded at me.

"Caesar salad," I said as politely as I could. "Please."

"Smart," Irma said. "Young man, I will start with a green salad with no tomatoes and no croutons. Ranch dressing on the side." She paused. "Now, how is the prime rib tonight?"

"Quite good."

"Less fatty than usual?"

"Perfection." The waiter nodded.

"It's pricey, but since Sunny is having a salad..."

"And would you like the rice pilaf or baked potato?"

"I'll take the rice." Irma smiled at him with regal benevolence. "You know, you speak quite well."

He nodded and disappeared into the back.

I took a drink and tried to tune out the peals of laughter from the kitchen.

"It's really true what they say about the black people here. They are much nicer than the blacks in Florida. It must be the lack of Haitian and Puerto Rican influence."

"We have Mexican Blacks here." Alan was slurring.

"That must be it." Irma smacked her lipstick.

Alan snapped at a waiter for another drink.

"Sunny, did you know Alan's brother is a rabbi? He's Orthodox, but I'll get him to perform the ceremony anyway."

"Alan never mentioned it," I said. Or his drinking problem. Or his past fiancés. Or Irma and her racism. I looked down and realized I'd polished off

11

my own Chardonnay without noticing.

I tried to picture myself circling Alan three times. Would the reception guests wait in anticipation for us to come out of the bedroom and display bloody sheets? Would Alan be considerate enough to stow away ketchup packets in his tuxedo for me? Would Irma come with us?

I looked at my arms. Bumps and welts covered my skin from elbow to shoulder. Rashes were often the first outward sign of a host of serious diseases. My throat tightened and my stomach ached.

"February is as soon as we can pull this together. Don't you think, Sunny?"

"It's already the end of October."

"That gives us almost four months."

"But I have to take the bar exam at the end of February."

"Sunny," she winked. "We already have an attorney. We do need a book-keeper, though."

"Irma, I'm a lawyer, not an accountant."

"Just until the kids are born."

I grabbed Alan's leg. "Alan?"

"At least you wouldn't have to risk flunking the bar again." Alan chewed slowly on a piece of ice, all that remained of his Dewar's refill.

Was the last time I'd thrown up in seventh grade or eighth? It didn't matter. The churn below my diaphragm signaled what was coming. With the thought of my Caesar salad, warm and wilted under the heat lamp with little droplets of spit from the wait staff mixed into the dressing, the bile rose in my throat. I excused myself just in time to close the bathroom stall and knot my hair behind my head.

Eventually, I was able to lean toward the faucet, put my face on the counter and rinse my tongue under the low spigot. My head pounded and my throat hurt. Why didn't Atlas warn me when I started dating Alan?

I left the bathroom to escape the smell of chemical flowers and leaned against the hallway wall. How could I return to Alan and Irma? While I tried to compose myself, I heard Irma return her prime rib, followed by Alan's potato.

As I turned in preparation for my journey back into Hell, a pair of hands, one on either shoulder, stopped me.

12

"Sorry, I almost knocked you over." It was our waiter. "I'd hate to send you away from your special night bruised up."

"I'm so..." I could only imagine my breath. "I hope they didn't offend you too much."

"Actually, we love it when they show up. It's usually so dull around here." He tried to stifle a giggle. "And it's heartening to know Mr. Fine has good taste in women."

We watched as the other prime rib, two-thirds eaten came by on a tray headed back to the kitchen.

"I knew when I first saw her she was bulimic." Irma's voice reverberated down the hallway. "She has that weird look around the eyes. You know, Alan, they have trouble getting pregnant. Then the babies are starved for food and sickly. Lots of problems."

"She's not bulimic," he replied. "Believe me."

"The real bad ones aren't stick thin because they can't possibly barf all the food out."

My abdominal muscles hurt too much to suck in my stomach. "I don't think I can go through with this," I said.

"You aren't married, yet," the waiter said.

"I'll go get her," Alan said.

My heart pounded even harder.

"Sit. She'll be back when she's done."

We have a phone in the kitchen if you want to make a call," the waiter said. "There's also a back entrance."

"I..." I said.

He put a hand on my back and led me toward the white light.

Somehow, I managed to dial my roommate, Kit, and found myself running out the back door toward the 7-Eleven on Manchester.

Sam

YOU LOOK LIKE YOU COULD USE A DRINK WHILE YOU'RE waiting to go wherever it is you're heading." The wind shifted and the bum's pungent body odor wafted in my direction.

I didn't much feel like talking, but seeing as we were the only two people outside the 7-Eleven, I was obliged to answer.

"I'm not really going anywhere now," I said.

"You're goin' somewhere." He nodded then closed his eyes and spun in a circle. "You're goin' somewhere when you know where you want to go."

At least I knew where I wasn't going; Miami, with Alan and Irma.

"I'm Sam," he said.

Since I sat with my bottom squashed on the narrow brick lip ledge beneath the window, I was technically loitering too. Transient rules of etiquette were, perhaps, in order. "Hi, Sam. Sunny."

"Not so much today." He looked up at the sky. "Might rain later."

It already had—all over my future.

Sam's cornflower blue eyes somehow sparkled beyond the sun-furrowed lines and layers of grime covering his face. "With a few bucks, I could go get something to cheer us up."

"Sorry, Sam."

"I could use something to eat." He gave a practiced forlorn look.

"I have no money." And I had no wallet, no driver's license, no cell phone

14

and no credit cards. Irma, no doubt, was rifling through my purse looking for a stash of Ex-Lax and diuretics to prove her case.

"Nothing?" His eyes pleaded. He wasn't nearly as old as he looked.

"Nothing." We were birds of a feather. I put my head in my hands and cried.

"Everything's going to be okay, Sunny." He sat on the pavement below the ledge and pulled out a harmonica.

I breathed through my mouth and listened to my companion play a bluesy riff. Actually, I was glad not to be alone at night in front of a convenience store.

Alone, once again.

If I'd had my bag, I'd have bought him some Boone's Farm, and me enough over-the-counter cold medicine to end it all. As it was, I didn't have fifty cents for a cab if Kit somehow didn't show.

Not that I was worried. Kit loved to be in the middle of a crisis, especially one where she could drive up and save the day.

"You from 'round here?" Sam's reeking breath brought me back into the moment.

"Not really."

"I live back over there." He pointed to an unlit, grassy patch wedged between the chain link fences of two rental car lots. We watched as a jet made its approach into LAX directly over his cardboard home. "It ain't bad if you need a place."

Was Sam simply being kind or a vagrant with a come on line as smooth as anything I'd heard at the bars? "Thanks, but my roommate will be here any second."

"When I have a bad day, I call my Mama."

"Where does she live?"

"In heaven." Sam picked up the harmonica and played an almost recognizable song.

Maybe I should have called Esther, but her "soul cure"— massive quantities of chamomile tea and tofu noodle soup—would work as well as a Band-Aid on an amputation. Besides, it would have taken her forty-five minutes with no traffic. And there was always traffic coming in from the Valley on Saturday night. Atlas was taping a

15

segment for his radio show and wouldn't be available. Calling Luna or my Dad was out of the question.

My best friend, Abby, would have picked me up in a second, but I wasn't about to spoil the engagement dinner she was enjoying with her fiancé's family by sharing the sordid truth about mine.

The bricks dug into the back of my thighs while I waited for Kit. *Kit's lots of fun and she'll do anything for you.* Abby had warned me on the day she introduced me to Kit who, as fate would have it, became both my roommate and co-worker. *But think about it before you let her.*

After discovering she'd shared my true (and not driver's license) weight to a group of her fellow paralegals at our law firm, I made a point not to share secrets or personal shortfalls with her again unless it was an emergency.

I fought back tears and Sam provided a dreary soundtrack until staccato beeps from a car heading toward us drowned out his music.

"I think your friend is here." Sam put down the harmonica to shield his eyes from the headlights. "Lucky you."

Kit barreled into the parking lot in her on-again-off-again boyfriend Philip's red Porsche. When he was out of town, she went out on the town—in his car.

"Sunny," she screamed over the CD player.

She flew out the driver's side door like a fireball in the naughty nurse Halloween costume she'd bragged about all Friday at work. Kit wrapped her arms around me and squeezed tight. "What the hell happened?"

"I...I..." New tears slid down my face.

"Cry it out, Sunny." She waved away Sam. "Shoo, shoo."

"Kit!"

"He's a bum!"

Sam smiled at me, then hoisted himself up and grasped his cart.

"Sam." If only I had some money to give him. "Thanks."

"To sunny days." He raised a smashed aluminum can in toast, and started off across the lot.

"See, everything's going to be okay." Kit climbed into the car and turned her pilfered spare key in the ignition. "You've already found a replacement for Alan."

"Funny."

16

"You gotta laugh these things off." As Kit revved the engine, she popped open the passenger door. "You're coming with me to a Halloween party. It'll cheer you up."

As soon as I closed the door, Kit cranked up the volume and roared out of the parking lot.

"I have no costume."

"I have a great little French maid costume I decided not to wear in the trunk."

By little, she undoubtedly meant a size too small for her which meant two and a half sizes too small for me.

"I also have no money and no purse." I screamed over the music.

"He took your Kate Spade bag?" Kit grabbed her wallet from its matching bag and threw two twenties in my lap. She eyed the blue dress. "Do you have to give that back, too?"

"No." I shook my head and turned down the music. There was no way I was telling Kit that Alan's mother bought it. It made far too tempting a Monday morning water cooler story. "I left my purse at Rapunzel's."

"I'd have run out that place, too!" She accelerated toward the 405. "You need to wash the taste of that place out of your mouth with a proper cocktail."

Sometimes Kit knew exactly the right thing to say. "Thanks, but I need to get my car at Alan's in the marina."

"Later." Kit shifted gears. "Shelby Nelson is meeting us at the party in twenty minutes. She just got dumped, too."

"I dumped Alan."

"Whatever." Kit checked her hair in the rearview mirror and glanced sideways at my ring. "How come?"

"It just wasn't going to work."

"What do you mean it just wasn't going to work?"

For all her easy-come, easy-go rhetoric, I doubted Kit would ever break up with someone who actually planned to marry her. There was no time to formulate a reasonable story she'd accept without too many questions.

"I'll tell you all about it later." I glanced at my soon–to-be-gone diamond. Losing the ring and its promise of forever would hurt a lot more than the breakup.

"That'll make a killer cocktail ring."

"It's a family heirloom. I'm going to send it back to him certified mail. Don't you think?"

"I say finders, keepers." Kit smiled. "I almost forgot to tell you, Philip hinted that he's looking for a ring while he's in Paris." She switched lanes. "Well, near Paris."

"That's great, Kit," I said with as much enthusiasm as I could muster. For the past two years, Philip promised her a ring after every break-up-makeup. Hopefully, this time it would be true.

She patted me on the leg then cut off two cars to gain access to a freeway on-ramp. "Let's go find you another one."

"I really don't feel up to it." Suddenly, my uterus felt as though it was being twisted and crushed by an invisible hand. "I think I just got my period."

She reached into her purse and threw a tampon in my lap. "Problem solved."

Kit relied upon the company of her less physically or emotionally fortunate friends to make her even more attractive at bars. Shelby Nelson was both, and I was utterly depressed. We were perfect sidekicks.

"Please, take Lincoln to Alan's. It's faster."

"No can do. It'll be fun."

If fun was watching Kit bob for apples and rich guys while Shelby mewled in admiration.

For a moment, I was tempted to go with her and drink myself into a coma, but I had to get back. Once Alan sobered up, he was bound to be furious. "You have to take me to my car. I need to get it before Alan comes home." I'd watched him kick the curb for two solid minutes after a client decided not to stock his sock line in their store. What would he do to my car?

"Leave that piece of shit Honda right where it is and come out with me. I'll take you to buy a new car tomorrow."

"Kit! I'm serious."

Kit whipped into a gas station and turned back toward the marina. "I was just trying to help."

I looked out the window, breathed through my cramps and tried not to cry as Kit screeched onto the brick turnaround in front of Alan's building.

"Drive past the door." I turned my face away as Kit halted just beyond the lobby. "Please!"

"My friend needs her car quick," Kit said in a booming voice.

"I'll take care of Miss Sunny." He reached his hand out and looked away as I tucked the Tampax into my bra and unfolded myself from the passenger seat.

"Thanks, Enrique." I ducked my head to hide my sniffles. I just need my keys, please."

Leaning out the window, Kit embraced me in a big hug. "Look on the bright side. You won't have to juggle a wedding and the bar exam at the same time."

"True." I willed the muscles of my face to remain expressionless. Since Kit failed at both law school and getting Philip tied down, it was hard to tell if she was being supportive or gloating. "Thanks, Kit."

"Text if you need me." She blew me a kiss. "And if you change your mind, you know where we'll be."

As Kit roared off toward West Hollywood, my relief at her departure was quickly replaced by panic. Allan and Irma couldn't be too far behind.

I ducked behind the valet stand. What would I say to them? What would they do to me? I spotted a pen and scratch paper next to a worn copy of Othello hidden below the kiosk. At the very least, I owed them a note.

Dear Alan and Irma,

I'm sorry. Don't worry, I will return the ring next week. You two deserve someone better. I hope you find her without too much delay. Good luck in Florida.

Thanks again,

Sunny.

PS: Could I please get my purse and stuff back? If you don't mind sending it COD that would be great. Thanks.

I folded the paper and handed it to Enrique as he held open my car door. "Enrique, please give this to the Fines."

"As you wish." He shook his head. "But they certainly don't like it when this happens."

Adam

MY THUMB RUBBED THE SPOT WHERE MY RING USED TO be as I proofed an overdue Motion to Dismiss. It might as well have been written in Sanskrit.

I dialed Alan's cell and got his voice mail again. "You've reached 310-555–5402. After the beep, you know what to do. If this is Sunny, burn in Hell."

I hung up. He was never going to forgive me.

The phone rang as soon as I replaced it in the cradle.

"Sunny are you done with the motion?" Rhonda White, self-proclaimed *savage bitch litigator* chomped on her nicotine gum. "It has to be on my desk by three or my world will come to a fucking end."

Rhonda was up for partnership in six months. I admired her relentless drive, even if every file she sent me to work on was marked *TOP PRIORITY* in red ink.

"Almost," I said.

"You've checked all the case citations?"

"I have..." *not quite finished.* I attached two affidavits to the motion and started revising the case citations so I could get on top of the pile of work spawning in my inbox. For a split second, I forgot about the Alan debacle.

Then, the intercom rang.

"Ms. St. Clair, an Adam Dey is in the lobby to see you."

"Adam Dey?" My pulse raced. The only Adam Dey I knew was an old friend of Alan's. Non-client visitors were unofficially unwelcome, especially for a first year on her second bar attempt. A personal visit of this nature was certain to generate gossip that would somehow end up in the top-secret *partnership viability* report. "Let me pull up his file and I'll be right out."

"Apparently, he's a friend of yours," Jillian, the head receptionist, said in a patrician phone voice cultivated by thirty-five years' worth of "Walker, Gamble and Lutz, how may I help you?"

She was well past sixty-five, but had the job security of a Supreme Court justice. It was a well-known (but unspoken) secret that she was the mistress of William Gamble and the mother of a certain love child named Bill Gamble Pogue, a homely and lecherous third year attorney with the firm.

When old Gamble died, his Last Will and Testament included a clause guaranteeing Jillian a job for as long as she cared to work. She chose to *maintain that personal touch* by answering the phones for a reported one hundred thousand a year, giving her extra access to every lawyer in the litigation department.

"Send him back, please. I thought you said Adam *De Lay*, a client." Butterflies hatched *en masse* from their cocoons in my stomach.

"Perhaps you'd like to come greet him, Ms. St. Clair." She lowered her voice to a whisper. "He's carrying a laundry basket full of your clothing."

"I'll be right there. Thanks, Jillian." I hung up. "Shit, shit, shit." The sound of my voice filled my tiny office. Had Alan and his mother sent an evil minion to embarrass me at work in front of everyone? By lunchtime, the secretaries would be clucking over a secret email entitled, *Sunny St. Clair's dirty laundry*. I desperately wanted my clothing back, but not like this.

I cracked open my door.

Kit's hyena laugh traveled down the hallway. Had Jillian already buzzed her with my predicament? Ever since Kit heard that Bill Pogue's marriage was on the rocks, and pronounced him *dateable*, she and Jillian had formed a potentially dangerous alliance.

I steadied myself by holding the doorknob and peered around the corner. For the moment, anyway, the secretaries were all tucked safely behind the gray walls of their cubicles. A row of closed doors lined the opposite side of the corridor. I started toward the reception area as fast as I could and still look nonchalant.

I almost made it.

Rhonda rushed out of Kit's paralegal cubicle with a handful of documents. "Whoa, Nelly. I meant to ask you about the Pulaski letter. I need that today, too."

"I'll have Pulaski done by five." I glanced at my chewed nails. "Gotta run. I have a potential client in the lobby." *Why did I say that?*

"Word to the wise." Rhonda twisted the largest bead on her graduated silver choker. "Don't let your social life get in the way of your career." She sauntered back into her almost corner office.

I took a deep breath to quell my panic and opened the door to the cavernous reception area.

We'd only met once, at a party, but there was no doubt it was Alan's boyhood friend, Adam Dey, who was seated on the leather sofa. Portraits of Walker, Gamble and Lutz stared down disapprovingly at his shaggy beard, blondish hair, faded jeans and T-shirt. The laundry basket next to him was like a flashing neon sign amidst the Oriental rugs, traditional furniture and Early American art.

"Sunny." He placed a copy of the Wall Street Journal back on the mahogany table. "How are you?"

"I'm fine, Adam, good to see you." My left thumb lunged for the AWOL engagement ring and my voice trembled as I reached out and shook his hand.

Jillian pecked away on the computer, pretending not to listen as she peered over the top of her bifocals at the laundry basket.

I began to itch as soon as I saw my cashmere sweater draped atop the pile.

"Please, Adam, come on back to my office." I had to get him in and out before he could do more damage. "And thanks, Jillian."

Her face crinkled with her saccharine smile. "Shall I hold any calls?"

"Just for a few minutes, please." *Shit, shit, shit.* I led the way to the door.

22

"Adam?"

Adam hoisted my laundry in his muscled, tan arms. He looked like he was in construction though I couldn't remember what Alan had said he did. If I walked far enough ahead of him, maybe no one would associate me with a workman carrying a laundry basket.

I stepped into the hallway, mentally crossed my fingers, and started the gauntlet walk. We passed the paralegal area, Rhonda's office, and made it beyond the ladies' room without incident. It wasn't until we'd rounded the corner nearest my office, that I heard the thud of the managing partner's heavy door behind me.

"Sunny?"

I didn't dare turn.

"Sunny. Hang on."

The voice didn't echo like Mr. Wakeman's fearful baritone.

Before I could glance reluctantly over my shoulder, beautiful and brilliant Jim Wolfe tapped me on the shoulder.

"Hi, Jim," I said airily, pretending for a millisecond that Adam wasn't two steps behind me.

"Sunny, I've left something on your desk. Can you get it to me by three?" He looked deep into my eyes, or maybe it was me looking deeply into his.

Maybe being single wasn't the worst thing after all.

We both smiled.

Adam caught up and stood next to me.

"Three?" I said, jarred by reality and simultaneous deadlines.

Jim looked into the laundry basket. He nodded as he turned to Adam and extended his hand. "Jim Wolfe."

"Adam Dey."

They shook hands.

Jim glanced at my folded clothing, at Adam, and knitted his perfect brow. "Sunny, call me with any questions."

Score one for the Fines. Everything I'd ever dreamed of in a man just watched me receive a basket of my laundry from a guy in a retro band T-shirt.

"Here's my office, Adam." I pushed him firmly through my doorway.

As I stepped in behind him, I scraped my bare shoulder on the brass *Ms.*

23

St. Clair nameplate. It clanged and fell out of its mooring beside my door.

Adam put the laundry basket on my desk, stepped into the hallway and grabbed the metal strip from the floor before I had a chance to sequester him out of sight.

"They slip right off." Kit appeared from nowhere and had her newly enhanced breasts in his face as he straightened up.

I resisted the urge to put my head in my hands.

"What?" he asked.

"The name plates." She smiled. "Because of the high attorney turnover."

"I see."

"I'm Kit Purdy." She reached out to shake his hand. "Sunny's paralegal."

Since when was she *my* paralegal?

"And you are?" she asked.

"I'm Adam Dey."

She glanced into the laundry basket. "An associate of Alan Fine, I presume."

"My shoulder," I grasped my upper arm. "Is it bleeding?"

Adam turned away from Kit and examined the red welt forming at the top of my arm.

Kit wrinkled her nose while Adam's back was to her. "Want me to stay?" she mouthed.

"I think it's just a scratch." Adam smiled.

"Oh, good." I checked my white silk tank for blood. "I'll check in with you later, Kit."

"Why don't I get some Neosporin from the first aid box?"

"That's all right," I said. "Thanks, anyway."

Kit gave Adam a suspicious glare and flipped her ashy hair. "Well, if you need anything, I'll be right down the hall." She pointed toward her office so Adam would see she was almost within earshot. "Tell Alan he really blew it."

"Kit's just trying to be protective," I said as soon as she was gone, but while looking out the window at my view into the twentieth floor of the high-rise across the street. "Sorry."

"I'm the one who should apologize." Adam glanced at the laundry basket. "I had no choice but drop your stuff here. I'm in the process of moving out

24

of town so..."

"I thank you for taking the time to return my things." What exactly were Alan and Adam up to? I snapped the rubber band I'd been stretching inadvertently around my ring finger. "He did get the ring back, didn't he? I sent it certified and insured, but I haven't got the receipt confirming delivery yet." Maybe that was why Alan sent him. "I'd never keep a family heirloom."

"I'm sure he got it or I would have heard about it." Adam shook his head. "You know, Sunny, I've tried to talk to him about the breakup, but Alan wouldn't even tell me where you live to return your stuff there."

He seemed almost nice, but I wasn't about to let my guard down. I glanced away from Adam, and into the laundry basket. Where were the rest of my things? I'd left at least three basket's worth at Alan's.

"If you want, I'd be glad to carry that down to your car." He reached for the plastic handle.

"No, No. That's okay." With my luck, the partners were meeting in the glassed-in conference room next to the elevators. As I slid the basket toward me and stowed it under my feet, I eyed the paperwork with Jim Wolfe's sexy scrawl all over it. I'd stuff a few items at a time into my briefcase until everything made it home.

Adam eased into my one client chair. "Sunny, are you doing okay?"

Maybe Alan wanted to know if I felt some remorse before he sent someone with the rest of my clothes. "Break-ups are always hard, no matter who initiates them."

"For sure."

I picked up a pencil and tapped it on my desk.

"You know, I tried to track you down at home, but I couldn't seem to get a current address.

"The utilities and landline are in my roommate's name." I didn't mention that my roommate was Kit. "How did you find me?"

"I called a St. Clair or two." He smiled. "I had an interesting chat with your sister."

"My sister..." I scratched my arms.

"I didn't realize Atlas St. Clair is your brother."

"I have quite a family."

25

"They seem pretty cool."

Adam's eyes were not only deceptively kind, but an unusual dark green, like the unlit shade of the banker's lamp on my desk.

"Can I ask how you ended up with my clothes?"

Adam sighed and picked up my starfish paperweight.

Would Alan's other friends stop by the office one-by-one just to torture me? My legs itched in concert with my arms.

"Sunny," Adam gnawed his lower lip. "Alan had a party the other night. Actually, it was a bonfire on the beach."

I scooted my chair back and lifted my sweater from the top of the pile. My jeans lay folded with *BITCH* written down one leg in large black letters.

"I'm afraid the rest of your clothing is gone."

"He burned my clothes?"

Adam nodded.

I couldn't scream invectives. I couldn't collapse in a heap then curl up in the fetal position. All I had left of my favorite clothing seemed to be the breakup-day underwear I'd spirited away in my handbag. I put my head in my hands.

"I'm sorry, Sunny."

The last thing I wanted was for Adam to see me cry, but tears rolled down my face, over my lips and dropped onto my desk.

Adam handed me a tissue. "I knew he was hurt and angry, but I didn't think he was going to go through with it."

I took a deep breath. What did I expect him to do after I ran out the back of the restaurant like a fugitive? At the very least, I should have told Alan I was sick and broken up with him later. I swabbed my eyes and nose. "I deserved it."

Adam shook his head.

"I've tried to call Alan and apologize, but he won't take my calls."

"I've heard his message."

"I feel so terrible. I'm not the kind of person who would normally..."

"Alan gets over it pretty quick." He half-smiled. "It's Irma that doesn't."

"This has happened before?" A shocky sensation traveled through my body. "How many times has—?"

"It's all right." Little dimples framed Adam's smile. "I had a feeling you

26

wouldn't be like any of the others."

"But..."

"I'm afraid I've gotta run, Sunny."

Adam stood and started for the door.

Obviously, he wasn't going to betray Alan by answering my question. "Thank you for saving what you could, and bringing it over." If he did report back to Alan, at least he couldn't say I'd freaked-out or made a scene.

"I'll walk you to the elevators."

As we started down the hallway together, two secretaries chatting with Jillian at the reception desk stopped talking and started listening.

"Thanks for coming. It was nice to see you again," I said loudly as we walked across the lobby to the bank of elevators. Luckily, no one was in the conference room.

"No problem." The doors slid open and he stepped on. "Take care, Sunny."

"You, too." Despite a futile effort to blink them back, tears welled in my eyes again. I had misjudged him. Why hadn't I thought to ask him what he did or where he was going? "Where are you moving to?"

The elevator door slid closed before he answered.

I looked down. Red bumps had popped up all over my body. Something was definitely wrong, and it wasn't just the breakup with Alan. I hurried back to my office. Despite my looming deadlines, I pressed autodial three on my phone and called the doctor.

The scheduling nurse deemed my condition a non-emergency and wouldn't squeeze me in until after Thanksgiving.

Atlas

YOUR RASH IS FROM NERVES." MY BROTHER ATLAS OPENED the armoire that served as a pie cabinet and located the handcrafted South American dishes that my mother Esther saved for special occasions.

"Are you sure?" What if Atlas and the nurse were both wrong? Would I be well enough to stand up in my best friend Abby's wedding?

"You'll be fine. I'll be your date if you stop stressing out and moping about your love life."

"What love life?" I'd accepted my destiny—no husband, four-legged children with whiskers and endless nights of tuna casserole watching TV shows that featured felines. At least, I had a brand-new Audi.

Kit had convinced me that a really nice car would more than replace Alan Fine and so far, she'd been right. A convertible with tan leather interior, turbo, and a great sound system, the Audi insured that at the very least, I'd be alone in style.

"Dad's gonna love your new wheels." Atlas placed a stack of plates on a mostly clean edge of the dining room table and headed back to the cabinet for salad bowls.

Proud as I was of my new acquisition, I parked at the end of my mom's cul-de-sac to avoid unnecessary commentary by my family. Of course, Atlas didn't have to look out the window. He saw everything without eyes. The itch started to creep down my arms. "It's leased."

"But, of course."

"I got a great deal."

"I'm sure."

"I'm not going to tell Dad until I absolutely have to."

"Why not? A little turmoil is good for him."

I resisted the urge to tear at my legs with my fingernails. Instead, I grabbed a handful of flatware from the drawer. I sorted the spoons that were the least crunched from the garbage disposal and set them on the table. If I wasn't ever going to have a husband, why shouldn't I have a nice car? At least I wouldn't have to suffer the humiliation of showing up dateless to Abby's wedding in my old Honda.

"It's a shame you can't marry me." He batted his blond lashes and smiled. "I'd be a great husband."

"I'm looking for someone a little more traditional, and less my brother. Straight might be nice, too." Besides, my dream man would wait until I actually said something before he answered me with a cryptic message or smart-ass comeback.

"That would take all the fun out of it."

"Stick with Drake." I smiled. "Is he coming for dinner?"

"He's getting ready for a meeting with the mayor tomorrow." A hint of something I couldn't read swept across his face. "I don't think he's ready for tonight's family extravaganza."

Nor was I. Atlas was wise to keep a catch like Drake away from the family insanity as much as possible. Ken would have ditched Barbie in a heartbeat after seeing Drake's blond hair, blue eyes, and chiseled features. Perhaps Atlas would let me borrow him so I could pretend he was my boyfriend for Abby's wedding.

"No impure thoughts. He's mine." Atlas slid a second placemat to the end of the table so Mom and Hugh could preside as co-heads. "Besides, no other guys will talk to you if Drake is on your arm."

I was supposed to be the engaged bridesmaid at Abby's wedding. Instead, I would once again join the throng of lonely single girls who rushed to the powder room at the first hint of a slow song. "I wonder if I should have given Alan a little more time."

"To do what? Move you in with his Mom in Florida and to more fully

29

realize his drinking problem?"

"It's just that I don't think I'll ever..."

"Sunny, it's time to move on."

"To what?"

Atlas rolled his head from side to side. A broad smile crept across his face. "You'll know when you find it."

"Sage wisdom. Sam the bum already fed me that one." Where was my sixth sense so I didn't have to rely on my brother's ethereal tidbits?

"Open your own Third Eye."

"An extra eye will make a great first impression."

The door from the kitchen swung open and our stepfather, Hugh, sauntered into the dining room with a tray of eggplant kebobs and a cucumber salad. He set the platter on the table with a flourish. "It's going to be a lively feast tonight."

Just once, I longed to come home for Thanksgiving dinner and find Hugh out back smoking a turkey on the grill. I dreamed of helping Esther prepare a salad with iceberg lettuce and familiar vegetables. We'd devour fluffy Potato Buds drenched in gravy and pass around white dinner rolls, then take turns slicing the red Jell-O-ring full of fruit cocktail with a chilled knife. At the other split-level homes in Thousand Oaks, such meals were already in progress, but, as per usual, we were having vegan surprise.

In third grade, Atlas announced that he could no longer eat things he could hear think. Esther, thrilled by his pronouncement, jumped on the vegetarian bandwagon. Since Luna barely ate anyway, my carnivorous needs were largely ignored after my parents split up and Dad moved to an apartment across town. For me, family dinners involved near starvation until I could drive through the In-N-Out Burger on my way back to my apartment.

I glanced up from a tray of veggies as Hugh flashed a goofy, inexplicable grin at Atlas. As Hugh caught me catching the look between them, he pulled a rubber band from his pocket, ran his fingers through what remained of his hair and pony-tailed the long part. Despite the fact that we were celebrating Thanksgiving ultra-vegan style, I could feel it was going to be weirder than usual.

I shook my head and swung the door open to the kitchen.

30

"Hi, Sunshine." My mother wiped her hands on her apron. "Table set?"

"Yes. What else are we having, Esther?" I stopped calling her Mom to her face on my sixteenth birthday. Family rule.

"A Russian feast." She took in a deep cleansing breath and drained the water from a pot of mung beans soaking on the counter. "Don't you think the faux feta mixes nicely with the cabbage?"

"What if I make a plain green salad?" I'd fallen asleep while studying and missed lunch. The Snickers bar I'd had as a snack wasn't going to sustain me through two hours of simulated eating.

"I already made a salad. Could you hand me a tomato, sweetie?"

I looked into a basket containing vegetables and fruit in an advanced state of decay. Esther liked to watch the colors appear as the rot set in, plus she swore the nutritional value increased as it ripened. I grabbed a firmish tomato and put in on the counter next to her.

Esther hummed some dated hippie tune from before her time as she arranged slices on a plate. Her ample hips swayed back and forth in time. Despite her diet, she looked a tad plumper than usual.

"We're just about ready." She handed me a platter. "Call Luna and take this to the table."

My room became Hugh's study the moment I moved out, while Atlas's departure meant a craft workshop for Esther. However, Luna's bedroom remained exactly as she left it the day she went off to college. While the rest of the world faced the harsh realities of weekend catch up, Luna came home and languished in her quarters enjoying a mental health day.

"Anything in particular on her mind today?"

"She's under a lot of pressure with the new business." Esther wrinkled her brow. "There are so many details to get it off the ground."

"How hard could it be to run an imaginary company?"

"Sunny, think about your karma when you say such things."

"I was thinking of Luna's." She had likely spent the day staring at the ceiling, planning how to leech more money from Esther and Hugh to get her gourmet water business or whatever it was, off the ground.

"Sunny, don't take your frustrations out on your sister. Alan was part of your learning process." She held her hands over her eyes and pretended that she too was psychic. "You should thank your spirit guides. They were

31

looking out for you."

"I'm sure you're right, Esther." Before my Mom could regale me with more New Age platitudes I yelled, "Luna, dinner."

With a tray of something photosynthetic, I turned for the dining room where Hugh and Atlas were deep in conversation. They stopped speaking when I backed through the door.

Luna appeared at the top of the stairs. Dressed in her usual array of black to compliment her cropped ebony hair, she gazed upon the first floor from the landing. "Sunny, I'm glad you're finally here. I have some legal questions I need answered."

Bilking money from unsuspecting relatives for a hopeless business endeavor was more of a moral issue, in my opinion.

Atlas bore a hole through me with his ice blue eyes. *Go easy on her.*

Why didn't he ever send me psychic messages about me?

She started down the stairs slowly, pausing with each step. Though she generally ate only when absolutely necessary, she'd added a noticeable pound or two around the middle. *The belly ring is going to look strained soon.* The words almost left my lips. Instead, I chipped a dry piece of something akin to pasta off the table with my thumbnail. It landed next to Atlas's plate.

He smiled.

"What's with the fancy new wheels?" Luna asked as she reached the bottom step.

Since her balcony faced the street, she must have been staring meaningfully out the window as I drove up.

"You got a new car, Sunshine?" Esther appeared from the kitchen holding a steaming bowl of faux feta-cabbage surprise and the mung beans.

"The Honda met an untimely death." *It was running rough prior to the Alan incident.*

Atlas tugged a piece of eggplant off a skewer, stuffed it into his mouth and sat back in his chair.

Esther motioned Luna to sit. "Sunny, I think a new car is a great way to get over a man."

"I didn't buy the car to get over Alan."

"Men are necessary only for procreation," Luna said. "There's certainly

32

no reason to mourn an inferior specimen like Alan Fine."

"So it's safe to assume you're sticking to cucumbers?" I glared at Luna, who, despite admittedly exotic looks, to my knowledge, hadn't had a date in years.

"We forgot the rolls." Hugh ran for the safety of the kitchen.

"The age-old dilemma, a boyfriend or a cucumber," Atlas gazed into the salad bowl, "both have their merits."

"Kids. My kids. Celebrate each other. No bickering." Esther flung her long, gray ringlets which just missed a dunk into the veggie dip. "Atlas, your show was great last night. I think you saved that woman's life."

"She saved herself by calling," Atlas said.

"What happened?" Luna scooted in her chair. "I missed that part."

"A young woman called in wanting to know if she should join the military or get married," I said. There was no point pretending I didn't listen to the show.

"Now, there's a dilemma." Luna raised an eyebrow. "I wonder what Sunny would do?"

"At least the pay is regular in the military," I said.

"Sunny, just because you bought into Dad's corporate fantasy and became a big attorney to make him happy, doesn't make it the only way," Luna said.

"I didn't do it to appease Dad." My voice cracked. "I love my job."

Luna tipped her head to the side.

"Find yourself another free lawyer, Luna."

"Ah, the sun and the moon. Yin and yang." Atlas smiled and shook his head. "As for the caller, the marriage would have led to a life of numbing boredom. The job will ultimately lead her down a harrowing but amazing path."

Hugh returned with gluten-free, taste-free dinner rolls.

"Perfect timing, Hugh." Esther bowed her head and reached out her hands.

I joined hands with Hugh and grudgingly clasped Luna's oddly puffy fingers.

"We thank you Heavenly Mother for the health, happiness and prosperity of the last year and, especially, the bounty of your womb. Amen." She teared up and then collected herself. "Sunny, please start the passing, would you?"

I put a meager spoonful of something on my plate.

Atlas dumped a healthy glob of fake feta and cabbage before him. "Esther, it all looks incredible."

Luna picked at her food and reluctantly swallowed a fork full of the brown goo. "What is this, Esther?"

"It's called Mash-Mush." Hugh hunched over his plate and shoveled it in his mouth. "It's a traditional Uzbeki dish Esther discovered."

I shook my head. Usually, about an hour after dinner, Hugh would make some weak excuse about a late edition Sunday paper and return with McDonalds on his breath.

Luna clandestinely spit something into her napkin, dabbed at her mouth and stared out the window at a nest of baby birds.

Atlas grinned at Luna, looked over at Mom and Hugh, and broke into a big broad smile.

Esther gazed at the table with her Earth Princess serene face.

"What's going on around here?"

"Esther, Hugh, I'm too excited to eat." Atlas dropped his fork onto his plate. "Just give us our good news now."

Esther gazed deep into Hugh's eyes.

Hugh nodded.

"I was going to wait until after the Apple Baba I made for dessert, but Hugh and I do have something to tell you."

Esther plinked her water glass with her knife, which usually meant the kick-off of Esther's latest humanitarian project.

Luna started for the bathroom.

"Luna, sit down, we won't make you fundraise again."

On our eighteenth birthdays, Esther stopped giving us holiday gifts and donated the proceeds to various causes. In recent years, she also insisted we raise money as well.

"What organization did you join now?" I lived in constant fear someone at my firm would recognize my mother or stepfather on the evening news as they were hauled off to jail from some undeniably worthy but embarrassing protest.

"This is more like who is joining our organization." My mother stood, held her hands palms up and then reached out to us. "You know how much

I love children."

"Oh, no." Luna put her head in her hands.

"Oh, yes," Atlas said.

"Oh, God!" My stomach turned. Esther wanted as many children as God-Goddess was inclined to implant in her willing womb, but three children were more than adequate for Bernie who had a vasectomy after Luna.

"Hugh and I are indeed having a sister or brother for you."

I pushed my plate away. Whatever meager appetite I'd drummed up was long gone.

"A brother." Atlas smiled.

Hugh put the fork to the water glass again. "Spectacular."

Before anyone could ask another question, Luna bolted from the table and rushed up the open stairway as though the new sibling was already on his way over to evict her from the shrine to her childhood.

We all watched in silence as she slammed the door.

"Luna seems a little more emotional than usual tonight," Hugh said.

My arms and legs not only itched, but tingled. Esther was forty-eight and to my knowledge, Hugh was sterile. "How exactly can you be pregnant, Mom?

"It's quite simple, Sunny. I went to the sperm bank and made a withdrawal."

I put my head in my hands. The mere idea of my mother's geriatric egg combining with the seed of a horny college guy short on beer money made me dizzy. And then, a worse possibility hit me.

And also Luna.

With a voice so shrill it would have caused hearing loss had she not been upstairs behind closed doors, she screamed, "You didn't Mom. You couldn't have."

"Oh, but she did." Atlas stuffed a big bite of something into his mouth and pushed back from the table. "I'll deal with Luna." Atlas marched up the steps toward Luna's room. "It's going to be an amazing new year."

And there I was, left in the thick of it, as always. "How did you...?"

I wasn't sure I wanted to hear the answer.

In one of their last great battles, Esther begged Bernie for another baby one week before the vasectomy. After five days of fighting, he made a

35

deposit in a sperm bank in case he had a change of heart and went through with the procedure. They split up within a year. Esther, forced to make do with the three of us, resigned herself to a smallish family. Or so I thought.

"The sperm bank called and said the deposit was possibly losing its potency. I couldn't bear to see any of my babies die without a chance at life." She patted her belly. "And, I wanted Hugh to experience the incredible blessing of fatherhood."

"Oh, my God."

Esther struck a Madonna pose. "Aren't the wonders of life endless and joyful?"

It was a wonder they'd procured Bernie's seed without him. It was a wonder this somehow seemed rational to the two of them. I wondered how I would make it through all this.

"Bernie and I made beautiful babies together." Esther stroked my hair and gazed at the sunset as it reflected from the bald top of Hugh's head. "It was meant to be."

Hugh beamed.

My head throbbed. "I assume you cleared this with Dad before you did it?"

"Don't worry, Sunny." Esther flung her curls grandly and patted her belly again. "We left some."

"Mom, he could sue." The lawsuit would be all over the evening news. My hopes for a date with Jim Wolfe, or anyone who followed current events faded in an instant.

"Possession is nine-tenths of the law." Esther smiled. "You should know that, Sunny."

"You have to tell Dad." I needed enough warning to get out of town for about nine months. "When are you going to tell Dad?"

"We'll start Bernie off with the Audi as a warm-up." Atlas shouted from Luna's open doorway. "Esther will be the grand finale."

I didn't correct him by saying main event.

Instead, I simply scratched my legs.

36

Bill

THE RASH YOU ARE PRESENTING, WHICH BY THE WAY HAS disappeared from one leg since the exam started, is from nerves. Dr. Kachina's words spun around my brain as my feet circled on the pedals of the stationery bike. *In general, I tell my patients to reduce stress and get regular exercise, but you…*I cranked up the volume on the TV set in front of me and took deep stress relieving breaths.

My legs felt stiff and achy as the bike kicked into hill climbing mode. It had been over three months since I'd made it for a lunch-hour work-out in the building's fitness center. I checked the digital time readout: Four minutes, forty-nine seconds.

Ms. St. Clair, I think you'd be well served by a specialist. I'll leave a referral and some Calamine samples.

My face blazed with the same intense prickly heat as the moment I'd glanced at the name in big block letters on the referral slip: *PATRICIA GOLDSTEIN, PSYCHOTHERAPIST.*

I pushed the up arrow, set the bike on level four, and cycled up my mental mountain.

Bill Pogue appeared out of nowhere and climbed on the bike next to me. His legs were bony, white, and covered with curly orange hair. His Harvard Law tank top clung to his paunchy mid-section. Rumor was he'd barely graduated from Southwestern. "Fancy seeing you here."

I kept my eyes on the TV screen. "Hey, Bill."

He gave me the once-over with a lecherous version of his mother Jillian's evil squint. "Did you just join?"

"I usually stop by later in the day." I scanned in vain for an empty spot across the room in the *executive* treadmill section.

"Didn't know you worked out," Bill said, setting his bike to level one and pushing off.

I tugged on my T-shirt so it covered my bottom.

"You look good and everything, but I guess I think of you more as a brainy babe."

A brainy babe?

Bill remained blessedly silent for thirty seconds as he stood on his pedals to conquer a level one hill. "Are you ready for the bar this time?"

A partner from the probate department scowled and pressed the incline button on his treadmill.

"I've been studying a lot." I lowered my voice hoping he might follow suit.

"Cool. Did you hear they may be cutting some first-years at the end of next month?"

"Really?"

"You worried?"

"Nah." I removed an earbud and turned to Bill. "What did you hear?"

"I've heard some things that shouldn't be overheard." He surveyed the room and flashed a lipless smile. "I've got tickets to the Laker game tonight."

Why hadn't I seen this coming? Word was he'd been on a rampage since his wife fled back to Tokyo and left her forwarding address in Japanese.

I looked down for a second to compose my *thanks but* speech. "Bill..."

"I hear the cuts may be in the litigation department."

My exercise-taxed heart thumped harder. How could I find out if it was true without spending the evening with him? "Could you maybe whisper what you heard?" It was bad enough to consider his sweaty, red face next to my ear. An evening together was unthinkable.

Bill leaned toward me. "I've got the W, G and L courtside seats."

I shifted my left hand so he couldn't see my ring finger. "Bill, if I weren't engaged..."

The men's room door swung open. Jim Wolfe appeared in the doorway and started toward the free weights in a faded Stanford T-shirt he'd no doubt purchased when he went there.

"I heard that's off." Bill's voice boomed across the room.

"We're back together," I mumbled.

Jim spotted me and gave a casual wave.

Would he come over?

"What?" Bill asked loud enough for the entire gym to hear my answer.

I had no choice. "We're back together."

As soon as the words left my mouth, Jim walked past the cardio area and into the weight room. He set his towel on the bench press machine.

I might as well have run over and kissed him goodbye forever. "Thank you anyway, Bill."

Bill climbed off the bike. His red hair dripped with sweat. "I'll try and let you know if your name comes up."

"That would be great." I pretended to stare intently at my monitor as Bill headed toward the locker room and Jim hoisted a barbell above his strong-looking shoulders.

I didn't let myself scratch until I got to the showers.

Jane

"YOU'RE ON THE AIR WITH ATLAS ST. CLAIR."

As my brother's voice crackled from the tiny holes on my computer speaker radio, I placed a mostly empty bottle of Baileys Irish Cream on my nightstand and pulled the covers up around my neck.

"Mr. St. Clair?"

"Call me Atlas."

"Atlas, this is Ben from Long Beach."

"Ben, Ben..." Atlas was silent for a second. "You want to know about your job."

"Wow." Ben paused. "I didn't think you were for real."

"But, I am," Atlas said.

"Am I going to get...?"

"Before I answer, I have one question for you."

"Sure, Atlas." Ben sounded tentative.

"How will this promotion really change anything? You hate being an accountant."

"I don't hate it. I mean, it's a great career. I make a good living and..." Ben choked up but caught himself.

"You've lived many past lives where necessity forced you to look away from your true desires. You can't do that again in this life, the price will be too high." He paused. "But, the promotion is yours if you want it."

"Really?"

"Do you really want it?"

"I guess I... I don't know."

"Think about it. And Ben...?"

"Yes, Atlas?" His voice was shaky.

"In the meantime, dust off the guitar you threw into the back of the closet and cut back on the drinking."

As I took the last swig of Baileys, I couldn't help but consider the merits of alcoholism. As my brother became more and more famous, I could check in and out of rehab on Atlas's tab. Wasn't it a time-honored tradition for the siblings of noted public figures to drown in reckless excess?

I set the empty bottle back on the table, but I was still thirsty. What I really needed was a cup of chamomile tea.

"Hi, Atlas. My name is Rose from Manhattan Beach."

Rose Underwood from law school lived in Manhattan Beach. What problems could she have? She was first in our class, happily married and had a full-time nanny to watch her kid.

"You know, Rose, you make simple life situations into terrible crises. Calm down and focus on the half-full, not the half-empty. I sense a number of loving spirit guides surrounding you. They will ensure the choices you make pave the way for your ultimate happiness."

"I just don't get it. I'm happily married. I have a great kid..."

Maybe it was Rose Underwood.

"All you need is a winter vacation and a cup of chamomile tea. My mother swears it brings inner peace. Try it."

I was on the verge of landing in a psycho ward, had a history of failure with men, and if I didn't get back to the books, a two-time bar flunkee. I was clearly beyond the healing powers of chamomile tea. Maybe it wouldn't hurt to call Patricia Goldstein and see what she had to say.

"If you have something on your mind, give me a call. 213-555–6161."

I picked up the phone, but my fingers ignored my brain and pushed Atlas's on air number.

It rang.

"You're on the air with Atlas St. Clair."

I panicked. What was I doing calling my brother on the air? "Hi," I said.

41

"This is Jane from La Mirada."

The radio barked back my "Hi" in a southern drawl. No question, I was definitely losing it.

"Turn down your radio, Jane from La Mirada."

I twisted the volume all the way down.

"Do you think I need therapy?" The fake accent became more pronounced as I spoke.

Atlas seemed to chuckle. "Jane, there's nothing wrong with you that you can't figure out yourself."

"Well, I also have this skin condition. I went to the doctor but all he gave me was Calamine and a referral for the..."

"You're fine. Call your sister. She needs you."

The line went dead.

I turned the volume back up. Was there any chance that there was a Jane in La Mirada whose sister had a serious problem?

"Well, that's all the time we have left. This is Atlas St. Clair signing off until next time. Remember, we can all use our inner vision if we allow ourselves to see."

Luna

THOUGH I MANAGED TO DRAG MYSELF OUT OF BED THE NEXT morning and limp in to work, I never could get a hold of my sister. She didn't return my texts and every time I dialed her number, I got her voice mail.

Instead of going to UCLA law library after work, I headed south toward Loyola for a change of scenery and a quick swing past Luna's place.

When I pulled up in front of her tiny beach cottage, Luna's vintage VW Bug was parked at the base of her front steps with the windows rolled down. Why hadn't she answered my calls?

I pushed the window buttons, put the top up and checked my door locks twice.

Luna appeared in her doorway. The breeze rustled through her hair and softened the severity of her black chin-length bob. "Well, look who's slumming."

"I was on the way to study and thought I'd stop by."

"Come on in."

"Didn't you get my messages?

"Had the phone off so I could focus on researching this amazing spring near Arrowhead. You can't believe the water report on this place." She tried to hand me a pile of paperwork. "I need you to look this over right away."

I set it down on a table without a glance. "You can't just turn your phone

43

off. What if an important business call or an urgent message came in from one of us?"

"Well, I did, and nothing earth-shattering happened, did it?" She ambled over to her slip-covered couch, moved aside some empty water bottles, and plopped down in the center. "Besides, I'm glad you're here because I'm going to need your official legal services soon."

Why had Atlas told me to call her? Her job situation was status quo. She didn't look sick, just pale, and she was always pale.

"What perfume are you wearing?" Luna scrunched her face and scooted back from the center of her sofa.

I sniffed the fresh floral scent at my wrist. It smelled better as the day wore on. "That new one by Stila."

"Hang on a sec." She shuffled across the bungalow to the bathroom, closed the door and turned on the tap.

A noisy group of teenagers passed by on the sidewalk. Their body jewelry jangled as they crossed Luna's yard.

I hurried over to the window with my keys and checked the remote car lock again.

Over the faucet, I heard the retching sound of water forcing its way out of her dilapidated pipes, the flush of her toilet and the squealing hinge of the medicine cabinet.

Luna returned from the bathroom in a minty haze. "Let's go for a walk. It's stuffy in here."

Venice Beach made me anxious and Luna knew it. "Sure, love to."

"We'll get a bite on the strand." She tossed a fringy black shawl around her shoulders that looked like the thrift shop cast-off of a retired witch. "I'm starved."

Luna closed the door without securing the dead bolt and took three Esther-like cleansing breaths before stepping down the brick walkway toward the street. Nothing was wrong with Luna.

Nothing new, anyway.

A stroll on the strand, even on a winter Wednesday, was a carnival of oily bodybuilders, skanks in string bikinis, over-friendly Rastafarians, and people talking to imaginary friends. Despite the smattering of Christmas decorations and sparkling lights, it still smelled of sunscreen and rotting garbage.

"What time is it?" Luna asked.

Of course, she never wore a watch and had stopped carrying her phone around, apparently. I looked at my high school graduation watch. "6:15. I can't stay too long."

"You know, you have to pass the bar this time. I'm really going to need legal counsel soon."

What she needed was a job, not a lawyer. I took my own deep cleansing breath. She was being nice and I had to be, too. "Anything I can do."

"Did you ever think that being a lawyer isn't what you're truly meant to be?" Luna pulled at the fringe on her shawl.

When we were kids, Bernie often asked a similar question. "Are you going to be a doctor, a lawyer or an engineer?"

Atlas would smile and say, "Famous radio personality." Luna would shrug and mutter some dreamy comment about ballet dancing or living in France. I had to say something reasonable or we'd all face an hour-long lecture on fiscal responsibility. I'd look pointedly at Luna and Atlas, who both seemed unconcerned that Bernie's ears flared red, and answer, "Lawyer."

Bernie would nod at me. "At least I can count on one of you to earn a living."

"At least I earn a good living," I said to Luna as I gazed toward the beach. "Besides, I love the legal profession."

Her right eyebrow peaked. "I was hoping you'd think about going into business with me."

We walked in silence as the sidewalk broadened into a pedestrian walkway spanning the width of an alley. Beach huts tucked between modern houses and old brick apartment buildings lined the thorough-fare. The smell of dinner interlaced with evening flowers in the front yard gardens.

I watched a young mom shove a spoonful of baby food to her cooing toddler through the floor-to-ceiling window of her Dwell-inspired great room.

"That's my dream house," Luna said, her skin reflecting slightly green in the waning light.

"If that's what you want, I hope you get it." She was as far away from

45

living in a beach mansion as I was from serving on the Supreme Court.

"Sunny, you should try living for your dreams sometimes."

"Have you talked to Esther, recently?" I asked, changing the subject.

"We had a long talk this morning. She's going to turn Hugh's study into the nursery, at least for a while."

I shook my head. Even our new brother couldn't even evict Luna from her room.

As she started off ahead of me, her black capris stretched across her broadish bottom.

"Hey Luna!" A hawk-nosed old man looked up from his guitar and tipped his filthy beret. "How ya holdin' up?"

"Pretty good, Leon. No complaints."

A contortionist, perched on a concrete bench, waved a foot from over his shoulder as we made our way down the strand.

"Good luck this weekend, Horatio."

He gave her the thumbs-up from between his legs.

"Would you believe he makes almost as much as Dad?"

"Speaking of which, has Esther talked to him yet?"

"Didn't say anything to me about it."

"Aren't you worried about how he'll take the news?"

"What can we do?" Luna shrugged, spotted something down the strand, and suddenly increased her pace.

I could barely keep up.

What if Dad wants the sperm?" I huffed behind her. "What if he has Mom arrested?"

"You worry too much."

"I shouldn't worry that our mother is a sperm bank robber?"

"Oh, shit."

Had the reality of Esther's crime sunk in? "Oh, shit what?"

"Oh, shit. Hot Dog on a Stick is closing."

"Hot Dog on a Stick?" I chased behind her as she broke into a full run. She hated junk food, especially hot dogs.

Luna, out of breath, rushed over and tucked under the half-lowered red, blue, and yellow security awning. "Joe, you can't be closed, it's not 6:30."

"We're slow, love. I thought you weren't coming tonight." Tattoos

46

covered Joe's arms and peeked up over the neckline of his circus-striped employee tank top.

"Is the fryer still hot?"

"For you Luna, anything."

Since when was my sister a regular at Hot Dog on a Stick? No wonder her rump looked wider. Something *was* wrong.

Joe reached into the refrigerator, grabbed two hot dogs impaled on sticks and submerged them into a bucket of batter.

"Better make another one for my sister. Or do you want a cheese stick, Sunny?"

"A hot dog will be fine." I never dreamed I'd hear those words from anyone in my family besides Bernie.

The man dipped a third hot dog in the coating and immersed it in the deep fryer. He winked at me. "Would your pretty sister like lemonade, too?"

"Lemonade would be great, thanks." I watched that he didn't touch the rims as he filled the cups with ice. He didn't strike me as a hand washer.

"Trudy," he yelled to the back. The sound of running water came to a halt. "Bring a pitcher of lemonade from the back."

A pretty girl emerged from the back with a pitcher and filled our cups. "Here, Daddy."

"Thanks, love."

"Doesn't he totally remind you of Bernie?" Luna asked.

We laughed. My father had never, ever, called either of us *love* even though we knew he loved us. He just didn't want us to know.

Joe handed us the drinks and turned to the fryer, removing the sticks all at once. He handed two to Luna and one to me. "Let them cool for a second, ladies."

Luna reached into her pocket and pulled out a ragged ten.

"I'll get it this time," I said.

"It's on the house tonight. You've been keepin' us in business lately, Luna."

I watched Luna devour the molten hot dog before it had even cooled to hot. My sister who hadn't touched a hot dog or a carbohydrate in years was suddenly a raging carnivore?

"Thanks, Joe," she managed through a steaming mouthful. "See you soon."

47

I watched, dumbfounded, as she guzzled the lemonade and bit another healthy hunk off the top of her second corn dog, cooling it between her teeth by blowing air in and out of her mouth.

As Luna devoured her dinner down to the sticks, inhaled the remainder of her drink, and wiped her mouth on her sleeve, I nibbled on the breading while I waited for mine to cool down to a reasonable temperature.

She seemed calm, even blissful as we headed back along the strand. Then, as we neared the turn to her street Luna threw her shawl at me, darted into the alley and barely made it to a trash bin before she heaved.

"Luna! Are you okay?"

Before she could answer, Luna threw up again.

"Even the most diehard processed food fanatic can't ingest that so fast and expect no stomach upset."

"Damn." She wiped her mouth with the paper sleeve from the hot dog. "This happens every time."

Had Luna developed an eating disorder? What if it was something worse? Was this why Atlas told me to see her?

Was Esther actually keeping the room to care for my sister as she weakened, sickened and the life force slowly flowed from her?

The last time I'd seen her barf, she'd gotten carsick all over me in sixth grade. How would I handle caring for her through an illness?

"I'm dying for some chamomile tea," Luna said.

I put my arm around her waist and helped her walk. "Whatever you want, sweetie."

As we made our way toward her house, tears began to sting in my eyes.

Finally, I couldn't take it anymore. "What is it Luna? What's wrong?"

"Evening sickness." Luna lurched forward and threw up into the sewer grate, but when she finally looked up she was smiling. "The thing is…Baby Hughie is going to be an uncle almost as soon as he's born."

~*~

You've reached the confidential line for Pat Goldstein, Psychotherapist. Please leave a message and I'll get back to you as soon as I can.

"Hi, this is Sunny St. Clair," I said, trying to sound casual. "I was referred to you by Dr. Kachina's office. I'm calling because I have this nervous rash I want to talk to you about. Actually, I probably should also come in because a lot is going on in my life, but I probably need to schedule this a while out. I'm really busy and sort of broke and..." The machine cut me off before I could leave my number.

There was no way to erase my jumbled message.

"It's Sunny St. Clair again. Guess I got cut off. Please call me." Jane from La Mirada might not need a shrink, but Sunny St. Clair from West L.A. definitely did.

Abby

WHEN I STEPPED INTO THE GRAY STONE CHURCH, thousands of roses and nearly as many scented candles intoxicated me with the heady scent of true love.

And my lack thereof.

I'd looked forward to Abby's New Year's Eve wedding for almost a year. A year when I'd had a diamond on my finger, the promise of a certain future, menstruating family members, and a medical record that didn't include the word *LOONEY*. At least my Auld Lang Syne would be more exciting than watching Kathy Griffin trying to grope Anderson Cooper while the ball dropped in Times Square.

I spent New Year's Eve afternoon in the bride's room watching in awe as every tendril of Abby's honey blond hair was fussed over, curled, and painstakingly arranged into an effortless looking French Twist. I could barely take my eyes off her as she transformed from an everyday beautiful girl into a stunning bride-to-be, simply by stepping into her grandmother's size-four vintage French lace and seed pearl wedding gown.

My Nana was four-eleven and had a double D cup. Her moth eaten bridal-wear was mail-ordered from Sears and lay molding in a trunk in Esther's attic. Not that there'd be much left of it, if and when... I pulled a curly lock of hair and watched it *boing* as I let go. "You are absolutely breathtaking, Abby."

"I can't wait until it's you," she said.

"I think I gave up my chance."

"No way." She bestowed upon me the coveted bridal smile. "I'll be the first guest to dance at your wedding."

Easy for her to say. Abby and Charlie were paired as dance partners in eighth grade cotillion. They waltzed effortlessly from high school boyfriend and girlfriend into college sweethearts, and, soon, husband and wife. She was a princess waiting for the preordained moment when she would marry her prince and live happily ever after.

Kit breezed in from the lobby and stared open-mouthed at Abby, but didn't say anything. She turned to a mirror and examined her plumped cleavage in the black, strapless bodice of her bridesmaid's dress.

Her boyfriend, Philip, couldn't get back from Brussels, Butte, or wherever he was currently working, but Kit seemed relatively unconcerned. She'd already scored some first quarter points with Guy Jackson, Charlie's college roommate, and a third-string Detroit Lion with a tight end.

When she was done admiring herself, Kit looked me up and down. Luckily, she knew to hold her tongue. In a dazzling collection of narrow-hipped bridesmaidens, I was the fuller-figured gal who threatened to ruin the pictures if the dress pulled too tightly across my hips, or if my arms looked like tree trunks—a problem I'd solved by wearing a double set of Spanx.

Without a word, Sylvie Parker, Abby's mother, walked behind me, pinched the edges of my dress together and coaxed the zipper the rest of the way up.

Abby smiled. "You're beautiful, Sunny.

"Who is Alan's lucky stand in for tonight?" Kit stopped herself from touching her up-do which had fallen once already.

"Atlas."

"Oh, good." Kit patted down a scrunched layer of tulle. "I really need to talk to him."

Kit used Atlas as a love bookie, assaulting him for advice on which horses to put the big money on and which to skip, though it was hard to imagine she much followed his advice.

"Your little brother is Atlas St. Clair?" L'Aerie the makeup artist, *née* Larry, blew a final mist of shimmery powder on Abby's cheeks, then set down the jar and flew toward me. "He's so amazing."

Abby smiled. She knew the Atlas phenomenon drove me crazy. "They're twins."

"Don't speak again until you've made it down the aisle, bride." L'Aerie shook a finger at my breathtaking friend, then squeezed a tan blob from a tube and covered my face. "Is Atlas coming tonight?"

"I don't feel his presence, yet."

L'Aerie's eyes grew wide. "Are you psychic, too?"

It didn't take otherworldly abilities to know that Atlas always ran late. "Not exactly."

Abby stifled a chuckle.

Kit stepped behind her and began to fasten the pearl buttons into the silk loops that ran from the base of Abby's neck to well below her bottom.

"Not so rough, Katherine. The pearls will break." Sylvie Parker checked the length of the gown for damage.

"Sorry." Kit's smile looked more like a grimace.

Abby caught my eye. She'd apologized to me over and over after Sylvie insisted Kit serve as maid of honor. Though Abby had been my best friend since our first semester as dorm mates at USC, she'd known Kit since birth. When Kit's mother died in a car accident, Sylvie practically adopted her. We both knew there could be no other maid of honor. I walked over to Abby and hugged her without actually touching her. "I'm so happy for you, Mrs. Charles Crawford."

Abby grasped both our hands. "I love you, guys."

For the first time ever, I saw tears of joy in Kit's eyes.

"Bridesmaids!" The wedding coordinator rushed in waving her clipboard. "I've made a last minute switch and I need you in the foyer." She led me out by the flabby underneath part of my arm. "You are, again?"

"Sunny."

"Sunny," she repeated as though she hadn't singled me out to walk slower and not clomp my feet. Twice. "I've decided to change the procession order. You go first."

"First?" I pointed to Sylvie Parker's current best friend's daughter. "She should go first."

The wedding coordinator shook her head and pushed me up to the front of the line. "The balance and height, it's just not working with you in the middle."

The other bridesmaid fell in behind, followed by Charlie's statuesque cousin. Kit hung toward the back.

"Much better," she pronounced. "Groomsmen, stay as you were."

My new escort was Abby's nondescript cousin Ted who gave a little wave from his hip.

I looked down at my French manicure and my lonely ring finger.

Other than the fuzzy mustache which, I decided, fell into the hipster category, he wasn't bad looking.

I smiled back at him as Charlie made his way over from the front doors of the church and stood next to Guy. He pulled a pack of mints from inside his jacket and passed them around.

Kit popped an Altoid into her mouth and tucked the pack back into Charlie's tuxedo jacket. "I need to talk to you for a minute."

"Obviously, this isn't a good time, Kit." Charlie turned toward his brother.

"Just for a second," she said tugging his sleeve until he followed. "It's important."

Hopefully she was planning some sort of surprise for Abby and not harassing Charlie with questions about Guy Jackson. Out of the corner of my eye, I watched Charlie dig the toe of his patent leather loafer into the grouted corner of the stone wall as he listened to Kit. He never looked at her face as he shook his head a few times and walked away.

A moment later, "Jesu, Joy of Man's Desiring" filled the church. The groomsmen filed to the right hand doors. As Charlie rejoined his entourage, he peered back at Kit in the open doorway to the bride's room then turned away quickly when Sylvie Parker appeared beside her.

~*~

Tiny crystals shimmered off Abby's dress with the light of each passing candle.

Mr. Parker lifted Abby's veil, kissed her briefly and handed her to Charlie.

Mrs. Parker made tiny choking sounds as Kit arranged the train then stood motionless, looking toward a stained glass depiction of Jesus on the cross.

"Isn't Abby a gorgeous bride?" Ted whispered, tickling my ear with his mustache.

"Amazing," I whispered through my bridesmaid smile.

As Ted and I stood together with our arms entwined, I barely noticed time pass. It seemed like mere seconds from the procession to the moment Abby and Charlie extinguished their single candles and lit the brilliant center candle of unification until the joy of their fateful kiss. Tears ran down my face as the newest Mr. and Mrs. Crawford took the first steps together of their married life.

"I was glad to be paired with you," Ted said, drying his eyes unabashedly. He held my hand and we walked back down the aisle as a couple until we got separated in the crowd that had gathered in the foyer.

I spotted Atlas with a starstruck L'Aerie and Edmund who had him pinned in the corner.

"Doesn't your sister look breathtaking with the right makeup?" L'Aerie asked as I joined them.

"She is breathtaking." Atlas nodded and smiled. *Edmund and L'Aerie aren't even gay. Business ploy.*

"Ugh," I said, stifling a chuckle. "I have to go do pictures."

"I'll see you at the reception."

~*~

An hour and countless photos later, I finally reached my spot at the head table. Atlas had finished his salad and was working his way through mine.

I reached over him, grabbed one of his heart-shaped Godiva chocolates, and popped it in my mouth.

"Heartbreaker." Atlas raised his wineglass to Abby and Charlie then glanced at Kit as she pushed closer to Guy on the dance floor.

Charlie took Abby's hand and led her out for a dance. They sailed across the room with the effortless grace of true love. I couldn't help but wonder if I'd ever find my Charlie?

"Will you ever find your Sunny?" Atlas asked. "That's the bigger question."

I lifted the fork from Atlas's hand and reclaimed the last bites of my salad. "I know exactly who I am."

"Really, Jane from La Mirada?"

"I wouldn't have to pretend to be someone I'm not if you'd just talk to me the way you talk to everyone else. Why didn't you tell me that Luna was pregnant?"

"What would you have done if I had?"

"Helped her."

"By freaking out and acting like Dad?"

"I wouldn't have done that."

"Sunny, Luna needs you. And believe it or not, you need her."

"Luna needs a winning lottery ticket or, better yet, a job." I searched the room for Ted. "What I need is a family who at least strives to be half-normal and a new boyfriend."

"So you say."

"And what do you mean by that?"

"Atlas St. Clair. We're all dying to meet you at my table." One of Sylvie Parker's oh-so-proper friends rushed over and grabbed my brother by the hand.

I was left with an angry lump in my throat and a handful of red-wrapped Godiva.

I scanned the crowd and finally spotted Ted.

He waved and started toward me until an elderly aunt pulled him in the opposite direction.

I stuffed the chocolates in my clutch and set out for the ladies room. As I made my way past the guest tables, old ladies smiled and mouthed "hello." I was a wedding day celebrity. I nodded to each one and finally made it out into the lobby and down the hall to a ladies' lounge with a row of self-contained toilet rooms. Patrons could tend to necessary business without concern that an untoward noise or unseemly odor would be traced to their red-soled pumps, dangling a telling inch from the floor.

I closed the wooden door to my personal sanctuary, arranged some toilet paper on the seat, and lifted my skirt carefully.

Will you ever find your Sunny?

The door to the restroom opened and closed. I waited silently in my stall so I wouldn't have to chat up some senile relative while I had mascara running down my face.

"Sylvie didn't miss a detail," a voice said, then ran the tap. The wicker towel-bin snapped open and closed.

I tiptoed to the edge of my stall.

"Of course not. She's been planning this day for a good twenty years."

55

I leaned my head against the wood and peered through a narrow slat. A handsome woman in an aubergine cocktail dress was brushing color on her thin lips.

"Rumor has it the Crawford wandering eye is an inherited trait."

"Charlie?"

"Seems so."

"What did you hear?"

"Laurel Moss came early. Apparently, she saw something curious in a parked car in the church lot."

"As in?"

"The young lady was wearing ivory tulle."

"Not surprised." The gray-haired woman shook her head. "I do hope Abby holds up. She's such a sweet thing."

"Sylvie'll see to it. After all, she's finally adding a Crawford to the family tree."

"I'm sure you're right. If only the Crawfords had a daughter."

"Stop dreaming, Ruth."

They giggled. Compacts snapped closed, and their heels clicked in unison toward the lobby.

My fingers and toes felt cold. There had to be some sort of mistake. Maybe Charlie had to retrieve a dress from the car or it was some sort of optical illusion. Two bridesmaids were married, the other his cousin.

That only left Kit.

Even she wouldn't go that far.

There had to be a logical explanation.

I forgot to glance at my hair or makeup before I started back to my table.

As Charlie and Abby swirled around the parquet, Kit sat on the other side of the raised dais, looking somber.

Guy headed toward her with two glasses of wine. On his way past the dance floor, Guy stopped Abby for a kiss on the cheek. He was roughly the same height and description as Charlie. Predictably, Kit had already taken Guy for a test drive. A wave of relief washed over me as I made my way back to my brother. Whoever Laurel Moss was, she needed glasses.

I sat down before my surf and turf and smiled at Atlas as I sliced some steak and stuffed a steaming chunk into my mouth.

"Don't torture me, Sunny. I'm just trying to help you." He wiped the mascara smears from under my eyes with his thumb then blew a kiss to Abby as she waited for Charlie to rejoin her at the table.

"I just want to be happy, Atlas."

"But you search for it in the eyes of everyone else."

Abby smiled at us.

I thought I saw an odd look sweep across Atlas's face but it disappeared into his crooked smile. "This has gotten way too serious for New Year's Eve. Let's dance."

Ted caught my eye from the edge of the dance floor while he chatted with some friends. "Maybe I should wait a while in case..."

"Ribbit." Atlas laughed and extended his hand to Kit.

~*~

Abby held the bouquet above her head and approached the podium.

Ted, who'd made his way over to where I was, pressed his hand against my back and nudged me toward my trampling death.

"Bouquet tosses are not for me." Even with the promise of Ted, I didn't savor the idea of being pushed, clawed, and clomped by a swarm of former debutantes in sharp-heeled pumps.

"Go, ahead." He looked deeply into my eyes and smiled. "You never know what the Big Guy has planned."

The Big Guy?

"I'm in no hurry to get married," I said. The truth was unimportant, especially at first. The magazines always said a wedding was the best place to meet a guy unafraid of commitment. As an added plus, Ted was Abby's cousin.

Atlas's back faced the dance floor. As usual, a crowd was gathered around him and I couldn't read his face for a sign.

"You can do it." Ted pushed me on the dance floor and gave what looked like the Black Panther solidarity fist.

I took my place toward the back with a group of fiftyish divorcées clutching wineglasses.

Ruth, with the stylish gray bob, whispered to a friend, then gestured in my direction. Had she spotted me coming out of the restroom? What if she thought I was the bridesmaid in the back of the car? A cold sweat moistened the nape of my neck.

An elbow dug into my side.

"Excuse me, dear." An attractive middle-aged woman in a purple cocktail dress pushed me. "You're still young. I need to catch this thing."

"Gwen, don't push her out of the way. My Ted seems to have his eye on her." Ruth appeared at her side.

"All's fair in love and war," Gwen said.

I was pushed forward into the crowd by Ted's mother's friend.

"Here we go," Abby said into the mike. She turned around and tossed the bouquet backward.

After a hopeful moment filled with bows, hair, flailing body parts, and the combined stink of perfume, hair spray, and failing deodorant, there was a scream of delight.

Standing in the spot where I'd been shoved from seconds before, a seven-year-old flower girl held up her bouquet in triumph.

I turned and glanced back at Ted.

He was checking his fly.

Peter

I GLANCED AT THE PHONE AGAIN. IT HAD BEEN OVER TWELVE hours since we counted down to midnight, Ted kissed me, we said goodnight, and he vowed to call "soon."

Not that I really expected to hear from him quite so soon.

In the meantime, Guy's formalwear made a breadcrumb path to Kit's bedroom and her empty bridesmaid's dress stood like a mound of vanilla ice cream, the bodice like dark chocolate drizzle.

My stomach growled. I left my study materials on the couch and searched the refrigerator for something more interesting than an expired package of ham and a jar of pickles. I'd already blown my diet for the weekend. How much collateral damage could a pint of Haagen-Dazs, a bit of whipped cream, caramel sauce, and nuts do? And the banana was healthy. If I started on a diet first thing Monday morning, I could lose two or three pounds by the time I had my first date with Ted.

I grabbed the car keys and headed for the store.

The terms of my car lease specified that the interior and exterior had to be in good condition or I would be penalized. I'd intended to have the car cleaned regularly on my way home from work, but bad traffic and long lines kept me away. As I turned right on Sawtelle, empty frozen yogurt cups collided with plastic spoons that were brown with congealed chocolate and strawberry non-fat. I couldn't put off a wash any longer.

There was an open car wash on Olympic, so I pulled in, hopped out before the vacuum guys could associate me with untidy new wheels, and rushed in to pay.

"Lady, you didn't leave the keys." An attendant chased me inside with his pad and a pen. "You want The Works on that Audi, don't you?"

"How much is The Works?"

"Includes Armor All," he bellowed, so the manager would hear his pitch.

"Just a wash will be fine."

Everyone in the checkout line turned to view me, an unfit auto mother, neglecting her metal baby.

"You sure?"

"Alright. Go ahead." I handed him my keys then tried to blend in by examining a wall filled with air fresheners. I lifted a paper lemon off the hook and took a nauseating sniff.

"Not so good?" A deep voice asked from beside me.

I relaxed the muscles in my face so I wouldn't look like I'd sucked on the lemon, then snuck a sideways glance as I reached for a paper pinecone.

He had hazel eyes.

"What's your favorite?"

"Enchanted Forest, I suppose." As I replaced the pinecone back on its display tree, my hand slipped. A harvest of air fresheners toppled to the ground.

"You made your own little enchanted forest," he said, watching me crouch down for a second before handing me a pile of musk-scented trees, green castles, and a choke-cherry-scented paper silhouette of a naked woman with giant breasts and high heels.

"Thanks for your help," I said, my face flushing as we walked together, or maybe just at the same time, to the counter.

"Ladies first." As he stepped back, his left hand grazed my back.

No ring.

I decided the year was off to a promising start as I handed my credit card to the cashier.

She looked at the imprint then turned it over to check the signature. "Short for Sunshine?"

"I go by Sunny."

He glanced over my shoulder at my Visa as he fiddled with a Porsche key chain.

Why couldn't Esther have named me Jane?

"Sunny St. Clair. Sounds like a movie star." He offered his hand and held on to mine for an extra second or two. "Peter."

I giggled as I signed my credit card draft.

The cashier rolled her eyes.

Peter pulled a soft-looking brown wallet from his brushed twill trousers and placed a platinum American Express card on the counter. Peter Woods.

Delineating only the P and the W, he signed fast, put his hand on my back, and held open the door. A whoosh of moist car wash air blew my hair into his face.

"Sorry." I tried to knot my mane behind my head.

"No problem." He touched a loose curl and flicked it lightly. "I like your curls."

His strawberry blond hair was cropped short.

"It's kind of a pain to manage."

Peter looked deep into my eyes and smiled.

I put my shoulders back and stood up straight as we strolled under an awning to watch the workers labor in the sun over a row of expensive cars.

A Mercedes, a new Honda Accord, a Dodge Charger, and a BMW convertible lined the blacktop. The only other car was a Range Rover with a car seat in back. Was he a ringless daddy?

A worker waved a towel over his head by the Rover.

"Come on Cedric." A woman grabbed the chocolaty hand of her little boy who was amusing himself by rolling M&M's back and forth on the concrete and smashing them into the cracks.

Peter leaned toward me, narrowly missing the chocolate smear destined for his white shirt.

The mother scoured Cedric with a wet wipe from her tote bag then whisked him into his car seat.

"I would never let my kids make a mess like that."

"You have kids?" he asked.

"Oh, no. I meant if..."

Peter turned to watch as a worker pulled my shimmering Audi into the last

61

open drying spot.

"Yours?"

I nodded.

"Cool car."

The monthly payment had been well worth a moment like this.

A worker whistled by the Mercedes sedan. A tall man, who looked eerily like Abe Lincoln, tipped the attendant, folded himself into the car and drove off.

That left the BMW, the Charger, and the Honda.

"Do you live around here?" I asked, feeling anything but scintillating.

"I'm in the hills." He eyed the worker running a final check on the Dodge.

I glanced toward the BMW to see if he would look at it too.

He did.

The worker assigned to the champagne-colored convertible waved his rag in the air.

Peter reached into his pocket and pulled out a five and a business card. "Sunny, listen, I'm afraid I'm in a hurry." He handed me his card and touched my arm lightly. "Call me." He sauntered over and handed the bill to the worker. He climbed into the Beemer and waved as he rolled out of the parking lot.

As soon as I was out of rearview, I glanced at his card. *Peter Woods Enterprises*. The post office box was in Encino, but the area code was 310.

A banana split was suddenly out of the question. I ran my hands through my now beautiful curls as I planned my low-cal grocery list and waited for my cool car.

~*~

The blinking light from our landline answering machine filled the room when I returned home. I put my bag of groceries in the kitchen as I listened to the messages.

You have two new messages.

Saturday 4:23 P.M.: Hi girls. It's Abby. Charlie and I wanted to thank you again for everything. An airport loudspeaker blared in the background as Charlie chimed in. Hey Ted, if you're there, way to go buddy!

Charlie! Abby giggled. He'd never do that. We'll call as soon as we get back. Love you.

Saturday 5:01 P.M.: Kit, Philip. I got the message that you've lost your cell phone again. Please find it and call me back when you do. In the meantime, I made reservations for dinner on Saturday the sixteenth when I get back. Wear the black dress. See you, babe.

I shook my head. Not only was it unsurprising that Kit had lost her phone again, but that she was in bed with some guy, and missed talking to Philip about what could be her long-awaited proposal dinner. I jotted a note on a piece of paper in red pen. *Kit, there's an important message for you on the machine. Please listen ASAP.*

I started toward her bedroom door with the paper and a piece of tape. What if she listened while Guy was in earshot? I went back into the living room and added, *from a Philip Gates.*

The headboard banged rhythmically against the kitchen wall, so I decided to leave the note on the table by the phone instead.

Bernie

MY CELL PHONE RANG MONDAY EVENING AS I WALKED IN THE door from work.

Ted Parker.

"Hey, Ted," I said, managing to sound cool and collected as I settled on the couch to slip off my pumps.

"How was the rest of your weekend?" he asked.

"Nice."

"I hope you got outside. It was beautiful."

"Sure was," I agreed.

"I took my church youth group on a hike near Carlsbad on Sunday." He spoke slowly, enunciating each word.

Church youth group? Did he know I was Jewish? St. Clair always threw people off. At least I knew why he didn't call on Sunday morning. "I haven't been hiking in—"

The doorbell rang. "Ted, can you hang on for a second? Someone's at my door."

I popped off the couch and peeked through the curtains expecting a solicitor. Instead, my father was on the landing, forty-five minutes ahead of schedule.

My father thumped again. "Sunny!"

"Coming, Daddy."

His conference on genital warts must have let out early. My father was the keynote speaker at a symposium on annoying but non-fatal sexually transmitted diseases. I suspected his wealth of knowledge hailed less from his day-to-day OB/GYN practice than his after-hours research.

"Ted, I'll just be a second." I'd waited a whole weekend for his call. I covered the mouthpiece with one hand as I flipped the dead bolt and twisted the doorknob.

Bernie opened the squeaky aluminum screen and locked me in an arm's length hug. He ran his hands through his wavy salt and pepper hair before adding a half-hearted air kiss.

"I'm just finishing up a phone call." I motioned him to sit on one of the matching leather cigar chairs Kit bought at a scratch-and-dent sale at the Pacific Design Center. "Sorry, Ted. My father just stopped by."

"Do you have to go?"

"In a minute."

"It's nice you have such a close family. Is everyone as colorful as Atlas?"

Bringing Ted home for dinner at Esther's was out of the question, at least until we were married. "They're an interesting bunch."

My father raised an eyebrow and dumped a stack of notepads shaped like birth control pills with matching pens onto the dining room table.

If you could keep him quiet, at least Bernie looked socially acceptable.

"Anyway, where were we?" I wasn't anxious to analyze my family with "exhibit A" milling around the living room.

"I was telling you about my youth group hike yesterday. I'm the outdoor activities director at my church." Ted said.

"That's great."

Bernie pointed to his watch, headed for the kitchen and opened the refrigerator. He stuffed a slice of ham into his mouth, chewed for a second then spit the mouthful into the trash.

"I'm an outdoors and sports fanatic," Ted continued.

He needed to cut the small talk and ask me out quick or Bernie was going to freak out waiting. "It's been a while since I've been hiking, but I really enjoy the outdoors," I said.

"Oh, really?" Dad shook his head then leaned under the kitchen tap for a palette cleansing drink.

My one and only hiking experience coincided with my short-lived stint as a Girl Scout. I signed up just in time for the yearly camp-out by forging Esther' signature. I knew she'd never agree to let me participate in an activity that required conformist uniform wearing. After convincing Bernie that I needed fifty dollars for a Weekly Reader series entitled, "One Hundred Epic Works of Literature for Third Graders," I purchased my coveted green ensemble and an approved GSA camping set then headed for the overnight hike.

If I hadn't come home from my "sleepover" at a friend's house with virulent poison ivy, Esther might never have suspected I'd earned my outdoor cooking and nature badge in one evening. As punishment, she banned me from organized after-school activities for the rest of the year. She couldn't bring herself to expose me to Bernie's wrath for lying about money, so she went to the library and checked out *War and Peace, A Tale of Two Cities,* and *The Complete Works of William Shakespeare.* Together we skimmed for pithy phrases. Bernie was delighted when I advised Luna to "Get thee to a nunnery."

Clearly, Luna ignored the Bard's advice. For my part, I never had the occasion or the real desire to hike or camp again.

"I'd love to take you on a hike sometime," Ted said.

But maybe with Ted...

"I have to come up to L.A. this weekend for a leader's conference on Sunday. How about Saturday?"

"Sure." What was a leader's conference?

Bernie motioned for me to wrap it up.

"Ted, can I call you back a little later or tomorrow and we can finalize plans?"

"I'll just come up first thing Saturday morning and we'll go from there."

"Sounds fun."

"Get your camping gear organized."

As though I had any. "Great."

"Jesus, you're always on the phone," Bernie said as I hung up.

"I have a date with someone new."

"You don't need to date."

"I do if I ever want to get married."

66

"Marriage is for morons." Bernie tugged a white cloth hankie from his pocket and honked into it loudly. "Besides, you're a big-time lawyer. Get changed. I'm hungry."

I tried not to smile. Dad had never called me a big-time lawyer to my face. He didn't quite know about the first bar results, but hopefully, I'd pass it this time and he'd never know. After all, my test results paled in comparison to the information Luna and Esther had in store. "I just need to throw some jeans on. Give me a second."

Maybe I would mention the car after I passed the bar.

Bernie glanced out the window. "Do you think the Mercedes is safe parked in this neighborhood?"

"Mercedes?" I glanced out at a gleaming E320 sedan parked directly in front of the Audi. "You bought a new Mercedes-Benz?"

"I'd never buy a new car. Stupidest thing you can do."

My stomach churned.

And then churned a little more when he added, "I made the brilliant move of picking up this baby from my new baby."

My father had been sampling Mercedes and women for years. His medical practice provided a steady stream of prospective females from which to choose, but he was running out of car dealerships. Every few months he'd make the rounds, looking for a second car and never finding one cheap enough to justify the added insurance cost. Bernie was asked to leave two different showrooms and never return without a signed cashier's check.

He eyed the street. "Well, I guess the moron with the Audi doesn't seem worried. He left the sunroof open."

"I'll be back in a minute." I hurried to my bedroom and shut the door. At least the moron had activated her alarm system.

"Meet me outside." Bernie clomped across the hardwood and out the door.

I forced myself over to the dresser for a pair of jeans and a top. If I was a big time lawyer, why was I so afraid of my father? He'd forget that I was a double idiot when he heard about Luna. I scratched my legs and arms, threw on my clothes and forced myself out the door and down the stairs. "Sorry it took me so long."

Bernie pointed to his Mercedes. "Sweet, huh?"

I didn't care about the details of the car or its purchase though I was sure to hear them repeated *ad nauseam* for years to come. "Congratulations, Dad."

"Would you believe this baby was gathering dust in a garage? Never suffered so much as a scratch." He had the audacity to lean against the Audi, albeit lightly, as he admired the gun-metal metallic paint on his new car.

Please don't set off the alarm.

I looked into the front window and feigned interest. "It's beautiful."

"I hit the ball over the fence this time. Found a low mileage German touring sedan fully loaded. The widow came at no extra charge."

I rubbed my eyebrow with my finger but stopped when I noticed my father brushing a bushy brow with his pinkie.

"In for her annual exam." Bernie gave a little wink. "A young widow. Couldn't bear to drive the old guy's wheels. She made me a screaming deal. No pun intended."

"Must have been fate," I said to derail him from the inevitable TMI moment.

"Someday, when you've paid your dues, you might earn the right to drive a nice car." Bernie pushed his muscular frame off the Audi while I prayed again that the alarm wouldn't sound. "Overpriced piece of shit."

The car was true to me and remained silent.

"Hop in." He opened the back door of the Mercedes and pulled out a stuffed carryall.

"Why the luggage?"

"Penny's meeting me in town later." He climbed into the driver's seat and lowered a pair of Ferrari sunglasses from atop his head. "We're staying at the Four Seasons for a few days."

"The Four Seasons?" How had this Penny transformed my father from the world's most penurious vacationer?

"The conference is paying for the room."

I opened the passenger door and stretched out across the supple leather. The stale odor of Penny's late husband's forever-extinguished cigar permeated the passenger cabin.

"Hand me my cell, would you, Sunny?"

As I pulled the phone from the console and gave it to my father, I realized I'd left my cell in the apartment.

He was dialing before I could tell him I needed to run back inside. "Hi, darling."

Darling? Maybe I did need to meet her.

"What time can you get to the hotel?" Bernie, who seemed to be in a love trance as he listened to her answer, slid the car into reverse.

There was a lurch.

Followed by a horrible metal crunch.

I rocked forward against the dash then careened back into the passenger seat. The alarm wailed like an angry baby. The lights flashed.

"My car." All three of us yelled in unison over the *MEEP, MEEP, MEEP.*

"Your car? This isn't your car, it's mine." Bernie screamed at Penny and me.

"My car." I pulled at the door handle.

MEEP, MEEP, MEEP.

"I'll call you back." Bernie killed the engine. "Sunny, what the hell are you talking about? Your car?"

I lifted the lock and released myself from the passenger cabin. "It's mine."

A wave of disgust crossed Bernie's face as surveyed the interlocked fenders. "I haven't even made a payment."

"Neither have I."

"What?" He rubbed a patch of navy blue paint from his fender. The Mercedes was otherwise unharmed, but the front of the Audi was smooshed.

"My car." I hugged the Audi. "It's ruined."

He shook his head. "What the hell were you thinking, buying a—"

"Leasing."

He threw his hands in the air. "You can't afford a Goddamn Audi, much less the maintenance."

"Maintenance is free for thirty-six thousand miles."

"Didn't you learn anything I ever taught you?" He shook his head. "You're just like *That Woman.*"

"I'm nothing like Esther." My lips trembled. "And, I'm an adult, you know."

"So you went out and bought a car to prove it?" He walked around to the driver's side. "Give me the keys."

My father surveyed the Audi then hopped into the driver's side.

"Unfuckingbelievable," he muttered as he turned the key. "Come on."

"What about the Mercedes?"

"It'll be here when we get back."

My Dad had mutilated the front of my perfect new car and now he was going to take it for a test drive?

I opened the passenger door, climbed in and stared out the window. "Where are we going?"

"Don't worry about it."

We sat in silence as my father backed up carefully, then zoomed toward Santa Monica Boulevard. He weaved in and out of traffic, fiddled with the sound system, the climate controls and set the cruise. "Hmmppfh."

My hair whipped into my face, but I didn't dare move or utter a word.

He made a few sharp U-turns. "Not bad." He accelerated and headed west toward the ocean. "The safety record on these isn't bad, but they're finicky. What kind of rip-off price did you get suckered into?"

I cleared my throat. "Well, I really shopped around, then waited until the end-of-year lease incentive and made sure about the warranty. They gave me twenty-five hundred for the Honda."

He would never pay me for the damages if he thought I'd bought the car on the spot.

"Not bad, not bad."

"I knew you weren't dumb enough to walk in and ask the salesman to rape you. Those car guys always see you coming." He made a hairpin left into a Red Lobster parking lot.

"The Red Lobster?"

"I have a coupon. I won't have any money after I pay Penny for the Mercedes."

Technically, he was also responsible for the damages to my car. How exactly was I supposed to ask him for his driver's license and insurance information? I summoned all my courage. "Daddy, should I call my insurance company in the morning?" I said in as meek and non-threatening a voice as I could muster.

"Of course you don't call the insurance company. I teach you until I'm blue in the face and still you know nothing. You're a lawyer for Christ's sake. I have a patient whose husband owns a body shop. You'll take it there."

70

"What if I need a rental car?"

"Do I need this aggravation, Sunny?"

"Sorry, Dad." What was I sorry for?

"Why didn't you tell me you were looking for a new car? I'd have helped you negotiate, or made you a deal on the Probe."

~*~

Bernie dropped me home and hurried off to the Four Seasons before I had a chance to rifle through his medical bag for a sedative.

My phone, which was face up on the coffee table, showed one missed call.

From: Patricia Goldstein Psychotherapy.

I listened to her message:

I understand you feel a need to delay our meeting, so I'll check back within a few weeks if I haven't heard from you. In the meantime I have a little exercise for you. I want you to make a list of the reasons you might be resistant to coming in, and we'll talk about it when we meet.

I looked down the hallway into Kit's room, hoping she wasn't home, or wasn't in a snooping kind of mood.

Kit opened her door and popped her head out. "You left your cell on the coffee table."

Ted

WHEN MY ALARM RANG EARLY SATURDAY MORNING, I POPPED out of bed ready for the best therapy of all—a day with Ted. I showered and put on makeup without having to worry about looking Saturday night perfect. Since my hair would take an hour to dry and style, I settled on a red bandanna, tied hiker-girl style around my head.

I went down the checklist I'd copied from an article on outdoor dates— khaki hiking shorts, pale pink T-shirt to reflect and not absorb light, new boots. I didn't have a chance to wear them around for a week to break them in as the clerk recommended, but they felt pretty comfortable anyway.

Maybe I would like hiking.

The doorbell rang at the stroke of 8:00 A.M.

"Ready for some fresh winter air and sunshine, Sunshine?" Ted asked as he leaned against the doorframe. His legs looked cute in his khaki hiker shorts.

I smiled. "Please, call me Sunny."

"Sorry, I thought I heard your Dad call you Sunshine the other day."

"He does, but I wish he wouldn't." I didn't mean to embarrass him and now I was embarrassed. "Would you like a cup of coffee? I was about to make a pot."

"Never touch the stuff."

My stomach grumbled. "Can I get you something to eat?"

72

"I loaded us up with gorp and snacks."

Gorp? I'd pictured our date starting at some roadside diner known amongst the outdoorsy set as *the* place for heaping plates of flapjacks and eggs. It was just as well. I'd only lost one pound on my Ted-date-diet. "Give me a second. I'll just grab something for us to take with."

"It's January. Throw in some long pants and a rain jacket, too."

There wasn't a cloud in the sky. "The weather looks perfect."

"Rule one of hiking: be over-prepared." He tapped his hand against a leather sheath on his belt that housed some sort of huge Bowie knife and a compass.

The mountain man thing did have a certain sexiness.

"I'll be out by the truck re-checking the supplies."

The truck? I glanced out the window. A blue Toyota with a camper shell was parked in front of Bernie's Probe, which I was temporarily saddled with, in lieu of a real rental car. Was there a chance Ted had some sort of sporty sedan for everyday use?

"We should go." Ted headed for the door. "There could be traffic."

"I'll only be a second." I hurried to my bedroom, threw a pair of sweats, clean undies and an anorak in a bag. On my way to the truck, I grabbed a bagel, slathered it with cream cheese, and popped open a can of Diet Coke.

"Lookin' good." Ted surveyed my gear as I reached the truck. His eyes fell to my breakfast as the napkin uncurled from around the bagel.

"Would you like me to grab a bagel for you?

"No thanks." He stared quizzically.

"How about a bite?"

His eyes grew big. "Isn't it Kosher?"

"I have no idea, but if it is, all the better, I guess."

He took a hesitant nibble along the edge. "I don't know many of the rules of Judaism." He pronounced it jew-day-ism.

"If you keep Kosher there are some foods you don't eat. But anyone can have a bagel."

He scrunched his mustache. "I hope I brought enough of the right foods for you."

"I don't keep Kosher, Ted."

"Oh good, then we don't have to worry."

73

Three hours and two small blisters later, I filled my fist with another handful of peanuts, raisins and M&M's. Gorp was really good.

"Let's get moving." Ted sped up on the dusty trail. "We're running way behind schedule."

"Hang on, Ted." Sweat dripped down the center of my back. I already felt out of breath, but didn't dare pant on a date. I took a ladylike glug from the water bottle and reattached it to my hip with a special plastic loop that held the top to the container. "Maybe we could stop for lunch soon?"

The strings from the sleeping bag attached to the bottom of my pack slapped my calves as I hiked. The packs seemed awfully full for a day hike.

"Sunny, we really need to get a move on, or we'll never make the falls before dark. How about stopping for lunch in about a mile? I know a spot where the view is heavenly."

I didn't want to complain, but perhaps I should have bought my boots before Friday and worn them around the house some. "You wouldn't happen to have a Band-Aid or two, you know, just in case?"

"You're carrying it. I never hike without my medical kit." He slapped the pouch of my enormous backpack. "I should lighten your load a little." He reached in, pulled out a cooking pot and an extra bottle of water and handed them to me to stuff into his pack.

"Thanks, Ted." I re-cinched the tie.

"We'll get you into prime hiking shape yet."

Did that mean he wanted to take me hiking again? I slugged up the path over a dusty golden hill with renewed vigor.

"It seems like we have a lot of stuff for a day hike."

"You just never know, it could rain, you could sprain an ankle, we could decide it's so incredible here, we want to stay the night. As long as you have supplies, everything is cool."

I looked at my stiff leather boots. No way my ankle could move, much less twist, and there still wasn't a cloud in the sky. Loud fast flies zipped past my ears. I'd never realized that there was so much nature in Ojai. "I wish I *could* stay but I have a lot of studying to do."

"You couldn't get me to study on a day like this. A beautiful sunny day, a beautiful Sunny." He clasped my hand. "Hiking is the nearest way I know to get closer with God."

The article in outdoorwoman.com warned of this. *Beware, nature boys don't see the outdoors as a bunch of sticks, weeds, and wild animals. He feels confident and manly with that knife strapped to his belt. Your strong silent hiker may let his guard down in the outdoors and let his sensitive side emerge.*

"You know, I don't have a chance to get out and hike too much, but I have to admit my most spiritual thoughts happen outdoors." It seemed kind of corny to say, but Ted smiled, so I smiled back.

He picked a perfect yellow flower that had sprouted in the middle of the trail, ran it under my chin and handed it to me. "It says in Romans, that God is evident in nature. You can't look outdoors and not see the hand of the Creator."

"I've never heard that particular passage." I sniffed the sweet scent and smiled back at Ted. My other spewed proverbs by the Dalai Lama, Buddha, even an occasional Hare Krishna tidbit, but the New Testament rarely figured into her repertoire.

Ted stopped for a moment, reached over and pulled a stray strand of hair from my eye. "Sunny, have you ever considered allowing Jesus Christ into your life?"

Normally, I tried to avoid these sorts of conversations. "You know I'm Jewish, Ted." It wasn't that I wouldn't consider other religious traditions if it was important to Ted and things worked out but...

"As you probably realize, Jesus was born into the Jewish heritage."

I tried to remember anything I'd learned in my one year of Sunday school. "Jews feel that Jesus was a great man and maybe a prophet. We really respect him."

"When you come down to San Diego, I'd love for you to meet the kids in my youth group. They'll adore you."

Was he asking for a second date?

He clasped my hand and we hiked in silence like a couple.

It wasn't that I couldn't believe in Jesus. Luna was basically Buddhist, and Atlas had a whole new religion he followed without even a name. Perhaps we could get all the bases covered so one of us could beg mercy for the other two, if need be. "How much further to the waterfall?"

75

"Another mile or so. Trust me, you'll love it."

My blisters hurt more with each step and my stomach needed something more substantial than trail mix—and soon.

We marched on.

Ted hummed a song I didn't recognize.

I tried not to check my watch, but did anyway. It was already 2:30 P.M. My heels felt on fire and wet at the same time. The burning, raw skin ached with every stride. "Ted, I'm really sorry to make a big thing of this, but I could use the Band-Aids if you don't mind. I have blisters from these darn boots."

"My perfect spot is just up ahead."

I trudged onward in silence, trying not to let the pain show on my face.

Ted pulled a plant from the brush beside the path. "Licorice." He sniffed and put the dirt-covered root under my nose.

"Mmmm." I almost took a bite out of it.

He looked down at my boots. "Did you break them in before you wore them?"

"Sort of, just a few days though."

"And now you're paying the price, sweetie."

He called me sweetie.

"They really hurt?"

I nodded.

"Then we can't let you suffer. Take off your boots over there." Ted pointed to a wide, flat rock that faced a bubbling stream. "Dr. Ted's going to fix you up just right. He removed my backpack and set it upright against a pine tree.

I unlaced my boots. My right boot, like a vacuum seal, made an un-sucking noise as I pulled it off my swollen, aching foot. The circulation rushed back into my left foot as I removed it from the leather. My sweaty socks stuck to my blisters.

"Let me see those tired dogs." Ted reached for my feet.

I stifled a scream as he peeled my socks off and set them out to dry in the sun.

"We'll fix these guys up in a jiff." He examined the giant oozing blisters at my heels. Ted poured water on my feet from an old canteen and carefully patted them dry with a towel he produced from deep in his backpack. He slathered antibiotic ointment and some configuration of moleskin on my heels and massaged my arches gently. "There you go—Good as new."

Ted. Sunny and Ted. Not a bad ring to it.

"Apple?" Ted reached into his pack, pulled out two Red Delicious and threw one in my direction.

I took a big bite and watched Ted check and recheck his watch as he paced back and forth on the path.

"I'm so sorry to slow things down with my blisters."

Ted stopped dead in his tracks. His eyes stared past me. "Don't move." His voice dropped to a whisper.

"What?"

"Don't move and don't turn around."

"What is it?" My heart thumped, but I didn't flinch as adrenaline coursed through my veins.

Ted bent slowly and picked up a long stick from the ground beside him. A split second later he lunged past me to the back of the flat rock where I sat. "Got him."

A giant snake hung at the end of the stick.

I screamed as Ted eased himself off the boulder and examined the writhing snake.

"It's just a bull snake, but I have to admit, I thought I saw a rattler at first." He bowed his head a little and muttered something that sounded like a prayer as he walked over to the trail and tipped the snake onto an exposed bit of dirt. The serpent slithered away at a frightening pace. "It's kind of too bad it wasn't a rattler. We could have added the meat to our menu."

Snake meat?

That was my last thought before everything went dark.

I don't know exactly what happened or how, but when I came to, my head rested in the crook of Ted's arm.

"You'll be okay in a minute." He poured me a sip from his Nalgene bottle. "Lie still."

"What...?"

"Heat and shock." He kissed my forehead. "Put your head back on the sleeping bag. "We'll have lunch here."

"Maybe for our second date, a meal in town might be a better choice."

"Rest. I'll take care of everything."

I watched from my sleeping bag pillow as Ted laid out a feast of cheese and crackers, apples and honey, a plastic tube marked *Peanut Butter*, and Hershey's chocolate kisses. "Only one thing missing." He searched for a moment and produced a large log of Kosher Salami. "I brought it for you."

Ted sliced off two hunks with his pocketknife and handed one to me. "Eat up. You need your strength." He then took a hearty bite of his chunk without removing the casing. "I think I could learn to love Jewish food."

Even though I hated salami, I smiled as I pulled the plastic from around my slice and tried to nibble a bit with my nose closed. "It's great."

"As soon as you feel better, let me know. We still have a chance to make the waterfall."

We ate quickly and then I watched as he packed up the remainder of our lunch, popping a peanut butter covered apple slice into his mouth. I didn't care at all about the waterfall, but Ted had bravely defended my life. "I'm sorry for slowing us down so much."

"It's okay." He squinted toward the sky. "But I think it's going to rain."

~*~

The rain fell fast and hard, jabbing like tiny pins all over my body. Wrapped in my anorak, huddled under a tree, I watched a tent emerge before my eyes.

"Hop in." Ted unzipped the front, which he'd carefully directed away from the wind. "See what I mean. You can never be too prepared."

"What do we do now?" I crouched into the entrance of the tent and deposited my dripping backpack in the corner. "I suppose a campfire is out of the question."

Ted smiled shyly. "We'll keep cozy in here."

"How will we get back to the truck?"

"I don't think it's wise to attempt a four-mile hike in the dark during a storm, so let's enjoy our unexpected evening under the stars."

"Okay," I said.

Okay it wasn't. Ted's definition of cozy involved more than just freeze-dried beef stroganoff, marshmallows, and hot chocolate. I expected inspirational camping songs or ghost stories. Instead, I was treated to Ted's personal rendition of *The Call of the Wild*.

The moment he flipped off the camping lantern I felt his lips moosh against my face. He pulled at my T- shirt. "Oh, Sunny."

"Ted, no." I removed his hand from my breast and pulled my sleeping bag up around my neck. "I don't fool around on the first date."

After Alan, it was a firm rule.

I managed to keep his hands at bay while we he kissed my neck and ran his tongue from my shoulder blade to my chin like a love-deranged monkey.

"You taste so good." He kissed me hard and then shuddered. "You're so beautiful. You smell like fresh rain."

He smelled like wet fur.

"Please, please." He moaned over the patter of rain as it rumpled the tent fabric. "Sunny, I want you so much. It's so right. I know you must feel it, too."

Ted, who was inspired by the creations of God and Jesus when he visited the outdoors, had transformed into a wild beast. I felt no safer in the tent than outside the zippered nylon with the identifiable predators. "Ted?"

"Hmm?" His tongue paused a moment.

I held his face in my hands and looked into his eyes. "I'm very attracted to you, but you're going too fast. I don't usually spend the night with someone on a first date."

Ted leaned forward and kissed each of my eyes. "Sunny, look at everything that's happened: the flat tire, your blisters, the snake, and a miracle rainstorm out of nowhere. It was all by design. You *have* to see that."

"I'll admit a lot of unexpected things did happen today." Was Abby's cousin just another horny toad, disguised as a prince?

Ted put his arms around me, buried himself in my chest and made a pout that morphed into a suckle. "It's all I ever hear, 'not yet Ted.' I thought you were different."

"Excuse me?" My neck felt like a glazed donut.

"I didn't mean it like that." He put his arms around me and pulled me close. "It's just, you have so much spirit. I just want you so much I can barely stand it." He ran his hands over me then hugged me tight. "You're so soft."

"Ted, I didn't say never." We were stuck in the middle of nowhere together. I didn't want to be mean. "Just not yet."

Ted unzipped my sleeping bag all the way and pushed his body close to mine. "So good, so good," he moaned. "Doesn't it feel so good?"

"Yes, Ted, but I have to... I have to pee."

Ted sighed, then handed me a roll of toilet paper and a flashlight. "Hurry back."

Luckily, the rain had stopped as I unzipped my way into the cool night in my Adidas sweats and T-shirt. Scanning the campsite for shiny pairs of eyes, I spied a split trunk tree close to the tent, but not so close that Ted might hear any inappropriate bodily noises.

I squatted backward over the forked limbs and managed to keep my shoes and panties dry as tinkle splashed to the ground in a thundering flood certain to arouse the curiosity of sharp-toothed beasts. At least I wasn't having my period. I'd read somewhere that mountain lions were attracted for miles by the scent of blood.

Something rustled in a nearby bush.

I wiped, tossed the toilet paper behind the tree, hauled my pants up and ran back to the tent. Perhaps, Ted was safer after all.

"Come here." He had zipped our sleeping bags together. "I'll take care of you, sweetie."

I did like the feel of his hairless chest and sinewy arms as he spooned me. "Just behave, okay?" I ignored the lump he pressed against the top of my hamstring, and I closed my eyes.

He kissed my hair as I tried to go to sleep.

I couldn't sleep with his hot breath wafting in my face.

Ten minutes passed and only my arm was asleep. I shook it then tried not to react to the pins and needles.

"You look like an angel." He whispered, rolling on top of me and pressing his chest into mine. Our teeth banged together as he rolled his tongue around my mouth like a washing machine agitator. He lifted up, put his hand in my shirt and kneaded my right breast. The weight of his body squashed my left one like a pancake.

"I need you. I need this," he whispered between sweeps through my mouth. A hand burrowed between my legs. "I want you so much. Oh, please."

"Ted." It came out as a moan, though I'd intended to sound stern and forceful.

He rubbed against my leg. His boxers no longer contained his intentions. "See what you've done to me?"

I closed my eyes and ignored the excess production of his salivary glands. "Please, please."

We wrangled as we kissed. Ted kept pressing against me and rubbing. He begged and begged. Never had anyone beseeched so passionately, for so long.

I don't know whether it was the sheer force of his desire, the biological effect on me of Ted's constant friction, or the fact that I felt like prey trapped in a nylon web accepting the ultimate will of nature, but I finally gave in. "Do you have any, you know, protection?"

"I do, I do." He lunged for the outer zipper of his pack and opened a squashed but sealed package of Trojans. *Always be over-prepared.* How long had he carried the box around hoping for a lucky camping trip?

He dropped his boxers, fumbled with the package and dropped the condom onto the floor of the tent. "Darn. I guess I'd better get another one."

I nodded. Was it too cruel to back out?

"Could you not look? It's making me nervous."

"Sorry." I stared down at my sweatpants. Maybe it *was* too cruel.

Ted flipped on the flashlight and tore open another. His erection made a substantial reflection against the wall of the tent.

I couldn't decide whether to take off my clothes or wait for Ted. With the snap of latex, a thought of Jim Wolfe flashed through my head. What if I was stuck in a tent with him instead? I closed my eyes and pretended Ted was Jim.

"Here we go." The sleeping bag rustled as Ted moved toward me. He pounced on top of me, lifted my shirt and pulled off my sweats in one frantic motion.

There was no time to position myself in a figure-flattering way or move out of a bad slice of moonlight. Ted was nursing my left breast and pushing my legs open like a wishbone before we'd even kissed again. He held his penis like a sword and rammed it too far forward, readjusted, struck again and hit the side of my leg.

I took a deep breath, reached my hand down, and guided him to the right spot.

"Oh Lord, thank you." He pushed into me for five epileptic seconds, uttered a giant "Yiahhhhhhhhh," then broke into a sweat and collapsed on top of me.

Quick Draw McGraw. I'd never truly understood what it meant before.

He'd been so concerned about my well-being all day but he didn't seem to realize...

"Ted?" I pushed on his chest to prevent suffocating.

Ted rolled off and turned away. "I'm sorry, Sunny."

I didn't want to insult him. "It's okay."

I heard the rubber stretch as he removed the condom and placed it somewhere I didn't want to think about.

"It happens." It was selfish of me to think of my pleasure when he was so obviously embarrassed by his performance. I rubbed his back.

He recoiled.

"I shouldn't have pushed it. I knew it was wrong."

"Ted, it's really okay." I'd read that men's self-esteem could be affected long term from these situations. "Maybe we should try again." I didn't want to in the first place and there I was offering myself again, but it seemed like the right thing to do.

"I'm sorry, I'm so sorry," he said into my ear over and over as he rubbed his body against mine.

I felt him grow again as he pushed his groin against my stomach. "But you feel so good..."

The second time was not as quick, though I wish it had been.

~*~

The next morning, Ted barely spoke as he pulled the metal stakes from the ground. The tent collapsed in a heap.

I sat on a nearby rock and stuffed the sleeping bags back into their separate sacks. "Is there anything else I can do?"

"You've done enough." Ted packed away our temporary home as though it had never existed.

I fought back tears and confusion as I swallowed a handful of trail mix crumbs and washed it down with a plastic-flavored gulp from my water bottle.

"We have to get moving." He loaded his pack and looked past me down

82

the trail. "I need to check in at my leader's conference by ten. As it is, there's no way I'm going to make it."

I laced up my boots and prepared to load the pack on my back. It was only 6:00 A.M., after a sleepless night a rigorous hike was still ahead. Did post-coital humiliation qualify me for rescue helicopter pick up? I checked my cell phone. There was no signal.

Ted started on the trail before I even snapped the hip belt around my waist. He looked as ragged and depressed as I felt.

"Wait up, Ted, I'm going as fast as I can."

Ted examined something in the brush and kicked his shoe in the dirt. "I'm sorry, Sunny."

"You don't need to apologize again." I readjusted my scrunched shirt from under the waist belt of the backpack. I didn't try to hide that I was winded.

His voice quavered. "I guess even Samson couldn't stand up to Delilah."

"It's okay. It happens to everybody." He was more embarrassed than I thought. "The second time was better."

"I'm so weak."

He took off down the path.

I chased behind praying I would wake up in my bed with fleeting memories of a Ted nightmare. As I jogged down the trail, the moleskin lifted from both of my ankles and wadded into lumps at the bottom of my socks.

Ted's legs, which looked muscular and cute on the way up, seemed fuzzy and bony as he raced ahead of me. His butt stuck out. Sweat stains formed half-moons under his arms.

I couldn't wait to get home and take a shower.

"Ted," I called between side cramps.

He was far enough ahead that he didn't seem to hear me.

I hiked the last mile of the trail totally alone.

When I finally reached him, Ted silently removed my backpack and tossed it into the bed of the truck. Tears streamed down his face as he opened my door and went around to the driver's side.

For the first time in my life, I seriously considered hitchhiking. Instead, I slid into the passenger seat and tried to think of something more fitting to say than *I really want to die*. "Ted, we're just human."

"And easily swayed by the weaknesses of the flesh." He closed his eyes and bowed his head in prayer before turning the key in the ignition. "It wasn't supposed to be like this."

I put my hand on his shoulder. As he recoiled, a jolt rushed through me. Maybe Ted wasn't suffering from performance anxiety at all. The words flew out of my mouth before I could censor them. "Ted, are you... I mean, were you... Have you never...?"

He began to sob. "I'm turning twenty-seven next week and I'm still not married. I just couldn't wait anymore."

My first time, I was seventeen and a senior. Clark Stapleton, a Junior College engineering major, told me to get undressed and prepare to make love. I dutifully removed my clothing, folded them on his bedroom chair, got under the covers and waited. As Clark described the technical details of the event destined to take place in mere moments, I suspected it wasn't going to be like in the movies.

He removed his clothing under the covers so as not to scare me then guided my hand to "his member," which was not nearly the banana-sized appendage I'd expected. "I know it seems large to you, but actually I'm just average." He kissed me clinically and proceeded with his demonstration of the facts of life.

I was bored, but not ashamed.

"How can I face them today?"

"The leaders?"

"I'm so weak. I'm such a hypocrite. I meant to wait until I got married, but you were so close, and you smelled so good, and the rain, the tent."

He weaved into the next freeway lane.

For the rest of his life I would be his secret shame. My stomach churned. What could I possibly say that would make him feel better? "God will forgive you."

Ted looked dubious and stared straight ahead unblinking.

I looked out the side window as Ted pushed his preset radio buttons to a Sunday sermon that, of course, had to mention the word fornication.

The distance from Ojai to West L.A. never seemed longer.

If only my splitting headache could have started twelve hours earlier...

Kit

"THANKS AGAIN FOR THE HIKE," I MUMBLED.

Ted stood with me at the threshold of my apartment. He held my bag of damp clothing.

I pushed my front door open and prayed for a painless goodbye.

Kit sat on the couch, facing us.

No such luck.

"I was half an hour away from calling the police." She glared at Ted like he was a convicted rapist.

He grasped the doorknob and gazed down at his boots, unable to make the quick escape he'd certainly planned. "We got trapped in a rainstorm."

"I'm sorry, Kit. Ted was running late this morning for his conference so we didn't think to call on our way back."

She gave my dirty sweats and tangled hair the once-over and resumed her evil eye gaze on Ted.

"Sunny was totally safe." Ted stammered as he avoided Kit's accusing glare. "We set up my tent to wait out the storm. By the time it ended, it was too dark to hike down."

Kit raised an eyebrow. "I thought you were dead."

"Sorry." Ted fiddled with his pocketknife. "There's no way to predict the will of nature."

Kit took a dramatic sip from her oversized coffee mug. "I was up all night."

The door to Kit's bathroom flung open. Bill Pogue's bloated belly glistened with water drops. Only a too small towel prevented the horror of full disclosure. "Hey, Sunny."

My jaw went slack. "Bill?"

"Bill was worried too." Kit half-smiled. "Weren't you, Bill?"

"It's nice to see Sunny out and about again." He winked. "Kit, how about some java?"

I glanced at Bill who'd begun to air dry into his greasy self as Ted cowered by the door.

Kit shook her head. "Ted, if Sylvie hadn't reassured me you were an experienced outdoorsman, I'd have called out a search party last night."

"You called Sylvie Parker?" I felt ill. The Parkers would think *I* was a dangerous beast.

"I've really gotta go." Ted turned for the door. "Sorry to scare you, Kit." He hung his head and didn't look me in the eyes. "Sunny, allow the Truth into your life."

"Byyyeee," Kit said as Ted scampered out to his truck. She shook her head and started for the kitchen. "Coming with the coffee, Bill."

I closed the door and slumped to the floor.

"How could you, Kit?"

She shrugged. "He's not married. His wife went back to Japan and took her rice steamer with her. How could you spend a whole evening with Ted?"

She set off for the bedroom before I could formulate a response.

Eventually, I forced myself into the bathroom and tried to drown myself in the shower. When that didn't work, I settled for rubbing my skin raw with oatmeal soap and a loofah.

Before the sting of cleansing and the ache of rolling around in a tent settled into my body, I climbed into bed for a nap. I had nightmares where Abby threw condom packets at me as she cried in disgust.

~*~

"He who lies with the lamb gets dirty."

"What?" I opened my eyes to Kit standing over me, wearing men's boxers and a Detroit Lions T-shirt. Noontime sun flooded my bedroom.

She shook me again then popped a handful of grapes into her mouth. "I figured biblical quotations were your new thing. Get up."

"No." I put the pillow over my head. The ache of pulling and tugging had settled into my breasts and crotch.

"Get dressed. We have a massage appointment in twenty."

"Kit, I'm not going anywhere."

"I pulled a lot of strings to get two last-minute spots."

"I need to study."

"Study tonight." Kit started out of my room. "Get dressed."

When Kit wanted to do something nice, I had no choice but accept. Still, I didn't want to go out with the sin of Ted all over my body. What could I possibly wear that could mask my shame?

Kit sashayed over to my bureau and pulled out the purple yoga pants and matching hoodie she'd given me as a present a Christmas ago. She shook her head as she pulled off the sales tags. "Wear this."

There was no point arguing that the pants made my legs look like water balloons, so I dutifully slid them on and tied the jacket around my waist. I felt like a grape.

"Much better." She looked me over as she pulled my hair back and pinned it up with a clip from my dresser.

At least I was in no danger of attracting any more virgins for the rest of the day. The memory of Ted licking my neck like a puppy should have sent me a giant warning signal. I felt a guilt-tsunami even though I reminded myself that the sex was Ted's idea.

We headed out to the cars.

"I'll drive." Kit jangled her keys as she passed Bernie's Probe. She would sooner die than be seen in such a car but she'd sleep with Bill Pogue for a close-up look at whoever had played last night at the Bowl.

Kit slid behind the wheel.

"What exactly did you say to Sylvie Parker?" I tried to sound nonchalant.

"Your chin looks red. Were you squeezing again? We should try and get facials while we're there."

"What did you say to Mrs. Parker?" New acne bumps erupted on my face as I spoke.

"I didn't go into the details. Why?"

Kit never didn't go into the details.

She zoomed toward Beverly Hills.

"Does Sylvie know I was out all night with him?"

"What did you want me to do? Call the police?" She leaned on the horn. "I was worried. Your note said day hike."

"It's just that I don't want her to think..."

"What's she going to think? You were with *Ted*. He boycotted the senior prom on moral grounds, for God's sake." She changed lanes to get around a Jetta doing the speed limit.

We drove in silence the rest of the way to Beverly Hills.

Kit slid into a space only a mere step from giant green doors with *GLOW* sprawled across the front in golden cursive. "What a spot! Like Doris Day in those old movies." She hopped out of the car. "They were booked for the lunch service, but I'm going to check on the facials." Kit pulled open the giant golden handle.

"I assume they take credit cards?"

"It's on me." Kit opened her purse and pointed to several hundreds in her wallet.

"Thanks, Kit." Even though her paralegal salary was almost half of mine, her trust fund allowed for endless indulgences that I couldn't afford.

I followed Kit inside.

A stunning receptionist with too much makeup for Sunday morning, and auburn hair extensions gave us both the once-over. "Welcome." She had no inflection to indicate she meant it.

"The reservation is under Purdy—Sunny and Kit."

"Sunny Purdy?" She flashed Kit a smile full of bleached teeth. "You must be new."

"Kit Purdy. I'm a regular. And you are? I haven't seen you here before. The owner is a close family friend."

"I'm Sunny St. Clair." I interjected. Kit's name-dropping wasn't going to help, and I couldn't take any more stress.

"I'm Jennelle." She smiled at me. "Great name. Are you related to Atlas?" She extended her hand.

I nodded.

"I love his show."

Kit flipped her hair. "We'll both have a Pellegrino, and I know where the robes are." Kit took off to the changing lounge.

"She's nice when you get to know her," I whispered to Jennelle before following Kit down the hall. *Was* Kit actually nicer once you got to know her?

"Why didn't you tell me about Ted?" I asked as we changed into thick cotton robes and matching slippers.

"I knew you'd figure out he was a geek soon enough." She stuffed an extra pair of slippers into her tote. "I couldn't believe you accepted a date with him in the first place. All he does is preach. What a bore."

"It wasn't exactly boring." *Why did I say that? Why did I say that? Why did I say that?*

"Oh, really?" Kit grinned.

"You should talk. Bill Pogue?"

"Bill *Gamble* Pogue." Kit giggled. "Actually, it wasn't worth the gamble. He's hung like a mouse." Her laugh echoed. "Now, I know why wifey fled the country."

Kit's disclosure put me at ease and I edged right into her web. "The hike was fun, and Ted wasn't totally boring. He caught a snake."

"Who caught the snake?"

I felt my cheeks heat up.

"Did you...?" Kit asked.

"Did I what?" I asked like a hapless fly, doomed to thrash in her web while I waited for her to eat me. "Don't we need to get out to the lobby? Our appointment was for five minutes ago."

"You fucked him!" Her voice resonated like a megaphone.

"I..." I rushed toward Jennelle. "You don't happen to have any openings for facials as well, do you?" I screeched more than said, as I ran down the hallway.

"He was Pasadena's most renowned virgin!" She laughed from deep in her throat. "Oh, my God, this is great!"

"Shhhh." I put my hand over Kit's mouth to stifle the sounds, but her choking noises grew even louder.

Jennelle tried to pretend she hadn't heard and gazed meaningfully into the appointment book.

As soon as I let go she barked, "You devirginated Ted Parker?"

Jennelle concealed a giggle. "We're booked, I'm sorry."

"When you didn't come home, Sylvie told me not to worry about your being up in the mountains with him." Kit coughed through her laughter. "Her exact words were, let me think... As you know *Katherine, he is very outdoorsy and unusually pure.* I guess he wasn't so safe with you, tiger."

Jennelle lost her composure and laughed outright.

"It wasn't like that." What was I going to tell Abby? How was I going to get to her before Kit did? And the office? Who wouldn't Kit tell at the office?

"Abby's going to die."

"Kit please, I'm begging you. For once, keep this to yourself. You can't tell Abby!"

"Was it any good?"

I shook my head. "He begged. It was horrible."

"Sure, Jezebel. This is great. You probably forced him."

"No, I just gave in after hours of endless pleading." I fiddled with the ties on my robe. "It lasted about three seconds."

I didn't dare mention the second time.

Kit smiled at Jennelle.

"Was he really a virgin?" Jennelle blushed. "I'm sorry to interrupt, but virginity is a better excuse than sorry, can't hang on more than three seconds. I went out with a guy like that."

"He cried afterwards."

Jennelle shook her head. "Typical."

"Maybe he *has* been putting one over on the whole family. Lina Adams would know. She went out with him a couple times after college. Can I use your phone, Jennelle? I left my cell in the locker."

"Kit, please."

"Just kidding."

"Kit, swear to me you won't tell Abby or spread this around the office." Could Ted have made the virgin part up? The box of Trojans seemed pretty old and banged up. But the second time wasn't so fast. Either way, it was humiliating.

"Sunny." Kit hugged me tight. "Don't take it so hard. You've just lived every man's fantasy. Have you ever heard of a man agonizing over taking someone's virtue?"

"But he's Abby's cousin."

"So?"

"Look at it this way, Ted will never forget you." Jennelle checked herself out in a giant golden mirror. "Personally, I'd take that as a compliment."

A beautiful, tan, muscular man appeared in the hallway and strutted toward us. "Hello, Kit."

"Hi, Hugo. This is Sunny." Kit pulled me along. "It's her first massage. She's a virgin."

I glared at Kit.

Hugo smiled and winked.

I tried to smile back. If he was the masseur, I might be able to forget Ted, for an hour anyway.

"You're in for a treat, Sunny. Marty is the best." He swept his arm toward a hallway marked *Massage Corridor*. "Come on back, ladies."

Maybe Marty would be cute, too.

"Here we are, ladies. Kit, get comfortable while I drop Sunny off with Marty." Hugo held open the door to his room.

Kit plopped onto Hugo's massage table. "And don't fret about Abby. She'd forgive anyone for anything."

"Sunny." A deep voice called from the next room. Marty emerged and extended her big fleshy hand. "Nice to meet you."

Her mustache reminded me of Ted.

Conrad

KIT BURST INTO MY OFFICE. "YOU HAVE TO SEE THIS!"

"Hang on," I said.

Peter Woods' secretary came back on the line. "Mr. Woods is unavailable. May I take a message?"

Kit perched on my desk, bouncing with excitement.

"I'll try him later, thanks." I hung up the phone. I wasn't about to add more fuel to Kit's fire by telling her about my next date.

"Ready?" She dropped a manila envelope in front of me. "It's a biggie." She pulled out a photo and flashed it in front of me.

I couldn't believe my eyes. A naked man lay sprawled out on the distinctive blue, green and red plaid carpeting of the Walker, Gamble and Lutz offices. A nude blonde perched over his face, while a second woman with long, black hair attended to him with her mouth. The sparse dark hair on his legs and his slim mid-section provided the only clues to his identity.

"Jesus, Kit. Where did you find...?"

"We're having a contest called *Name the Attorney*. Winner takes all. The pot has grown to fifty bucks, so far."

"Kit! You can't..."

"Bev guessed Michael Williams in real estate. Monica thinks its Henry Blum. I'm going with Nick Beebe."

"This is *so wrong*," I couldn't take my eyes off the photo. Other than a decent tan, he had no distinguishing features that weren't obscured by his companions' writhing bodies. "I have no idea who it is." I tried to glance away.

"He seems pretty hung."

"Kit!" I couldn't stop looking.

Kit's smile grew. "Come on, guess!"

Of the one hundred fifty male lawyers at the firm, at least seventy were both Caucasian and slim enough to be the man in the picture. If the photo was taken in the summer, forty could also be that tan. If you factored in the dark hair, there were around twenty strong possibilities. "I suppose..."

Someone rapped on my door.

I whisked the photo into my top drawer and Kit popped up from the edge of my desk.

"Come in."

Forty pounds overweight, ghostly pale, and definitely not the lawyer in the photo, Conrad Slater, opened the door and ran his fingers through his few remaining strands of gray hair. "Ms. St. Clair. Ms. Purdy."

"Hi, Mr. Slater," Kit said with a sugary voice reserved for senior partners. "I've gotta run but I'll need that document back ASAP, Sunny."

"Bye, Kit." Conrad twisted his wedding band as he watched Kit wiggle out of my office in her tight skirt. He turned to me. "Ms. St. Clair, I have a matter for you to handle." The fumes from his three-martini lunch seemed flammable.

"Of course."

Conrad Slater forced his girth into my narrow client chair. As his belly wiggled, dandruff flakes cascaded from his shoulders onto the file in his hand.

"Sandy, you've prepared a motion for the court to approve a settlement, right?"

He could have looked up my name. I didn't bother to correct him as I nodded. Even though I drew a complete blank, I'd learned never to admit what I didn't know to a partner. Everything could be looked up or figured out, but ignorance always resurfaced at review time.

"Great. We just reached a settlement. I need the client's sworn declaration drafted today so it can be filed tomorrow.

I eyed the pile of work on my desk. "No problem."

"Be sure to review the file carefully. When you draft the motion, include the details of the case, the expected lifetime medical costs of the injured parties, and an explanation as to why the settlement is reasonable. Also, it's absolutely crucial that you note our client's limited assets so the court will approve his contribution of fifty-thousand."

I reached into my drawer for a fresh note pad.

The back of the brunette's head, hard at work on the mystery lawyer, poked out from the back of the drawer.

"Ms. St. Clair, are you listening?" He stifled a belch.

I pressed the *ON* button of my recorder. "Of course, Mr. Slater. I was taping so I wouldn't miss any procedural points."

"Good thinking, Sandy."

How had Kit discovered the photo?

"When you've finished, have Helene prepare the document immediately. I want to see the declaration before you fax it to the client. Have him sign it and return it today. This *must* be filed by tomorrow. My daughter is getting married in San Francisco next week and I have no intention of flying back on Monday to try an already-settled case."

"Congratulations, sir." I moved the papers marked *URGENT* and the hodge-podge of grunt work needing my immediate attention over to the credenza. "I'll get right on it."

"Sandy, I'm depending on you." Conrad patted the file as he heaved himself out of my chair. His slacks pulled across his rump as he lumbered out of my office and down the hall.

I sighed.

Kit bounded in a second later. "So, what's your guess?"

She'd obviously lurked in the secretaries' lounge until Slater was out of sight.

"Settle down." I glanced at the file.

"Come on. Where's the picture?" She headed toward my chair, scooted me back and pulled open my desk drawer.

"Where did you get this?"

"A little birdie."

"I'm not getting involved." It could only turn out badly.

"Suit yourself." She grabbed the photo and started for the door. "If you would lighten up a little and enjoy life's simple pleasures you wouldn't need a shrink." Her platform shoes click-clacked as she hurried down the corridor yelling, "Elizabeth. You've gotta see this. You're gonna die."

I needed Pat Goldstein more than ever, but when would I even have time to go? I shook my head, picked up Conrad Slater's case file, and scanned the paperwork.

In the course of his employment as the owner of a mid-sized business, Mr. Richard McKeen rear-ended a van, which exploded on impact. Two people were killed. Five others sustained third-degree burns, three of them children.

The lawsuit was to be settled for six million dollars, less one-third for attorney's fees, split amongst the victims.

Four million split amongst five badly injured people didn't seem enough for ongoing medical costs plus a lifetime's pain and suffering. Perhaps there were mitigating factors.

The vehicle manufacturer was held partially liable, as a design flaw in the fuel line was blamed for the explosion. Our client's insurance carrier would shoulder the remainder of the settlement, save for a fifty-thousand-dollar contribution from our client, Mr. McKeen. Slater argued that McKeen had only fifty-thousand and no other liquid assets. Neither drugs nor alcohol were involved.

I picked up the file, leaned back in my chair, and looked at the attached image of the scorched truck—an ominous, yet insufficient, warning of the horrific photos that lay below.

Though his face was heavily bandaged, I saw into the brown eyes of eight-year-old Jesus Rodriguez. His glazed stare begged for a life he'd never know again. His tightly wrapped chest and hands were nearly lost in the web of tubes keeping him alive.

Singed clumps of hair framed the blackened, blistered face of Maria Elena Rodriguez, twenty-four—a year younger than me, and burned beyond recognition.

I closed my eyes, unable to bear the sight of another child mangled by flame.

Four million dollars was perhaps fair compensation for one, or even two

95

of the injured parties. But how much surgery would Jesus, Maria, and the other child endure just to survive? What would their lives be like after this?

The firm representing the plaintiffs was a third-rate personal injury mill that specialized in a Hispanic clientele, the vast majority of whom had no knowledge of the American judicial system.

Was facilitating rush deals with law firms intent on quick, big dollar settlements the reason I became a lawyer? Tears ran down my face as I tried desperately to replace the charred remains of the accident scene with the lurid image of my co-worker and his bimbos. I couldn't look at the remaining images.

I typed the contents of the declaration in an email to Conrad Slater's secretary, Helene.

An hour later, with a fresh coat of makeup to mask my horror, I knocked on Conrad's door with the document in hand.

There was no answer.

I knocked again with more force.

"Come in." There was a rustling in his office as I opened the door. Conrad stood by his couch as though he'd just bolted up from an afternoon snooze. He wiped the side of his mouth.

"Mr. Slater. I'm ready to fax this to the client. You wanted to review it first?" I handed him the declaration.

"Yes, of course." He grabbed his bifocals from the desk and reviewed my work. "Hmm. Richard McKeen's assets are listed properly. Nothing liquid. Looks good."

I forced a smile. "Thank you, sir."

He handed me the paperwork. "Nice job, Sandy."

My hands shook as I walked the document to the fax room. Even though Jim Wolfe's office was across the hall, I didn't try to catch his attention. I sent my correspondence to the client.

It took almost an hour before I could block out the screaming in my head and plow through the other urgent matters of the other privileged clients who could afford the superior legal representation of Walker, Gamble and Lutz.

I spent the remainder of the afternoon with a knot in my stomach waiting for the sound of the fax girl as she headed toward my office with her cart.

Finally, my phone rang.

"Ms. St. Clair? Richard McKeen here. I'm calling in regards to the statement you faxed over to my office."

"Yes, of course." Clammy sweat drenched the base of my neck and forehead. *How can you sleep at night*? How would I?

"Ms. St. Clair, I've gone ahead and signed the last page of the document, but I'm faxing corrections on pages one and two that need to be made to make it an accurate sworn statement."

"I'll make sure the changes are made." I willed my heart to stop pounding. I tried not to hate him. It wasn't his fault that the truck exploded when he hit those poor people.

"My assets do not total five hundred thousand."

You've already weaseled out of your fiscal responsibility. There's no need to make things sound worse.

"I've made some small wording changes that I thought might be important, but the main change lies in my assets. The most recent assessment of my net worth totals over one point one million, not five hundred thousand."

"Really?" My breath came easier. Perhaps the judge would reject the settlement and demand more for the Rodriguez family from McKeen's business. "Thank you, Mr. McKeen. I'll make sure it's taken care of."

"Call me Richard."

"Thanks, Richard. Go ahead and make your changes, sign the last page in front of a notary, and fax it all back if you will." Maybe, I wasn't working for the bad guy after all.

"I'm sending it now."

I ran upstairs to the fax room to wait. Even a little more money would help those poor people. Maybe I could take on some plaintiff's work, someday. I glanced across the hall at Jim Wolfe's office, armed with my best smile just in case he appeared in his doorway.

He didn't.

When the fax arrived, I ran it back to Slater. Luckily, he was in his office, awake.

"I'm sorry to bother you, but I have some questions on the declaration from Mr. McKeen. It just came over the fax and he's made a few changes. I thought I'd better..."

"What's your question?" He walked over to his desk, sat down, and stared at his monitor. He never looked at me.

"Mr. McKeen signed the final page, but he insisted that some minor changes must be made to the sworn statement to make it truthful."

"Like what?" He dug an index finger in his ear.

I smiled thinking of the extra half-million in assets. "There are a couple of wording issues and he scratched out something on page two."

Conrad yawned, then opened a pack of Tic-Tacs and poured half the contents into his mouth.

I walked over to his desk and placed the papers before him. "He miscalculated some of his assets."

"Hmm?" Conrad sat upright and grasped the fax from my hands. He leafed to the Declarations page.

"Shall I redraft the document and have him sign it again?"

"Huh? Uh, no." His smile looked forced. "Listen Sandy, you've done enough on this. I'll handle it from here." As he patted my shoulder, I got an unpleasant electric shock.

He picked up the phone and swiveled away from me.

"I'll be glad to do whatever else you need, sir."

"No need. No need. I have to make a confidential call if you'll excuse me, Sandy."

"It's Sunny."

He wasn't listening.

As I crept from his office, I almost bumped into Kit.

"Hey, Kit?"

"Huh?" She was distracted with her manila envelope.

I pushed her down the hallway out of Helene's earshot. "Have you done much work for Conrad Slater?"

"I try to avoid it." She lowered her voice. "Helene's such a ditz. Why?"

"Was he easy to work for?"

"Depends on how shit-faced he is."

Maybe that was it.

Cousin Abby

I TRIED PETER WOODS' NUMBER AGAIN, THIS TIME FROM A blocked office line instead of my cell. A decent date would take my mind off work, and the rapidly approaching bar exam.

"Mr. Woods is unavailable." This time, the voice was male. "May I take a message?"

"Is this his assistant?"

Why didn't he give me a cell number?

Don't call boys. The Universe will send the right one to find you. Esther's voice floated through my brain.

"It is. Can I take a message, please?"

"When do you expect him?"

"I don't have that information. Where can he reach you?"

I willed away the beginnings of an itch by taking a deep breath of musty air. This wasn't the Dark Ages anymore. There was no reason not to leave a message. "It's Sunny St. Clair calling. Please have him call me at 213–555–5101 or 310–555–2155." I hung up and started back across the UCLA law library to a massive oak table.

I unwrapped another Tootsie Roll and stuffed the wrapper into an empty Diet Pepsi can. To cap off the remaining five minutes of my study break, I balanced my checkbook. After the Audi payment, the student loan, rent, Visa and monthlies, I had enough extra for an appointment with Pat Goldstein.

I closed my check register and went back to the Real Property section of my review program: Covenant of Seisin, Covenant of Right to Convey, Covenant against Encumbrances. *The Covenant of Warranty is a covenant wherein the grantor agrees to defend on behalf of the grantee any lawful or reasonable claims of...*

A pair of soft, manicured hands covered my eyes. I felt the lump of a square-cut, two-carat, platinum engagement ring and matching diamond-encrusted band.

Abby.

"Covenant of Quiet Enjoyment... I don't think that was intended to include candy gorging." She looked at my array of wrappers, soda cans, and sunflower seed husks. "I was going to take you out for lunch, but I wouldn't want you to get sick."

"I'm so glad to see you." Visions of Ted, naked, and panting on top of me flashed through my mind as I stood. I felt like a harlot hugging Mother Theresa as I wrapped my arms around her slim frame. "When did you get in?"

"Late last night. Charlie had to go into the office this morning, so here I am." Abby tossed a fragrant necklace of browning flowers over my head. "Goes great with your textbooks."

If she only knew I'd now been "lei'd" by two members of the Parker family.

"How did you find me here?"

"I stopped by your place. Kit said you left at the crack of dawn." Abby's bright eyes lacked the telltale dark circles of jet lag, and her skin was tanned to a perfect golden bronze. She pointed at my garland and giggled. "I didn't bring one for Kit. The last thing she needs is another lei."

"You can't even imagine." The thought of an enthusiastic but diminutive Bill Pogue was more than I could bear.

"I'm afraid I can."

"Did she at least tell you that Philip is taking her out for a *special* dinner tonight?"

"*The* special dinner she's been bragging about?"

"I really hope so."

"An engagement ring would solve a lot." Abby looked pained for a second, but smiled.

Kit was lucky to have her for a friend. So *was* I. I felt nauseated, and it wasn't from the candy over-consumption. "I missed you. How amazing was your honeymoon?"

"It was great." Abby scanned the library. "Let's get out of here. Macy's is having a big sale."

"I'd love to, but I have so much to do." I glanced at my laptop. How was I going to tell her about Ted?

"I didn't drive all the way over here to watch you study and eat junk." She scooped up the pile and tossed my assorted wrappers into the trash. "I'll bring you right back, promise. It'll air out your brain."

"An hour is all I can spare," I said as I followed her out to her Mercedes SUV.

I avoided eye contact and made small talk as we looped into downtown Westwood, entered Macys and wound uneventfully through the cosmetics department, china and into linens for Abby's bridal returns.

I didn't get tripped up until the shoe department.

Abby scanned the size sevens, pulled a darling pair of tan suede square-heeled pumps from the top shelf, and set them in my lap. "These would be great with that Ellen Tracy suit we found last year."

"If only I still had it."

"The bonfire?"

I nodded.

Abby shook her head. "I still can't believe Alan did that."

"Desperation causes people to do crazy things."

"Fashion only lasts a season or so." Abby patted my shoulder and headed to a sale table. "But you might have been stuck with Alan for a lifetime."

"I suppose." Would she be so blasé if we were talking about Ted? I had to say something to her before Kit slipped. "Abby?"

She didn't seem to hear me as she reached toward the top rack.

"Cute boots," she said and flashed a sly smile. "Not so great for hiking, though."

I was suddenly short of breath. "What did she tell you?"

There had been no way to anticipate that Abby would stop by the house and see Kit before I had a chance to talk to her.

"Ted emailed us."

"It wasn't Kit?"

"For once, it wasn't." She smiled. "Ted was very excited."

If only it could have been Kit.

"I didn't have a chance to warn you that Ted has a bit of a tendency to proselytize." Her eyes crinkled as though she were about to smile or maybe frown as she examined a sole for the price.

"Ted's very nice." I couldn't say it. I didn't want to say it. I had to say it. "I didn't mind the religious stuff so much, but I don't think we're a good fit."

"It's okay. I didn't really think he was for you."

"I'm sorry."

"No need to apologize." Abby grabbed my hand and pulled me over to two upholstered chairs. She pushed me into one and lowered herself into the matching twin without breaking eye contact.

My mouth opened, but nothing came out.

"Sunny, I know the whole story."

"I'm going to kill Kit," I finally managed.

"Sunny," Abby grabbed my hand.

"I'm going to kill her." My ears felt hot. "Why can't she ever keep a confidence?"

A tortured look crossed Abby's face. "Don't know."

She'd been the victim of Kit's mouth long before me. "I'm just sorry that I didn't get the chance to tell you first."

Abby hugged me. "Truth is, I already knew."

"What do you mean?"

"My mom."

"Your mom?"

"Aunt Ruth told her."

"Ted's mother, Ruth?" I looked for the closest trashcan. I could taste the sour mixture of Starburst and bile rolling up the back of my throat.

"Actually, Aunt Ruth is delighted. She's desperate for grandchildren and she's been worried all this time that he might be gay."

This was getting worse and worse. "You are kidding, right?"

"Apparently Ted broke down and told her that day. Some sort of penance

102

thing. She's so happy she keeps calling my Mom and going on about how he's a changed man, even with the guilt."

"Now I really want to die."

"No need. Mom says he's much easier to be around. She says he's even toned down the rhetoric a little." Abby glanced at a tiny chip on her manicured big toe. "You're sort of the hero of the Parker family right now."

I still felt sick to my stomach.

"Relax, Sunny. It was bound to happen. Ted's looking for a Pollyanna Paris Hilton." Abby tucked a strand of golden hair behind her small ear and perused a rack of size fours. "Clearly he's gotten himself all frustrated looking for a woman that doesn't exist."

And what if the perfect woman existed, but tragically, was his first cousin? I couldn't help but smile, despite it all. "Abby, how many of your friends has he tried to go out with?"

"Kind of a lot. Most of them thought he was cute until he scared them away with his fire and brimstone lectures." She raised an eyebrow. "Apparently, he's been working on his approach."

"He might need to work on it a bit more."

"This time, I think *you* may have converted *him*." She giggled. "Even if you didn't, he'll have his evening of wanderlust with my best friend to treasure long after he's been totally absolved of the guilt by whomever is in charge of that sort of thing."

"Oh, Abby, I really am mortified."

"Don't be silly. Someday, he'll look back fondly on his night with you when he's finally found that vampy minister's-wife-in-training he's searching for." She grabbed my hand. "Come on."

I stood, but I was still too stunned to move.

"You'll do what I say. You ravaged my innocent cousin."

"It wasn't quite like that." I said following her like an obedient zombie toward sportswear.

She pulled a poufy skirt from a nearby rack and handed it to me. "They're all the rage in Europe."

"If anything, I need work clothes." Not that I could afford anything.

"Why didn't you say so?" Abby asked, heading to the next department.

I followed behind as she pulled an array of skirts, tops, and coordinating

103

accessories, then draped them over my outstretched arms.

"You *have* to try this on." She handed me a Tahari jacket and skirt that would more than replace the one I lost. "If it works, we'll grab the shoes."

"Abby, I can't..."

"Come on." Abby headed for the dressing rooms and deposited the bounty on a hook in an extra-large room with a three-way mirror. She sat, and I dutifully stripped.

I pulled the first dress over my head and modeled.

She checked me from the back. "Next."

The "no" pile grew until I reached for the suit. I knew it was perfect even before I tucked a pale pink silk blouse into the waist and looked at myself in the mirror. The skirt hit at a perfect spot above the knee.

"Spin around." Abby checked me out from the back.

I turned in a quick circle.

"Sold."

"I can't afford this."

"You don't have to. It's a gift. From me and Aunt Ruth."

"There's no way I..."

"You don't say *no* to my aunt, and you won't say *no* to me. It's a late Hanukah present."

"But?"

"You have no choice. Meet me in the shoe department."

I changed back into my jeans and met Abby at the checkout counter just as she handed over her new *Mrs. Abigail Crawford* gold card.

Who could blame Ted if he was in love with her?

Who wouldn't be?

LeJuan

WHEN I GOT HOME FROM THE LIBRARY, THE LANDLINE message light was flashing.

SATURDAY 4:30 P.M.:

Kit it's Stan. We won't be there 'til seven. We just found out my man Lou's getting called up from the minors. He's looking forward to a celebration with you before he heads back to Oakland in the A.M.

Techno music blared down the hall from Kit's room.

Somehow she'd missed the call. Philip had to be on his way over. She couldn't have double-booked a night like this.

Though officially I wasn't speaking to her, I bolted down her hallway. "Kit." I rapped on her partially open bathroom door. "Kit, you missed the message on the machine."

"What message?" Kit pinned another hot roller into her hair.

"Some guy named Stan and his friend Lou are running late."

"Oh good, I don't have to rush my makeup."

"Kit! What about Philip?"

"Why are you suddenly worried about him? No ring, no commitment."

"It's Saturday the sixteenth."

"Well aware."

"It's your dinner with Phillip."

"What the hell are you talking about?"

105

"The note I left by the phone when Guy Jackson was over. From Philip?"

"What message from Philip?" Her voice raised an octave. "He calls my cell."

I suddenly realized she hadn't said a word to me about the dinner since I left the note on the table. "Your cell was lost again when he called."

"Shit!" she said as I tore down the hall, scanned the table, ransacked the drawer below it and scoured the floor.

A paper edge peeked out from under the couch. "Oh, no!"

Kit, who had followed me, pulled the paper from under the couch leg and read the vague message. Her face flushed.

"You haven't spoken with him?"

"No, he was in Amsterdam. Well, near Amsterdam. He didn't say anything more about it. I assumed he was coming home from the airport to crash and that I'd see him tomorrow."

"Unless there was a change in plans, he should be on his way from the airport to take you to dinner."

"Sunny, why didn't you tell me when he called?"

"You were indisposed. Guy Jackson."

"Guy Jackson." Kit shook her head. "That was amazing."

"Kit, Philip said to wear the black dress. He sounded really excited." *For Philip, anyway.* "It seemed like..."

"The black dress is at work." Kit mumbled.

"Did he really say he was shopping for a ring?"

"He mentioned it," she said, gazing at her ring finger as though in shock.

I shook her. "You have to cancel your other date, fast!" The irony of Kit's situation didn't even occur to me.

"Can't." Kit ran her fingers through her hair. "What are we going to do?"

"We?" I shook my head.

"You have to help me out." Kit gazed dreamily at her finger. "You have to pinch hit."

"I can't do that."

"Please, Sunny. My friend Stan is a *sports agent*. He and his girlfriend Sheree set me up with this pro baseball player. Kit shoved a handful of cookies into her robe pocket. "He's really cute and he's going to be famous."

"I have to study tonight."

"Study until they get here." She looked at her watch. "What time's Philip going to be here?"

Actually, I'd never been out with a professional sports anything. Peter hadn't exactly called, either.

"I have to get ready. Please. Please?"

Kit had an almost fiancé, a work affair, and a pro-football fling. I had nothing. "Doesn't Lou expect you?"

"He won't care, he's never met me."

I checked my watch. "You better get dressed fast."

"Thanks. You'll have fun." She turned for her room.

"What should I tell them?"

"Tell them I'm otherwise engaged." She swung back around and kissed me on the cheek. "Wear *your* little black dress and some lipstick."

"What are you going to wear?"

"My other black dress. Philip will never notice." She smiled and started toward her bedroom.

My dress was, of course, a victim of the bonfire. I sighed, and headed toward my closet to try and rustle up something presentable.

~*~

LeJuan, Lou to friends, was cute. I mean, he had kind, brown eyes, he was tall with broad shoulders, and his skin was a beautiful shade of mocha.

He glanced at his Tag Heuer and gazed down the hall of Stan's apartment. Stan and Sheree were lost in the bedroom looking for the wallet he'd "accidentally" left at home.

"When does training camp start?" Or was that football?

"Not sure." He rubbed a scuff out of his Kenneth Cole loafers. "They haven't officially called me up."

"I thought Stan said you went pro."

"That's what Stan's hoping." LeJuan stretched his lanky arms and reclined into the plaid sofa. A gust of mildew overwhelmed the sultry haze of spicy cologne that hung about him. He tugged a gnarled pillow thread loose.

Stan's apartment lacked the cool modern flair I'd expected from a big time sports agent. In fact, an exact replica of his couch had graced the hallway of my college dorm. "How long has Stan been representing you, LeJuan?"

"Since last month. He's about to get me a big contract."

"Does he have any experience?"

"He knows some folks."

"Well, if you need any legal advice, I probably know some people, myself."

"You a lawyer?"

I nodded. Saying so was one of the great perks of the job.

"You got anyone offa death row?"

"I'm not that kind of lawyer. Mostly, I help insurance companies not pay out claims." I banished Jesus Rodriguez' bandaged face from my conscious.

"Cool."

"What position do you play?"

LeJuan smiled sheepishly. "First base."

"Do you bat, too?"

LeJuan laughed.

I glanced down so he wouldn't see me blush. I'd entirely ignored baseball since I was picked last in fourth grade. "What time does the movie start?"

"9:30." LeJuan peered down the hallway toward the closed door. "This always happens when Stan and Sheree get together. It's gonna be a while."

We sat in silence.

He checked his watch again.

I twisted my silver charm bracelet around my wrist.

"You oughta come watch me play once Stan gets the deal worked."

"I'd like that."

"So your roommate's tryin' out to be a Laker Girl?"

"That's what she says." *To guys with a future in pro sports.* Kit might have slept with him or at least taken him dancing. She'd have gazed at him longingly as they swirled around the dance floor.

I wanted to apologize for being me, but I couldn't think of how to say it. "I'm sorry Kit couldn't make it."

"Stan says she's hot, but you're cute, too." He moved over to my section of the couch. A stale beer odor wafted from beneath the cushions.

"Thanks."

LeJuan grabbed my hand and led me toward a narrow balcony. "Let's check out the lights."

The view toward the ocean was obscured by a high rise on the opposite

108

side of the street. The balcony, a decorative afterthought, looked as if it couldn't support our combined weight. The railing extended less than two feet from the wall.

"Can we both fit?"

"If we squeeze." He tugged on the iron where it was bolted in. "There's no need to be scared."

"I'm not," I said as my heel caught an edge of the metal weather stripping and I tripped.

LeJuan caught me in his arms.

I closed my eyes and didn't look down.

After a few minutes, he edged sideways, moved behind me, and wrapped his arms around my waist.

I opened my eyes to a beautiful, romantic view of Westwood. LeJuan smelled good and felt warm.

"I'm a very good kisser." He nuzzled my neck. "Knowing Stan and Sheree, it's gonna be a while. Kissing's a good way to pass the time."

I didn't know how to respond. It wasn't that I *didn't* want to kiss him. "LeJuan, I..."

He turned me around, leaned down and before I could protest, kissed me softly. "How was that?"

"Nice. It's just..." Kissing two men in as many weeks definitely wasn't my style.

"It's just what?" He smiled.

What was my style, anyway?

He kissed me again.

This time, I closed my eyes and allowed the memories of Ted's slobbering to fade with LeJuan's competent kisses.

I should have been home studying or at least gloating that Kit hadn't used me again. Instead, I enjoyed the mostly gentlemanly attentions of LeJuan. I needed a few good kisses, and he *was* a very good kisser.

~*~

When I got home, a note shaped like a bloated birth control pill was taped to my door in Kit's loopy cursive: *False alarm. No ring.*

Otto

"SUNNY. PETER WOODS."

"Hi, Peter." I tried to sound businesslike so Kit, who was in my office, wouldn't suspect he wasn't a client, and he wouldn't suspect I was still awaiting his call. "Can you hang on a second?" I put my hand over the receiver. "Look over the file and I'll be down to your office in a minute."

Kit narrowed her eyes, sighed, and clomped off down the hall.

I was already paying for the ring incident and there was nothing I could do about it. On top of it all, I was forced to load her up with work. I removed my hand from the receiver. "Sorry, Peter."

"No problem. I was returning your call." He waited as though he wasn't certain who I was. "I've been out of town."

"We met at the car wash, a couple weeks ago. You gave me your card."

"Right, right. Hayvenhurst?"

He didn't remember me. I should have left a message right away. "No, St. Clair."

"I meant the car wash on Hayvenhurst."

"Olympic, by the air fresheners. You mentioned my hair."

He paused. "Of course. Sunny with the beautiful curls. Great to hear from you."

I tried to picture his face and light eyelashes.

"Listen, Sunny. I know this is last minute, but I'm headed over to Vertigo

110

Redux. Come by. I'll buy you a drink."

Vertigo Redux? "What time?"

"7:30?"

"I could stop by, but I'm afraid I won't be able to get home first and change out of work clothes." There was no way I could find something vintage '80s that was cool enough for Vertigo with less than a week's notice.

"No worries. I'll put your name on the list. When you get in, ask for Otto, and he'll bring you to my table."

He had his own table?

"Later."

Vertigo Redux? It was impossible to get in without the right someone. Clearly I'd found him. I bit the inside of my cheeks as I started down the hall. There would be even more hell to pay if Kit saw my enormous smile when I reached her office.

"Fuck," she hissed. "I'll be here 'til midnight." Kit sat hunched over a file; a stack of papers all but blocked her head from view.

"I'm so sorry, Kit. You know I wouldn't pile you up like this unless..."

"Where the hell are you off to?" Kit wouldn't look at me.

"Nowhere."

"At 7:30?" Her breathing was ragged. She'd raced down the hall seconds ahead of me.

"You were listening to my conversation?"

"I didn't mean to." Kit raised an eyebrow. "I thought I'd left my notepad on your desk, but here it is." She patted too hard on a legal pad.

"Then, you know where I'm going."

"I didn't hear that part."

"Some sort of '80s night at a club."

"Where?"

"Vertigo," I barely whispered.

"Redux?"

I nodded.

"You're shitting me." Her voice filled the room. "With who?"

"You don't know him."

"What are you going to wear?" Kit's cheeks blazed scarlet as she eyed my A line skirt and blouse. "You can't show up in that."

"I don't have time to change." Since she'd heard every word of my conversation, I could only attempt damage control. I didn't dare tell her I was on the VIP list.

She shook her head then glanced behind the door.

"I know..." she said, the excitement returning to her voice. "If we spray up your hair, my black dress will work. It's kind of retro."

The engagement dinner black dress hung waiting for a second chance. There was no way it would fit, and Kit knew it.

"It's a little big for me." She walked around her desk, lifted the clingy BCBG from the hook and tossed it into my lap. "Try it on."

I glanced at the tag. "Kit, it's a two."

"Try." Kit locked the door, sat on the edge of her desk and crossed her legs in anticipation. "Do it."

Despite the engagement ring incident, I wouldn't humiliate myself by bursting the seams on her dress just to make her feel better. It wasn't *all* my fault that Philip didn't pop the question. "It's okay. My name's on the list."

Kit's face dropped. "The VIP list?"

I nodded.

"So what does this guy do?"

"He's an entrepreneur."

"You mean a coke dealer?"

"Yeah, right." I couldn't wait to find out what he really did so I could drop it into a conversation.

Kit gave me the once-over, again. "At least take off your pantyhose and unbutton the top two buttons on your blouse."

I silently, dutifully, unfastened the top of my blouse and allowed Kit to scrunch and spray my hair. It was best to let her have the last word.

~*~

I stood outside Vertigo Redux amongst a throng of flawlessly dressed hopefuls. A pack of girls in black bustiers and ripped jeans pushed me aside and approached the velvet rope.

"Hi Rod." One girl blew the doorman a kiss. "Let us in tonight?"

Rod's square head looked incongruous with his white sport jacket, like Frankenstein with a guest spot on Miami Vice.

"Lookin' good tonight, Rod." The friend tugged down on her top so her

112

breasts popped up.

Rod looked her over. "Try again."

"Please, Rod?" a third whined. "Oh, please?"

An arm covered in plastic bracelets reached from behind and pulled the girl back into the crowd. "Shh. You'll ruin our chances for tomorrow." They turned en masse and clomped away on their high heels.

My tailored suit was certain to make a wonderful impression on Rod. Could he refuse me even though I was on the list? I probably should have stuffed into Kit's dress and tried to pass off the torn seams as *Flashdance*. "Excuse me, Rod?"

Rod pushed up the sleeves of his jacket and fluffed his retro Bon Jovi hair-do. He opened the red velvet rope to a dead ringer for a back in the day Charlie Sheen and a permed brunette in a bomber jacket. The man stuffed a wad of rolled-up bills into Rod's palm.

"Rod," I said a bit louder and feeling a lot more insecure. "I think I may be on your list."

He consulted his clipboard. "Name?"

"St. Clair. Sunny St. Clair. I was told to ask for Otto."

He scanned the list and unfastened the red rope for me.

A woman in a sparkling spandex dress gave me a dirty look from the wrong side of the velvet. Despite my attire, I was one of the chosen people.

Rod tugged a walkie-talkie from his belt. "Wait over there." He pointed to a dark nook inside the door.

Was I supposed to tip him? I fumbled in my purse for a few bucks. Luckily, he turned away to pick the next well-clad entrant before I had time to figure out the correct amount.

Prince lyrics vibrated through my chest cavity. An intoxicating mixture of perfume, cigarettes, and lust made my heart thump.

A moment later, a bald giant with a tattooed neck appeared before me. "I'm Otto."

"Sunny St. Clair." I shouted over a Flock of Seagulls.

"You related to Atlas St. Clair?" His voice was surprisingly high.

"He's my brother."

Otto smiled—I think.

"I'm supposed to meet Peter Woods. He said to ask for you." Being the

113

sister of a celebrity in a hot downtown club wasn't so bad. After all, weren't Frank Stallone and a few other 80's sibs livin' large back in the day?

Otto's stern smile faded into a line. "Follow me." The back of his neck read: *CARPE DIEM* or *CARPS DIE*. I couldn't make out the letters through the folds of skin. He headed toward a sea of beautiful bodies writhing in '80s designer clothes. "You know," Otto shouted over the music. "I tried to call your brother's show a couple times. Couldn't get through."

"I'll give you the hotline number." I put my shoulders back and stood tall despite my lack of leather pants, Lycra or chandelier earrings.

"Thanks." Otto led us along a narrow path overlooking the dance floor.

I spotted Peter's strawberry blond hair in the crowd below. I waved, but he'd already grabbed the hand of a redhead in a redder dress and pulled her onto the dance floor. His pelvis edged closer and closer to hers in time with the beat.

She ran her fingers down his back from his shoulders to his waist and dug a hand into his back pocket.

Otto shook his head. Splinters of colored light refracted off his shiny pate. "You been seeing him long?"

"We just met recently." I neglected to mention that it was at a car wash.

"What does Atlas say?"

"I don't usually ask my brother for advice on my private life."

"Why not?" Otto motioned to an empty table with a card that said: *RESERVED FOR PETER WOODS.*

"Apparently he feels I should figure things out on my own."

Otto shook his head. "Well, Peter's certainly The Man around here."

"Looks like it." I smiled.

"What would you like to drink, Sunny?"

"A Sea Breeze please." That seemed appropriately '80s.

Otto started off, then stopped and twisted his giant neck toward me. "If you need anything, I'll be at the bar."

"Thanks, Otto."

He nodded.

Seconds later, a waitress appeared with my not-so-eighties-priced drink.

I nursed my cocktail and waited. And waited. Why hadn't Peter come to check for me? I jotted down Atlas's hotline number, walked over to the bar,

114

and handed it to Otto. "Do you think I should go find Peter?"

"Nope." He tucked the paper into his chest pocket. "He'll find you."

"Otto, do you happen to know what Peter does for a—"

"Import-export." Peter materialized beside me, ran his fingers lightly down my arm and lifted my hand to his lips. "Sunny, good to see you." He dabbed his forehead with a napkin, then reached into his pocket and stuffed some bills into Otto's palm. "Thanks for taking care of her."

Otto nodded and disappeared.

"Come." Peter put an arm around me and guided me back to the table. His black silk shirt was slightly damp. "You're even prettier than I remembered."

I couldn't tell the color of his eyes in the dark of the bar.

A waitress appeared and set a cocktail before him.

"Keep the change, Trista." He handed her a rolled ten and examined my drink. "And another for Sunny."

The waitress nodded and turned for the bar.

"So you're a lawyer."

With his interest in my career, my waiting time angst began to subside. "As you know, I work for Walker, Gamble and Lutz and..."

"Do you do any criminal work?" Peter gazed at me as though I was the only woman in the room.

I smiled. The criminal side always sounded so glamorous to everyone outside the legal profession. "I mostly do business litigation and insurance defense, which can be very overwhelming at times. My firm just signed on a couple big clients and..."

"It sounds like you could use some R-and-R." Peter scanned the lounge area. "We should take a day on my boat."

"Sounds great," I shouted over Boy George. Kit was going to shit a brick when she heard I was headed off for a day of yachting.

"Can you excuse me for a moment?" He pecked me on the cheek and was halfway across the room before I could answer.

While I sipped my Sea Breeze and tried not to watch, Peter hugged a statuesque black woman and kissed her on each cheek. I thought I saw him put a hand into the back pocket of her leather miniskirt.

I prayed Kit wasn't right about him as Peter sauntered back to the table a few minutes later.

I took a self-conscious sip from a fresh drink that had appeared at the table.

"Let's dance." Peter grabbed my hand and pulled me out onto the dance floor before I could object.

I took a deep breath, slowly gave in to the beat, and tried not to look as awkward as I felt.

"You move nice." Peter whispered into my ear, his cologne was only slightly distinct from the hundred others mixed on the neon lit floor.

Dancers in fishnets, thigh high boots, and neon shorts thrashed and writhed in cages suspended above the throng.

Peter ran his hands down my back as the beat of *Superfreak* pulsed through my body.

"Peter." A woman in a black cat suit grabbed his hand and pulled us apart. "Mind if I cut in?"

"April." He kissed her European style as well. "You look great."

"It's business." Peter whispered in my ear. "I'll just be a minute." His lips grazed my ear.

Was I out with Hugh Hefner or Scarface?

"Sunny." Peter grabbed my hand. "Tell Otto we want a bottle of Dom. No more interruptions after this, I promise."

I started toward the bar with trepidation, as though I was headed before a judge. *Your honor, my client, and also my boyfriend, Mr. Woods, provides a necessary service to the retro club community and the models who depend on it. The clubs need his services to provide authenticity including but not limited to helping the models frequenting such establishments maintain the waifish standard of beauty expected in our society. For this reason, I believe my client should be offered community service as opposed to mandatory incarceration.* "Peter asked me to order a bottle of Dom Perignon."

Otto opened the refrigerator and produced a chilled bottle. He popped the cork and poured before I'd decided for certain that I didn't want any.

"Bottoms up." Otto handed me a champagne-filled flute.

"Perhaps the woman in the cat suit will appreciate Dom Perignon more than me."

"He wouldn't order it for her."

"Otto, I..."

"Drink. He won't be back for a few minutes."

I nodded and took a tentative sip of Dom Pérignon. The sweet amber on my tongue soon turned sour as I watched Peter place a tightly rolled plastic baggie between April's breasts. "I'm not thirsty."

"It would be a shame to leave half this champagne."

"I can't drink it."

"Nonsense. It's like water to him."

We glanced out onto the dance floor. Peter and cat suit woman, entwined in a slow dance, had their tongues in each other's mouths.

"It was nice to meet you, Otto. Give Atlas a call."

Otto pointed toward the emergency exit. "You better sneak out the back."

"Thanks, but the front door's fine."

"Mr. Woods won't appreciate a scene."

"He's already making one."

Otto shook his head. "Can't say I blame you, but..."

"It was nice to meet you, Otto."

"Take care, Sunny."

I made my way through the throng of dancers and tapped Peter on the shoulder. "Thanks for the champagne, but..."

April eyed my business suit.

Peter reached for my hand. "I was just on my way back."

"It'll never work with us." I slid my fingers from his grasp. "I don't do criminal defense."

With my head held high, I walked out the front door. For the first time in months, I felt great. As Rod unclipped the velvet rope, I even smiled to the less fortunate in line.

"Sunny!"

A cold chill ran down my spine. Was Peter coming after me? Was Otto trying to tell me Peter was dangerous and I was too proud to listen? I quickly glanced behind me, scanned the waiting crowd, and plotted the quickest route to my car.

"Over here!"

I turned toward the valet.

Jim Wolfe stood beside a black Mercedes.

117

Without a moment's hesitation I rushed over.

He grasped my hand as I nearly fell into his arms. "Fancy meeting you here."

A partner from the real estate department handed the keys to the valet and sidled up next to him.

"Bob, have you met Sunny St. Clair from litigation?"

"Haven't had the pleasure." He offered a too firm-I'm-just-pretending-I-think-women-are-equal-handshake. "Bob Thomas."

I kept an eye on the front door. "Nice to meet you, Bob."

"Leaving already?" Bob smoothed his hair-plug-thickened mane. His bomber jacket smelled of mothballs. "It's only 8:30."

I glanced over my shoulder for any sign of Peter Woods. "I have to get up early."

"Why don't you join us for a quick drink before you go?" Jim's smile turned my already weak knees to rubber. He was gorgeous even with his hair slicked back. The 80s-style shoulder pads in his cotton sport jacket somehow added to his charm.

"I...I..." What would Peter do if he spotted me with Jim? I gazed for a split second into his deep brown eyes. "I'd love to..." I lowered my voice, "but..."

"Terrific," Jim said.

Was there any way I could somehow steer us to a table on the other side of the club?

"They'll give away the cocktail table reservation if we don't get in soon."

Why? Did Jim have to ask me for a drink at this place on this night? Would Peter come after me in front of Jim or would he track down the name of my firm and put a contract out on me? Would a color photo of my mangled, bloody corpse slumped over a table appear on the front page of the L.A. Times?

"I'm afraid I just can't join you." I had to think of something, and quick. "My pregnant sister called. She's having some early contractions and she needs me to come right away."

"I hope everything's okay."

"She'll be fine, but she's scared."

"I'm sorry you can't stay."

Jim's smile broke my heart.

"Thanks." I had to say something that would tell him I was available. "I'd love a rain check, though." My heart pounded. "I haven't been out much since I broke up with my fiancé."

Jim grinned. "I'll keep that in mind."

~*~

"You left Vertigo Redux before nine?" Kit shook her head. "What's the matter with you?"

"I didn't like my date." *The coke dealer.*

"You were on the VIP list! You ditch him and find someone else."

"I was tired." I felt the pins and needles behind my cheeks and nose and turned for the bedroom before Kit saw the imminent waterworks.

"You're crazy."

She was right, but at least I wasn't crazy enough to ask her if she'd finished the work I needed on my desk by morning.

Dr. St. Clair

"YOU'RE CRAZY." MY FATHER EXAMINED THE MONT BLANC pen as he rolled it slowly between his fingers. "You can't afford to give a gift like this with what that car's running you. I would have been just as happy with a pack of Bics."

"Happy birthday, Dad."

"Hmm." He lifted a stack of lab results from the corner of his big oak desk and signed his name with a flourish of free flowing ink.

As kids, Luna, Atlas and I loved to play in Bernie's cavernous office while he caught up on paperwork. A pastoral rendering of domesticated animals in a flowing field of heather, a black and white photo series of barns under a country sky, and a large wooden rooster provided the perfect setting for a game of organic farm.

The office, designed to calm the nerves of the unlucky patient invited in for troubling news, hadn't changed in twenty years. I resisted the urge to Do-Si-Do on the area rug. "You ever think about redoing your office, Dad?"

Bernie looked up from a growing pile of papers bearing his signature. "Spend, spend, spend. If you could buy stuff for a living, you'd be the most successful gal in town." He rolled the ballpoint closed, cleared his desk and set the pen down so the light from his Tiffany lamp reflected off the gold clip.

He loved the pen.

"You could learn a thing or two from Luna. She never spends a dime."

"Luna doesn't have a dime to spend," I said.

"She's more shrewd than you might think."

Clearly, she hadn't filled him in on her latest shrewd endeavor. "Dad, we should go. The auto body shop is closing and I made dinner reservations for six." I'd spent far too long driving in oversized sunglasses and a hat so no one would recognize me in the Probe. I couldn't wait to get my Audi back.

Bernie removed his white lab coat and hung it on a brass horse head. He straightened the sleeves and fluffed the embroidered *Bernie St. Clair, MD.,* above the chest pocket. "Are your brother and sister coming? I haven't heard from either of them today."

"I'm sure Atlas will show up at just the right moment, as always. As for Luna..." What could I say? *You see, Dad, Luna is avoiding you because she's pregnant. Atlas is avoiding you because Esther is pregnant with your baby, at least genetically. If you hadn't crunched my car, I would have dropped your present into your mailbox like my siblings are doing right now.* I flashed my most convincing fake smile. "I'm sure we'll hear from her soon, too."

I'd lost my appetite. Bernie's feelings were hurt because they hadn't contacted him and there was nothing I could do. It just wasn't my responsibility to tell him about Luna. I wouldn't do it. Not on his birthday, not ever. I changed the subject. "How's your new girlfriend?"

"Menopausal." He winked and started down the gingham-papered hallway to the waiting room. "And I thought the young ones were horny."

Couldn't he smile and say "fine" like a normal father?

Bernie smiled as he let himself into the waiting room.

As I stuck my foot forward to catch the door before it closed in my face, a rough edge caught my pantyhose and an instant run zipped to my knee. When I bent over to examine the damage, I heard Luna's voice from the waiting room.

"Happy birthday, Dad."

I looked up and into the eyes of my sister seated beneath a watercolor of a mother hen surrounded by newly hatching baby chicks. If only I'd have let the door close in my face, I could have escaped through the emergency exit.

Luna closed a parenting magazine and placed it casually on an antique

121

metal milk jug. "Hey, Sunny."

An older lady smiled and gave Bernie the-aren't-you-lucky-to-have-such-dutiful-daughters-nod. She couldn't know she would need a flak jacket while she waited for her exam.

"Would it have killed you to call and say you were coming, Luna?"

I gave Luna the what-the-hell-are-you-doing-here stare.

She glared back at me, defiant.

I willed her not to stand. My heart thumped and my face prickled. "My car." I could hardly get the words out. "The place is closing soon." If I bolted for the door there was a chance I'd miss the fireworks.

"Calm down, Sunny." Bernie ran his hands through his hair and nodded back at the patient. "All you can think about is your damn car. It's my birthday." He peered into Luna's tote, searching for his present.

Luna's real gift was sure to overshadow my Mont Blanc pen.

While his head was in her carryall, she hoisted her bulk out of the armchair as though she was already eight months along.

My father gave her his perfunctory loose hug and reluctant air kiss. "You look good." He glanced over her left shoulder and eyed her rear. Then he noticed her belly. His giddy birthday boy smile fell.

Luna gave a startling re-creation of the Esther *Madonna* smile.

"Why don't I grab a cab?" I started for the door. "I'll meet you guys at the restaurant in an hour. I'll call Atlas and make sure he's on his way."

Bernie didn't take his eyes off Luna's womb. "Don't move, Sunny."

The knob slipped out of my sweating hand and the door slammed shut.

"What's going on?"

"Ask her." My voice squeaked. My brain screamed *run* to my paralyzed legs, but I couldn't move. I glared at Luna. "You tell him."

Luna stood tall, set her shoulders back, and took three cleansing breaths. "I've got a birthday surprise for you. She reached into her tote and pulled out a pre-wrapped tie box. "Here."

Bernie slumped as he reached for the present.

"I could also use a second opinion."

The older lady, who was no longer smiling, sunk behind her open magazine.

Bernie shook his head and stepped toward the office. For once, he held

122

the door for us before shooting into an open exam room. "For God's sake."

"Why did you drag me into this?" I hissed as I pushed Luna down the hall. "I'm going to kill you."

As I removed my hand from Luna's back, an electric charge surged through my fingers. *I'm scared. Help me.* I looked at her and shook my head. There was nothing psychic about it. Of course she wanted me to be the buffer. Who wanted to deal with Bernie?

"I'm sorry, Sunny. I couldn't do it alone."

"On the table. Now!" Bernie pried us apart by pulling Luna through the doorway. His face blazed red through his tanning salon bronze.

Luna lifted herself onto the exam table.

"It's *my birthday* for Godssakes."

I hovered in the doorway and dabbed my eyes as I considered another getaway.

"You." He pointed to the chair normally used by anxious fathers-to-be. "Sit."

"What did I do?"

"You thrive on this kind of tsuris. Sit."

I slunk over to the chair and tried to be invisible.

"How far along are you?" Bernie pushed on Luna's belly.

"Sixteen weeks."

"You're over twenty."

Luna's cheeks reddened. "Not possible."

"I've only been doing this every day for twenty-five years." Bernie pulled a measuring tape out of the exam table drawer and stretched it over the expanse of Luna's tummy. "Like I said, you're at twenty."

Luna looked frightened. "That's what *she* said."

"She who?"

Oh, no. Why didn't I expect this? Of course she'd been to Esther's favorite healthcare provider. I covered my ears, as though it would help. "Don't say it," I said.

"Tess Malone." Luna whispered.

"The goddamned midwife?"

Luna nodded. "Esther swears by her."

I glared at Luna. *Don't say it Luna, don't blurt anything about Esther.*

123

Don't do it. I'd never sent a stronger mental message to anyone, even Atlas.

"*That Woman.* I blame it all on *That Woman.*" Bernie stormed out of the room.

"Think he'll always call Esther *That Woman*?" Luna sounded like an old housewife at a bridge game. "He never got over the divorce, did he?"

I was in no mood for coffee talk. "How could you do this to me, Luna? How could you?"

"He never gets as mad when you're around." Tears welled up in her eyes. "I've been scared something's wrong. I needed him."

What if something *was* wrong with the pregnancy? Could Luna even handle a healthy baby? "Why didn't you at least tell me ahead of time?"

"You wouldn't have come. You barely mentioned dinner tonight. Dad would be devastated if I missed his birthday."

"And this isn't devastating for him?"

Bernie burst back into the room. "I'm too young for this, Luna. Both of you—follow me."

I helped Luna off the table and we followed Bernie down the hall as he muttered under his breath.

"Goddamn ultrasound cost a fortune and I'm giving out freebies to my own daughter."

He led us into a darkened room lit only by the glow of a computer screen attached to an elaborate machine.

Without a word, Luna climbed onto the exam table.

Bernie lifted her shirt and squirted a wad of blue goo on her stomach.

Luna and I shook our heads. We both knew better than to say anything.

He rubbed a paddle over Luna's belly. "What does a justice of the peace run?"

"Who said I was getting married?" Luna started to sit up. "Marriage is for morons."

Bernie, momentarily silenced by his own catch phrase, nudged her back down. He punched keyboard buttons at a blinding speed and gazed at the screen. "Son of a bitch."

"What is it?" Luna and I said in unison.

He shook his head.

"What's wrong, Dad?" Her voice trembled.

I shot out of my chair and instinctively put my arms around her.

Bernie shook his head again. "Just what I suspected."

"What's wrong?" I asked, tears suddenly welling in my eyes.

"Luna, you *are* just like *That Woman*."

"Dad! Leave her alone."

Bernie put his head in his hands. "It just figures she'd have twins."

"Twins?" Luna looked as ashen as I felt.

I stared at the screen. "Are you sure?"

He tapped a circle around two distinct images, like yin and yang nestled together.

"Even that idiot Tess Malone could see two fetuses and two placentas if she would dare use modern equipment."

Luna stared at the ultrasound, unblinking.

Bernie rocked as though he were in a synagogue. "Where did I go wrong?"

As though she'd come out of a trance, Luna rolled her head back, giggled, then started to laugh until tears streamed down her face. "Twins."

Bernie zoomed in on the babies, checking their statistics. "We might even have a boy here." His voice cracked a little.

Luna smiled.

I patted her in the hopes she might think something about the father that I might pick up. But I got nothing. Apparently, whatever psychic ability I had worked like the rusty antenna on an old television.

Luna folded her arms across her chest and reclined on the table.

Bernie shook his head again.

Luna sat up, wiped her belly with a tissue and pulled down her shirt. "I can do it."

"My daughter, the lawyer, buys herself a car she can't afford and then my daughter, the entrepreneur, gets herself knocked up with twins before she even opens her business."

"I was pregnant before Sunny bought the Audi."

"My faygelah psychic son is the only rational child I have." Bernie slumped onto his stool. "Where the hell is he, anyway?"

I was wondering the same thing.

"I need a drink." My father reached into his pocket, pulled out the keys to the Probe and threw them at Luna. "You can't drive your ridiculous

125

deathtrap of a car anymore. You won't fit behind the wheel in another month. Leave the VW here and take Sunny to the body shop to pick up her precious car. I can't take any more."

He walked out and closed the door behind him.

Luna eyed the keys to the Probe and smiled. "I think this went pretty well, considering."

Considering what? That I came from a family full of certifiable loonies? That we were victims of nature and nurture? That nieces, nephews, aunts and cousins would soon be indistinguishable?

Before I was doomed to two more weeks in Bernie's cast-off vehicle, I grabbed Luna's hand and led her down to the garage. Atlas was, of course, waiting by the Probe. A gift basket filled with Mercedes paraphernalia for Bernie sat on the hood next to him.

"Why didn't you tell me it was twins?" Luna waddled over and hugged him then leaned back and put her hand on her stomach.

"I wanted it to be a surprise for you." Atlas smiled. "Two down, one to go. Now, someone just needs to tell him about Esther."

"One of you guys will do it." I folded my arms across my chest and glared at him. "I'm not, I repeat, not, telling him about Esther."

They encircled me in a smothering group hug.

"I'm not." My words were muffled by Luna's newly huge breasts.

Mr. McKeen

I got to the office early Wednesday morning in the hopes that hard work would keep my mind off my family, at least until my afternoon appointment with the therapist.

"Sunny St. Clair. You're up with the roosters today." Delores, the ancient mail lady, shuffled down the hallway with a cart that doubled as a walker. Because of her bad vision, I often received the mail of Sam Cleary in the tax department. Yet, despite her seeming inability to see individual letters, she managed to note the arrival time of every associate in the firm with amazing accuracy.

"Good morning, Delores. Thought I'd get off to a running start today."

Delores lifted a foot, stuck her fingers into the instep of her orthopedic shoes, massaged, removed her hand from inside her shoe, and handed me a stack of correspondence.

"Thanks." I reached for the untouched edge of the bundle.

As I entered my office and dropped my briefcase, I noticed a message waiting ominously in the middle of my desk. *Call Richard McKeen ASAP.* What could he want? Conrad Slater would have corrected any of my freshman legalese when he finalized the document. The court had approved the settlement and the case was closed.

I took a deep breath just before McKeen answered his private line. "Richard. Sunny St. Clair."

"I've been waiting for your call."

"How can I help you?" I feared I sounded more like a nervous salesgirl than a corporate attorney.

"I've just received a copy of the motion sent to the court for approval, and I have to say I'm a little confused."

"Conrad Slater looked it over before it was sent to the courts so..."

Richard McKeen's silence pierced my eardrums.

"Ms. St. Clair?" He finally asked.

"Yes?"

"I received a copy of the document and it reflects none of the changes I made to my sworn statement."

"What?"

"I believe you heard me."

"That can't be." Or could it? I'd never actually seen the final draft. I steadied my voice. "There must be a minor mix-up. I'll run upstairs, double-check the file and get right back."

"I'll be waiting." His voice was icy.

I rushed to the nineteenth floor to straighten things out.

A red do-not-disturb indicator dot was placed discreetly next to Slater's plate. It was just as well; maybe Helene accidentally mailed McKeen the draft before the changes were made. There was no reason to get her in big trouble over a simple mistake.

I popped my head into Helene's cubicle, but she was away from her desk. All I could do was whisk the crumbs off her chair and wait while Helene and her three boys, rumor had it by three different men, smiled from an eight- by ten-inch photo on her return. Sweat collected at the back of my neck and under my arms. Could she lose her job over one sloppy error? Perhaps I could find the file, find out what happened, and then speak to her privately.

I scanned the headings on the file cabinets, pulled open the *closed files* cabinet and searched through the letter "M." There was no sign of the McKeen file. Perhaps it hadn't been closed out yet. I scooted the chair back toward Helene's cluttered desk and leafed through a mass of paperwork, careful not to disrupt whatever system she might have in place. In the middle of her droopy "to be filed" box, I finally spotted the manila folder I was looking for.

A few loose photos and the original declaration were stuffed into the back of the otherwise organized McKeen file. The front page of the revised statement was marked *Filed Monday, January 24* by the court. I read the declaration carefully. It contained all of Mr. McKeen's changes. A cold wave of relief swept over me. Somehow, the wrong copy was sent to the client.

From the looks of things, Helene was badly overworked. I unhinged the paperwork from the file and started to organize page by page.

"You don't need to do that, Sunny," Helene said, appearing beside me.

"I thought I could be of help." I tried not to sound judgmental or glance at her messy desk as I popped up from her seat.

"Whatever." She placed a mug of coffee and a candy bar on her desk and plopped her substantial frame in the chair. It let out a tired *psssshh*.

"By any chance, do you happen to remember anything about this case?"

"Huh-uhh."

"The client called this morning saying he'd received an unrevised sworn statement."

"I just sent what Slater gave me." Helene bit into a donut. "Better check with Mr. S."

I lowered my voice. "Helene, between you and me, it looks like the revisions were made on the copy sent to the court, but the client received the original draft."

Helene swallowed another mouthful destined for her ankles. "Sunny, I only sent what..."

Slater's door flung open. He emerged holding a *Time* magazine and the morning *Wall Street Journal*. "What brings you up to our fine floor this morning, Ms. St. Clair?"

"I'm just checking on the McKeen file."

"Helene's already closed it up." He continued toward his obvious destination.

I didn't want to get Helene in trouble, but what if the client called Slater next? "Sir, the client just called. He received a copy of the original document without the revisions."

Slater stopped and turned back. "What?"

"The copy of the sworn statement sent to him was not changed as he instructed." I tried to smile at Helene so she'd know I didn't blame her.

She seemed content to eavesdrop while she enjoyed her mid-morning snack.

Slater slapped the reading material under his arm. "Did you tell him it was a mistake?"

"Of course."

"I assume you've already discovered that everything is notated correctly." He reached for the file. "Fax McMeen a copy of the statement that was filed with the court."

"His name's McKeen, sir."

"McMeen, McKeen, whatever." He smiled. "You can handle this. You have nothing to worry about, Sunny."

When had he forgotten the client's name and figured out mine?

Slater walked back into his office, magazines in tow. "Helene, I need that letter dictated ASAP."

Helene finished off her coffee, slid her chair back from her desk and shuffled toward his office.

Pat

AS I SWERVED INTO *PAT GOLDSTEIN, PSYCHOTHERAPIST'S* high-rise parking garage, I narrowly missed a head-on collision.

"Everybody goes the wrong way down that one-way street." The parking lot attendant smiled as he handed me a parking ticket above a sign that read: *$5.00 Every Twenty Minutes*. "How long you gonna be?"

"Half an hour or so." I didn't want to say one hour or he'd surely know where I was headed.

"Park over there." He pointed toward a spot that read: *Fifteen minute parking only. Violators will be towed.*

I checked my watch. It was 4:29 P.M. My appointment started in one minute.

"Thanks." I whipped into the spot and ran frantically toward the lobby. Despite an urgent need to pee, I rushed onto the elevator. After an interminable thirty seconds, the doors opened and released me. It was 4:33 P.M. I rushed to the ladies room and twisted the doorknob.

Locked.

Without glancing at the floor directory, I bolted right. I could feel the bold lettering scream to me from down the hallway: *PATRICIA GOLDSTEIN, SHRINK. CRAZY PEOPLE WELCOME. VISA AND MASTERCARD ACCEPTED.*

I tucked my hair behind my ears, adjusted my bra strap and looked both ways as I approached her door. Hopefully, no one would see me enter.

Like the bathroom, her knob didn't budge.

131

I rapped on the door lightly.

Then harder.

As beads of sweat collected at my temples, I checked my calendar again. I'd waited so long for this meeting, I was desperate for her counsel, especially after my morning. I also needed her ladies' room key or I was going to wet my pants.

The law offices down the hall seemed my best chance for a restroom key. I dug through my purse and found a bent business card with my name. As I crossed my legs and pinched the card between the door and frame so she wouldn't charge me for a missed appointment, the door opened.

"Sunny?" I almost fell forward into her.

"Dr. Goldstein?"

"Pat." She pressed little square-framed glasses back up on the bridge of her nose and bit off a chunk of sandwich.

I uncrossed my legs.

"We do have an appointment now, right? I hope I didn't put it into my calendar on the wrong day."

"Running behind," she managed through a mouthful of turkey and cheese.

"Could I please use the restroom before we start? I was in a huge rush to get here and..."

"You'll need this." She reached into the pocket of her linen slacks and tossed me a key. "Take your time."

"Thanks," I said, trying to sound cool, balanced and unruffled.

Pat wiped a smudge from the door placard, which when I looked at it, showed her name and credentials in an understated script. The door slammed behind her.

I slipped back into her waiting room at 4:39 P.M. with my hair in a loose ponytail, a bit of pressed powder on my face, and relieved of the sensation that I might float away.

How was I going to start with Pat? What was I going to say to the managing partner about the McKeen incident? *Please, don't fire Helene, sir. The stressful pace of this job can sometimes overwhelm even the most seasoned secretary. I'm sure you realize she's a single mother with three young boys.* My guilt ebbed a bit as I pictured Mr. Wakeman's sharp features soften with my words. *Though I realize it's not my place to interfere with protocol, I hope you'll take into consideration the tight deadline she faced and...*

4:42 P.M. I dug through my purse for a mint.

4:46 P.M. Pat's voice was garbled as she left a message. She dialed another number. "New one. Sure she'll be a real wacko." Or maybe she said, "I sure wish I had a crunchy apple."

I looked at my ankles. A hint of rash dotted my legs. If all she did was help me stop itching, the meeting would be a success.

Her voice rose. "How about the Frog's Leap? Frankly, I don't care if it's Mad Dog 20–20. What I need is a drink, a soak in the hot tub, and a good fuck." She giggled. Her voice dropped to a whisper.

Pat opened the door to her inner sanctum at 4:57 P.M., broke off a square of chocolate and popped it into her mouth.

The aroma wafted straight to my stomach.

"Come on in."

If I passed out from hunger, was she going to charge me for the down time? I glanced at my watch.

"You'll have your full fifty minutes, Sunny." Pat made a sucking noise to free a piece of stray lettuce from her canine. "Sit anywhere."

"Thanks."

She pointed to a black leather, L-shaped sectional, which spanned half of a small room filled with primitive tribal art. "Take off your jacket."

I did as I was told, edged along a glass coffee table, patted down my skirt, and sat in the corner where the two sides of the couch came together. When I looked up, I was staring into the eyes of a life-sized wooden tribesman holding an angry mask before his wooden countenance.

I shifted to the left.

"Hmm." Pat jotted something on a note pad then plopped onto an animal print chair.

"Is this okay?" I stared at the zebra area rug while she jotted a note. "Should I move?"

"You don't like confrontation." She rested a high-heeled boot on the glass top of the coffee table, lightly nicking the sagging breast of an African fertility sculpture.

"I don't? Yes, I do. I'm a lawyer."

133

"Then why wouldn't you tell me it pissed you off that I kept you waiting?"

I looked defiantly at the man with the mask. "I wasn't angry, it's just that I had a tense day at work and I had to leave early to get here and the traffic was..."

"Do you often find yourself in the role of the appeaser, Sunny?"

"I'm not sure I would really characterize myself as..."

"Tell me why you were so reluctant to seek therapy?" Pat pulled a stray hair from a sizable diamond stud earring.

"I wasn't reluctant." I said with force so Pat would know I was unafraid of confrontation. "My insurance doesn't cover counseling. With my student loans and my car payment, I was saving up to pay the hundred seventy-five dollars an hour."

"I went up to two hundred dollars first of the year."

I felt my cheeks redden. "Oh."

"Do you think an extra twenty-five dollars should affect your long-term well-being?"

"No." I tried unsuccessfully to shake Bernie's voice from my brain. *At this price you'd better be crazy.*

"Why are you here today, Sunny?"

At least she wasn't wasting time. "I have this rash." I looked down at my ankles. "The doctor said it was from nerves."

Pat tapped the heel of her boot with the pen and jotted something that looked like *Hypochondria* on her notepad. "In what ways is your life out of control?"

"My life isn't out of control. I just itch all over." I scratched my leg raw to prove the point.

"I see that."

"I'm not a hypochondriac. I'm a lawyer at a prestigious firm." *Time is money. Talk fast.* Bernie's voice boomed in my head. Perhaps I was hearing voices, but maybe it *was* better to let it all out. I took a deep breath. "My job seems out of control, at least it did today. This lawyer at my office assigned me some last moment work on a case and the client..."

"This is good." Pat put a hand up. "We'll get back to your job in a minute, but I want to start at the beginning."

"Okay." I smiled.

She smiled back. "I was wondering about your name. It's a nickname, I presume?"

"Could we explore the itching problem? That's why I came."

"Sunny, I need to get some background so I can help you."

"My name is Sunshine." I whispered. "I hate it."

"Why do you hate your name?"

"My mother missed the sixties and I have to pay for it. Atlas and Luna don't mind, but for me it's so embarrassing."

"What do you wish you were called?"

"Something normal." I looked at my scuffed pumps. "Jane."

"Hmm." She nodded her head. "Why don't we go ahead and call you Jane—just for our session?"

"Okay."

"Jane, did you say Atlas as in Atlas St. Clair?"

"Yes, he's my brother."

She wrote another note on her pad and scooted in closer as though she was going to ask for his number. "Jane, do you suppose the rash could be your real feelings about Sunny bubbling up and manifesting themselves on you outwardly?"

When she didn't ask all about Atlas, I relaxed a little. "I guess, but it just feels like a rash."

Pat handed me a tissue box. "It's okay to cry."

I didn't feel like I was going to, but as soon as I grabbed the tissues, my eyes welled up and the downpour began.

"Jane, tell me what hurts?"

Despite some trepidation about Pat, I began to unload. "I love my family, but I'm not like them." I took a breath and tried to collect myself, but a volcano of words erupted all over the room. "I mean, I'm a lawyer in a top firm, well, I will be, if I ever pass the bar. I was even engaged to a normal guy, well, he seemed that way at first. Alan had a good job in a family business, and a great condo, and he was Jewish, and he loved me, even though he kind of drank too much and had a bizarre work relationship with his mother. I thought I could be in love with him, but I just wasn't and I broke it off, and now I'm not sure I did the right thing because I doubt I will ever find someone I really love that loves me back. Maybe it wasn't him that

135

was weird, maybe it was me." I heard the words as though they came out of someone else. I thought of my almost evening with Jim Wolfe. "He was probably my only chance."

"Do you really believe that?"

I grabbed another tissue and swabbed my oozing nose. "I don't know."

"Have you dated since the break up?" She angled the note pad so I couldn't decipher her notations.

"Sort of."

"Meaning?"

I wasn't about to regale her with the details of my past few dates. "The thing is, I'm really busy at work and sometimes my job is..." I paused. "I love my job. It's prestigious and the pay is good and... It's just that today, I thought that maybe this partner I work for... it turned out to be nothing." My stomach flopped as I pictured Helene scanning Jobs.com. "I guess I was just being paranoid."

She definitely wrote that on her notepad. "This is great, Sunny."

It actually felt good to let some of my worries out, so I kept talking. "Well, it's not just my love life and my work. My sister is pregnant and my Mom is pregnant with my Dad's baby but she is married to my stepfather and someone has to tell him and..."

"Tell your stepfather?"

"No, my Dad."

"Jane, I have an idea." Pat took off her glasses and rubbed her eyes. "It's a little exercise." She slipped her feet off the coffee table and walked over to her matching glass desk for a pad of paper and pencil. She handed them to me. "Draw a picture of yourself and all the people that are important in your life."

"I can't draw."

"It doesn't matter, stick people are fine."

"Shall I label them?"

"Whatever you want to do." Pat headed for the door. "I'll be right back." She slipped out of the office.

I stared at the blank page. How would a picture help her figure out what was causing my rash?

It took a moment to build up my courage, but then I drew a big circle. It morphed into my face and body, complete with stringy curls and chubby thighs. Atlas got a big smile and a piece of turquoise hanging from a string tied around his neck. Luna's usual grimace looked more like a straight line. Her twins snuggled together, smiling from her oversized belly.

As I got more into it, I dressed Abby in Ralph Lauren. Hugh looked more like Daffy Duck than a man. By accident, I made Esther gigantic, but didn't want to scratch her out. The baby swam the backstroke in her distended abdomen.

I made stick office people with sharp teeth, like little Chuckie dolls that leered at me from behind a desk.

Pat sauntered in seven minutes later, tucking her blouse into her slacks. "Done?"

"Almost." I didn't even care that she'd taken her daily constitutional on my hour as I put the final touches on Bernie and his Mercedes full of women. He looked like an exhausted bus driver. I put the pen down. "Finished."

"That was sort of fun." I slid my creation over to Pat, who was perched on the end of the couch. Putting Kit on a broom was strangely freeing. "I think I'm getting the hang of this therapy thing."

Pat eyed my drawing. "You are in the center of the picture, correct?"

"Wow, yes."

"You have no mouth and no feet."

"I don't?"

"The only fully formed people in the picture are these two." She pointed first to Atlas. "Your brother, I presume?"

I looked at the picture. Only Atlas and Luna were not dressed up stick figures. Luna's twins looked like real babies. Esther's fetus had a face identical to Bernie's.

"You seem to be floating on the intertwined hands of your sister and Atlas."

"I can't draw perspective."

"Perhaps you can. Who is the puppy-like creature?"

"Hugh. I didn't mean for him to look that way."

"Jane, you're holding hands with a distraught looking woman wearing much more clothing than everyone else. Who's she?"

"That's Abby." The wedding day rumor flashed through my mind. "She's happy in real life. She just got married to the greatest guy and..."

"Everyone else in your drawing appears nude, or at least the clothing you've drawn is transparent. Abby looks like she is wearing a thick sweater. Look at her mouth."

"Abby loves clothes. Besides, she's frowning at me."

"Why might that be?"

"Well, I accidentally slept with her virgin cousin."

Pat coughed as though stifling a laugh. "There appears to be a man floating above you in a car full of identical women."

"My father."

"And the women?

"His girlfriends."

"And who is riding the broom?"

"My roommate. She's upset with me because I thought her boyfriend was about to give her an engagement ring, but he really wasn't and it was sort of my fault because..."

"Who are these evil little creatures?" She pointed to my workplace tableau.

"My co-workers."

Pat glanced at a wall clock. "I'm afraid we're running short on time. How about Friday, same time."

"Friday?"

"From our discussion and your self-portrait, it is my recommendation that we start with three days a week. We can add more sessions if we need to."

"I can't afford that."

"You can't afford not to." She pulled out her schedule. "Does 4:30 work on Friday?"

"Could we make it 5:00?"

"4:30 is my last appointment for the day."

"Was I your 4:30 today?"

She nodded.

"I don't think I can get off work that early on a regular basis. I'll lose my job." I started to slink out of her office. "Can I get back to you?"

Pat shook her head as she examined the drawing. "I'll need payment for

138

today."

"Oh, right." I opened my bag and pulled out my fake Kate Spade checkbook. For once, I wished it didn't look so real.

"Would you mind giving me a number for Atlas? I need to talk with him about a patient." She glanced at my check. "Go ahead and write it below your address."

It was bound to happen. "Pat?"

"Yes, Jane?"

I felt suddenly annoyed at my therapy name. "May I take my picture with me?" I wanted to show Atlas.

"I'll need it for my file."

The elevator ride was a blur of self-loathing and intense hunger. I barely made it to the building snack bar for a large bag of M&M'S and a diet ice tea. I tore open the bag and poured a handful into my mouth. I ducked into an abandoned hallway and dialed my cell phone as I washed the chocolate down with a gulp of ice tea.

Atlas answered on the first ring. "Plain, peanut or one of the new fancy flavors?"

I started to cry. Bits of candy coating sprayed onto the mouthpiece.

"Come right over. I love to draw pictures."

Sunny

LESS THAN A HALF-HOUR LATER, I EASED THE AUDI INTO Atlas's dank underground parking lot and ventured into his Hollywood Gothic building. I climbed onto the old elevator, pulled shut the rickety metal gate, and closed my eyes. As the lift shuddered up to the tenth floor, a familiar panic settled in. What if the "Big One" was destined for the moment I traveled through the center of the 1930s stucco tower on my way up to Atlas's perch? Would I be squashed like a bug, or would the good craftsmanship of a bygone era doom me to a lonely, arduous death in a steel cage beneath a mound of Art Deco rubble?

The elevator stopped without incident on the tenth floor.

"No wonder the shrink thinks you're crazy." Atlas's voice filled the hallway as I peeled back the gate. He stood in the doorway of his apartment with a steaming mug of chamomile tea. "You're safe from *The Big One*. At least for today."

"Lower your voice." I scanned the hallway for open doors. As the token celebrity occupant in a once-desirable building, the starstruck neighbors tracked Atlas's every move. In a week, some tabloid cover would feature a blurry photo of me, haggard and wild-eyed, with a spliced-in snapshot of Atlas looking anguished. The caption would read: *Atlas St. Clair's secret torment. Twin sister on the edge.*

"When are you going to move out of this creepy place, anyway?" I peered into his one-room apartment. Other than a picture window that overlooked the neon haze of Hollywood, the place was a shabby shadow of its glorious past. "One good jolt would send shards of glass crashing down everywhere and kill you."

"One good jolt might bring you to your senses." He grinned and pointed to a wall of packing boxes lining the wall opposite his couch-bed. "Your wish is my command."

"You're moving?"

"Sit and drink your tea." He handed me the mug and led me to a chartreuse armchair. "I didn't tell you because it wasn't finalized. I'm moving in with Drake."

"Congratulations." I willed away a pang of jealousy. Atlas was about to live my dream. "What a coincidence. I may be moving too; into the funny farm."

"Perhaps we can figure out a way to keep you from being institutionalized." He walked over to his dining table, grabbed a roll of packing tape, and handed it to me.

"The shrink thinks I need at least three days per week."

"I'm sure she does." His impish grin did nothing to calm my fears. "Lucky for you, I'm offering 'lost our lease' rates on my counseling services." He pointed to a pile of empty boxes next to his sound system. "You can work off my fees."

"Where do I start?"

"The CDs. I'll pack the books." Atlas looked around and shook his head. "I hate to leave the furniture but Drake doesn't want it."

Atlas's Goodwill-issue armchair, futon bed and mismatched dining room set once graced Bernie's post-divorce apartment. He donated the lot to Atlas when he realized that the women, as opposed to *That Woman*, liked a bachelor to have an appropriate pad. He upgraded to build-it-yourself black melamine.

Atlas took a deep whiff of the third world aroma that permeated the apartment. "I'm going to miss the smell of Mrs. Chopra's veggie curry."

"Oh, please." I ambled over to Atlas's enormous music collection and grabbed a pile of CDs.

"Mark the first and last CD in each box. It'll make unpacking much easier."

I loaded the first crate and wrote Abba—Bush on the side with a black marker. Other than records, books and his clothing, there was nothing much to pack. It hadn't occurred to me before, but Atlas's Spartan chic was eerily akin to Bernie St. Clair cheap.

Atlas smiled. "We are all more alike than we dare admit."

"Perhaps the whole family needs professional help."

"So far, it's done wonders for you."

I felt my blood pressure rise. "That's not nice."

"Sunny, I you told you not to go to her. Why did you?"

"Isn't being born into the St. Clair family reason enough?"

Atlas removed a stack of paperbacks from the shelf. "Then why did you choose a path that started with this family?"

"Just as Esther's egg and Bernie's sperm were about to meet, I screamed, God, this is the really weird family I've been dreaming of. I've been a dutiful goat and a pesky fly. Now, give me what I want, I beg you." I stuffed another box full of assorted "C" and "D" CD's. "It's that kind of mumbo-jumbo that's pushing me over the edge."

"Sunny, if only you'd embrace who you really are."

"I'm from the only family on earth that thinks it's wrong to want a man, a good job, and a happy home."

"It's not wrong to want the right man, the right job, and the right happy home. Otherwise you're doomed."

"To what, a normal life?"

"Or worse."

"Maybe that would make me happy."

Atlas put down his books and came toward me. "Tell me that when you touch someone and feel their emotions and thoughts, you don't realize that *normal* isn't quite your destiny.

"It only happens sporadically."

"But it happens."

"Atlas, no offense, but I have no interest in setting up a palm reading business."

"How about the *business* of embracing the real Sunny?" Atlas put a hand up and made an expression not unlike Pat's. "Sunny, I have an idea, a little exercise."

"Very funny."

"Put the tape down and shut your eyes."

The last thing I needed was a reenactment of my picture-drawing incident with Pat.

"I'm serious."

"Okay, okay." I closed my eyes.

"Sunny, relax, focus inward and tell me about Pat."

"She was nice." I took a deep breath and tried to block my thoughts about her lewd phone conversation.

"I'm going to go into the kitchen. While I'm gone, open your Third Eye and use it to look at Pat."

Having spent my formative years milling around New Age bookstores with Esther, I knew that the big almond-shaped eye sat above and between the other two, but opening and using the thing was Atlas's department. "I can't do that."

"I'm not coming back until you do." A second later, Atlas was rattling around in the kitchen and I was left alone with my blind inner-eye.

I tried to focus on the spot from inside my head. *Pat. Pat. Pat....* It started to itch, then tingle. Would it open up and I could see out of it or...?

"Sunny?" Atlas's voice startled me.

Had I fallen asleep?

He smiled and grasped my hand. "Now, tell me about Pat."

"This is ridiculous. Why does it matter what I think about Pat and her..."

"Do it."

"Okay." I squeezed my eyes shut and focused on the tingly spot between my brows until I pictured Pat with bits of sandwich tumbling around inside her mouth. "She cares primarily about money and sex, in that order. She thinks I'm amusing, mildly neurotic, lonely, and gullible. She figures she can scare me enough to come in once a week, which will pay for the big screen TV she just bought. She's into leather and battery operated props." I opened my eyes.

Atlas hugged me. "Sunny, there's hope for you, yet."

I was exhausted.

"I want you to know, I got off the phone with Pat right before you arrived."

"She thinks I'm so sick she needed to contact family?" Why had I fallen for Atlas's game? Of course I was psychic when he was around. He could put anything into my brain.

"I didn't put anything into your brain and Pat didn't even mention your name. She was too busy asking for advice on her love life and the stock market." He winked. "I'd tell you more, but there's that patient-client privilege thing and all." He smiled. "Sunny, there's nothing wrong with you but a few of Bernie's genes fighting for genetic dominance in a DNA sequence filled with possibility."

Only in my family.

"Sunny, just listen to your heart."

I could hear it thump in my chest.

"I don't mean like that."

"Then help me."

He closed his eyes, rolled his head from side to side and then smiled. "Just don't confuse your love life with the love of your life."

"Meaning?"

"That's all I'm going to say." Atlas handed me a new box. "We have work to do."

I packed up CD's starting with "The" and worked until I finally loaded Zappa, Zebrahead and Zevon.

Atlas escorted me down the hall. "Everything will unfold as it's meant to."

I was definitely sick of hearing that one.

He kissed my cheek and slid the metal bars open so I could step into the dreaded elevator.

A door cracked open.

"Here's one you aren't sick of." Atlas's voice grew low and booming as the elevator groaned to life. "Beware the Ides of March."

Pogued

FEBRUARY CAME IN LIKE A LION AND CONTINUED TO ROAR.
With the bar looming it was going to stay that way. Despite Atlas's warning,
I simply couldn't imagine how March could be any more fierce.

Kit appeared in my office doorway with a foot-high stack of deposition
transcripts and plopped them on my desk. "Here."

"I just needed the summaries."

"They're on top." She dumped the pile on my desk, turned, and tottered
out the door on a pair of paycheck-devastating Jimmy Choos.

Even before I rifled through the first inch of paperwork, I had an uneasy
feeling. I soon discovered there were only three completed summaries. The
spines of the other nine transcripts appeared to be unbroken.

"Kit?" I took off after her in my stocking feet, but she'd already
disappeared into her office. I pushed open her door and rushed over to the
desk. "Kit, where are the other summaries?"

"I'm sorry, but I'm sick." She rubbed her stomach. "I've spent the whole
morning in the bathroom."

"With the stomach flu or the cocktail flu?" I was going to throw up myself.
"Why didn't you start on these three days ago when Rhonda gave them to
you?"

"I swear, I'm sick." Her eyes were red-rimmed and watery. "I can't keep
anything down."

She did look a touch pale. "Why didn't you tell me you couldn't finish?
I'm totally screwed."

"I'll make it up to you." She looked at me with her best pitiful expression then gagged a little. "I promise."

"I'll be up all night doing your work just so I can get to mine. Not to mention the studying I need to do. How can you make that up to me?"

"I'm sorry." Tears ran down her face. For once, she seemed to mean it. "I've gotta go home."

"Don't touch anything in the kitchen or my room." The firm gave me a paid exam study week and it started in the morning. I couldn't afford the flu on top of sleepless nights.

I went back to my office and resisted the urge to scream at the top of my lungs. Then, I dialed Rhonda's extension.

"Betty, it's Sunny. Can I speak to Rhonda?" My phone smelled faintly of men's aftershave.

"I'll check, Ms. St. Clair." She put me on hold for a second.

"Line's busy. Can she get back to you?"

"It's rather urgent." I took a deep whiff of the handset. It smelled warm and woodsy. Was stress making me imagine things?

"What is it, Sunny?" Rhonda came on sounding pissed.

"Sorry to bother you, but I'm wondering if...?"

"What do you need?"

There was no point in telling on Kit; it was my responsibility to make sure any paralegal assigned to my case got the work done, even her. "Kit needed a little longer to do the depo summaries than she expected. Can I get the Morgansen motion to you a bit later in the day tomorrow?"

"I need to have it on my desk for final review at nine." The line went dead.

Shit. I hung up and unlocked my bottom desk drawer. My emergency undies, skirt, and blouse lay folded beneath my spare cosmetics case, blow dryer, and hairbrush. At least I wouldn't have to slink home in broad daylight wearing yesterday's clothing like I'd had a one-night stand at the office.

My phone rang.

"What?" I snapped in voice intended for Kit.

"Sunny, it's Jim Wolfe."

*Jim...*I quickly collected myself. "Sorry Jim, I was in the middle of this unexpected..."

"No worries." He chuckled. "I'd sure hate to make your shit list, though."

"It sounds worse than it is." I giggled like an idiot. Maybe I hadn't made a complete fool of myself in front of Vertigo Redux. How about I tell you all about Kit over a weekend away, say right after the bar exam?

"Did you have any preliminary questions on the Harrison opinion letter?"

Letter? A wave of disappointment rushed through me as I shuffled through the papers on my desk. It was just business after all.

"I dropped it by this morning. Have you had a chance to look it over?"

I found it under Kit's pile of unfinished work in time to save myself from looking like an imbecile. "I'm looking at it now."

"I'm afraid I'll need it by morning. Sorry to drop it in your lap at the last minute, but it was unavoidable."

"I'm afraid I have a motion for summary judgment due to Rhonda by nine. I'll be here all night as it is. I'm glad to do what I can, but..."

"I didn't realize you were going to be here late." He paused for a moment. "Listen, don't worry about it. Would you mind walking it down to Pogue? I hear he's hard up."

Not as much as you might think. I resisted an urge to giggle. "Pogue? Are you sure?" I'd overheard some secretaries chatting in the lounge about "getting Pogued," which, by the tone of the conversation, had to do with working overtime to correct all the mistakes in his work.

"I don't think Pogue can screw it up too bad."

"I'd be glad to do any other work for you." At least I hadn't said something stupid like *I'd love to work for you.*

"We'll have our chance." And he was gone.

I sniffed the Harrison file. It smelled like my phone. I held the receiver to my ear and cheek for an extra moment then banged my head against the desk a few times before I took my missed destiny and placed it on Bill Pogue's desk.

~*~

Hours later, I sat suspended eighteen floors above the earth in the firm's library, listening to Bill Pogue sniffle and sneeze with Kit's unfinished work spread out all around me. If she wasn't home retching her brains out, there'd be hell to pay.

The human equivalent of a hairball, composed primarily of Italian sub,

Sun Chips, and grandmother's iced oatmeal raisin cookies, churned in my stomach. The gallon of Diet Pepsi I'd consumed to stay awake did nothing to dislodge the mass from my gut. I held in gas.

"Nothing like these library chairs on the back." Bill sneezed all over a computer keyboard I would need long before the germs had time to die.

"Uh-huh." I cracked my cramped knuckles. I didn't have time for idle chatter, especially with him. It was already 9:00 P.M. and I still had hours and hours of deposition testimony to scan.

Q: Mrs. Smith, when did the symptoms first appear?

A: I first noticed the rash in 1997.

A familiar cold sensation swept through my body.

Q: Isn't it true Mrs. Smith, that you didn't file suit until fall of 1998?

A: Well, the doctor said...

Q: Just answer the question.

A: Yes, sir.

I willed away my own itch.

"A massage would sure be nice right about now." Bill stretched and rubbed his paunch. Curly red hairs puffed over the collar of his dress shirt. "We could take turns."

It took all of my power not to tell him I'd sooner die. "Bill, I'm buried."

"It'll help you relax." He raised a bushy red eyebrow.

"I really can't take the time to relax."

Bill shrugged and went back to his computer.

Other than his sniffling, we worked in silence for about fifteen minutes.

"Ever had a close-up look at Wakeman's office?"

"Not since the day I was hired." I knew where he was going, so I played dumb. Until we made partner, associates were only invited in to Mr. Wakeman's for a serious reprimand, though rumor had it many young associates reviewed the "penal codes" on his giant desk after hours.

"Then you haven't experienced the first year ritual?" He scooted out his chair and stood. There was a smallish bulge in his trousers.

"Afraid not," I said without looking up.

He walked over and put a clammy hand on my shoulder. "Come on. I know you broke up with that guy." His library breath fogged my reading glasses.

"Bill!" I pulled away. "You're dating my roommate."

"Not lately."

He stood so close I was sure his germs were hopping on to my clothing. I edged back in my chair.

He raked his hand through his wiry hair. "I saw how you looked at me that morning when I was at your place."

"I, I..." I was dumbfounded.

He leaned his acne-scarred face toward me and puckered his lips. "I won't tell anyone."

I pushed him back with my hand and scooched my chair against the wall. Being Pogued apparently didn't involve work at all.

"Come on, it'll be fun." He grabbed my hand, which now would need washing. "It's not like Kit would care. She did half the tax department."

"That's not true." It was probably closer to forty percent.

The phone rang like a fire alarm and saved me from imminent disaster.

"Shit." Bill turned away and readjusted his trousers as he ambled over to answer. "That's gotta be Jim."

Life wasn't fair. I should have been on the phone with beautiful Jim instead of staving off germy Bill Pogue as I slaved away for Rhonda.

"Yeah, yeah. No questions. I've got it figured out. Nope, place is basically abandoned except for me and St. Clair." He shot a sour look in my direction. "Yeah, she's parked for the night. Okay." He hung up then stomped back to his desk and collected his file. "I gotta go meet with Jim before he takes off."

"At least you get to go home tonight." And meet with Jim.

Bill leered at my chest. "I'll check in before I go."

"No need." I pretended to scan depo testimony.

"Whatever." He sniffed and turned his back.

I ignored him.

The second he left the library, I rushed to the drinking fountain, rinsed my hand and scrounged through the librarian's desk for hand sanitizer to scrub the computer keyboard. I'd been Purdied by Kit and Pogued by Bill and the night was still young.

Jim

THE LIBRARY DOOR SWUNG OPEN NEAR MIDNIGHT. I JUMPED, but didn't turn from the computer screen. The last thing I needed was more of Bill Pogue.

"Sorry to startle you."

It wasn't Bill.

My heart thumped. "I was afraid you might be..." I tried to taste my breath as I spoke. Why didn't I snack on Mentos or Lifesavers instead of Nacho Doritos?

Jim Wolfe's white shirt still looked fresh even without his tie and the top button unfastened. Loose strands of shiny brown hair cascaded onto his perfect forehead. "I just sent him home."

"Thanks." I looked down. "I shouldn't have said that."

"I'm sorry you were stuck up here with him. It was unavoidable." He smiled, or rather, his kissable lips curled into a breathtaking grin. "I called to make sure he was staying in line."

"It wasn't bad until the last hour." It took all my will not to stare deeply into his eyes. I surreptitiously ran my tongue across my teeth to remove any errant food.

Jim moved closer and glanced over my shoulder onto the computer screen. He smelled like the lingering scent on my phone. "How much work do you still have?"

"I dunno. Somehow, I'll get it done."

"That much?" He smiled again. "Do a keynote search instead of a word search. It'll help narrow the results." He pulled up a chair and reached over me to type in the shortcut. His arm grazed mine. "See?"

Could he feel my heart thumping through my back?

"I still have to review all of Bill's work." He shook his head. "I may have saved myself all of an hour by assigning it to him."

Bless you, Bill. "I think you've been Pogued." It slipped out before I could censor my words.

"I was afraid that you might have been, too."

"I think I was. I mean, I didn't..." I felt the redness as it crept across my cheeks. "What I mean is I think I was the victim of an attempted Poguing."

"Was it as bad for you as it was for me?" Tiny creases highlighted his stunning brown eyes.

"It could have been worse. Your last call saved me from having to slap him. He suggested a study break in Mr. Wakeman's office."

"Pogue *would* try that one." He reached for my hand and pulled me up. "Come on. I'll teach you *my* study break trick."

I felt like a cartoon character, unmolding from the shape of a chair.

"Ready, set, go." He ran out the door and down the hallway.

"What are you doing?" The blood rushed out of my rear and back into my legs as I chased after him.

"They call it exercise. Hurry up, I'm beating you."

"Wait. I can't run in heels and my right foot's asleep."

"Excuses, excuses." Jim and his cantaloupe-round buns took off down the hallway. He had to look breathtaking in jeans.

I pulled off my shoes and set them by the wall, certain I'd fallen asleep and was dreaming.

"The coast is clear." He came around the corner, grabbed my hand and led me down the hall.

When our fingers touched, electricity surged from him into me and it wasn't the psychic kind, because it just shot south.

My heart fluttered as we raced around the plaid carpet on the eighteenth floor. I tried to maintain Jim's brisk clip until I felt a drop of perspiration roll down my back. Sweat was not an option. "I need to rest." I tried not to pant. "I'm out of shape from studying. I haven't been able to get to the gym more than two or three times a week." *In my mind, that is.*

I sat down and leaned against the wall, trying not to look as dizzy as I felt.

Jim stopped next to me and slid to the floor. He rested his head on my shoulder and closed his eyes as though he'd passed out.

My heart thumped harder. This *was* a dream. I was going to wake up and find Bill Pogue fondling my breast.

I squeezed my eyes closed. *Please, don't be Bill Pogue.* When I reopened them, Jim was gazing up at me.

He smiled. "I owe Rhonda a big thanks for making you work late."

I blushed. "Technically, Kit Purdy's to blame. She got sick just in time to worm her way out of nine deposition summaries I needed in order to prepare the motion for Rhonda."

Jim shook his head. "Kit Purdy..."

I raised an eyebrow and feigned nonchalance while I awaited a dissertation on her unbelievable extracurricular feats.

"It's because of her and that legendary mouth, that I haven't redeemed your rain check from that night at Vertigo. It wasn't easy to think of a way to spend time with you that wouldn't trigger an instant inter-office email." He ran his fingers lightly down my arm. "When I asked you to work on my project, I had ulterior motives."

It was late. I'd consumed toxic levels of aspartame. I was hallucinating.

I began to babble like a nervous idiot. "Kit can't keep a secret, but I've known her a long time and she has a lot of good qualities that..."

"You're really cute." He reached up and stroked my hair. "And funny."

I am?

I'm not sure whether he lifted his head, or I lowered mine, or it was both of us at the same time, but the next thing I knew, we were kissing. He didn't shove his tongue deep in my throat like a space probe, drool into my mouth, or bite unintentionally. He tasted sweet.

"I knew that would be nice."

"You did?"

"I pictured this moment the first time I laid eyes on you," he said.

"But, you were taken." He kissed me again. "Or so I thought."

We kissed again. And again.

I would like to say that he produced a diamond solitaire from his pocket, placed it on my ring finger, then lifted me in his arms and carried me across the threshold where we made mad, passionate love. Or even that we rolled down the hallway in each other's arms, whispering promises of forever until we could no longer avoid the epic consummation that was our destiny.

The truth is, the next thing I knew we were naked in the cot room.

Until that evening, I dreaded the thought of a night in that dour windowless space, but with Jim, the narrow cot covered in hospital white sheets with a single pillow felt like a feather bed. The drip, drip of the dreary tiled shower provided a soundtrack more inspired than anything Mozart could dream up.

Jim's hairless tan chest shimmered in the yellowish cast of the industrial lighting. "Come here." He pulled me closer and kissed my eyelids, my cheeks, my lips.

As I ran my fingers down his snag-proof back, a knot formed in my stomach. What was I doing? What if someone heard us? Would I be fired? How would I face Jim when I ran into him in the hallway if this was a one-night stand?

"Don't be nervous, Sunny." Jim smiled then stroked my hair and kissed me.

I ran my fingers across his chest.

Would we be a couple? Would everyone start referring to us as SunnyandJim? I resisted the urge to shower him with kisses. I didn't want to scare him off with too much passion.

"This has been coming for a long time, you and me."

It had?

He ran his hands over my body and smiled.

We made love.

There were no awkward hands or elbows in the wrong spots, nor fumbling with the condom, excessive perspiration, or post-coital pleas for God's mercy. Just a blissful blur of his lips, hands, tongue and that perfect body wrapped around me, inside me.

Afterwards, he dozed in my arms.

I crooked my head and stared at the expanse of Jim's amazing body, from his strong shoulders to his muscular thighs. I ran my finger over a mole on his left leg as I memorized his feel, his smell, and his freckled shoulders. Was this it, or the beginning of IT?

An elementary-school-issue wall clock ticked off the blissful minutes. I felt like Cinderella at the ball moments before midnight, only it was 4:00 A.M.

"Jim, Jim!" I shook him gently.

"Can't again. Tomorrow," he mumbled and hugged me tight with one arm.

There was going to be a tomorrow!

"I should get back to work." I needed to disentangle one leg, but I didn't want to move, ever.

"I've got work to do, too." He kissed my forehead and rolled off the cot. "But, I'm not quite done with you." He whisked me into his arms, and carried me over to threshold of the shower.

He turned the spigot and a stream of cold water tumbled down on us.

Jim put his lips over my mouth and stifled my scream until the water warmed up. "We can't live on love. The other partners frown upon this sort of thing, especially when they aren't invited along."

He said the "L" word.

He kissed me again and lowered me gently to the floor.

Water cascaded down my face and into my hair. "My hair!"

My blow dryer and brush were locked away in my office. I didn't have time for the hour-long ordeal of styling.

"I love it." He stared into my eyes as he shampooed in giant tangles, then rubbed soap up and down my arms, my shoulders, my breasts, belly and...

I soaped him up, too. "Here." I handed him the bar of soap when I got too far below his belly button.

He laughed, and rubbed against me. The soap transferred between us.

The clock ticked.

At the stroke of 4:30 A.M., our love palace transformed back into a dingy converted storage room in the bowels of an office that would soon fill with staff.

Jim grabbed towels from a metal cabinet, handed one to me, and dried off. In moments I would be alone, with wet hair and half of a motion for summary judgment.

I hated this part.

I rushed over to my discarded pile of clothing, grabbed my undies and bra and pulled yesterday's panties up over my still damp legs. My bra didn't

154

match and had a slight tear in the lace. My top was missing two buttons. I leaned under the automatic hand dryer to dry my hair before I sneaked back to my office like the servant Cinderella, transformed back into rags.

"Let's keep this between us, for now." Jim pulled me toward him and hugged me as the dryer clicked off for the fourth time. "Okay?"

What an idiot I was.

"Coast is clear." He kissed me once more, unlocked the door and peered down the hallway.

I scurried down to my office, threw on fresh clothing, reapplied makeup using the hand mirror I kept in my desk and headed back to my abandoned spot in the firm library.

I tried to concentrate and not think of Jim as I finished my work. Somehow, I completed the motion and had it on Rhonda's desk just before 9:00 A.M.

As I made my bleary drive west on the 10 freeway toward my apartment, I saw Jim in every car, on billboards, coming out of the convenience store, at the corner bus stop. Had I told him I would be out all week studying? Would he know to call me at home? Should I have left an Ann Taylor pump in lieu of a glass slipper?

I pulled up in front of my place, bolted inside and barely peeled off my clothes before I fell into a deep sleep and dreamed of Jim.

~*~

I awoke at 4:00 P.M., to the heady scent of fresh cut roses. A dozen red long-stems sat in a vase on the dining room table.

My hands shook as I pulled the card from the plastic holder. Could it be?

I recognized the loopy script as I pulled the note from the envelope.

Sorry about last night.

XO,

Kit.

How did I tell her I owed *her* the bouquet? I checked my phone for a message or a missed call. Had he thought of me? Was he even awake yet? Would a man who wasn't going to call have washed my hair? An after-shiver rushed through me. I headed down the hall to thank Kit for the flowers and not tell her about my evening.

I knocked on Kit's door. "Kit, how are you feeling?"

155

There was no answer.

I opened the door and was greeted by her unmade bed and a crumpled pile of clothing. Clearly, she was so sick, she went out.

But how could I be mad? I walked back to the living room, plopped on the couch, and tried to study: *Constitutional and Self-Imposed Limitations on Exercise of Federal Jurisdiction Policy of "Strict Necessity."* Fair apportionment reminded me of Jim. Sale consummated made me think of Jim. Domiciliary state implied a marriage with Jim. I picked up my laptop and moved to my desk.

Was he going to call?

The phone finally rang two hours later. Our landline, that was.

I flew off the toilet, pulled up my jeans and ran for the living room, but the machine answered before I could. "Sunny and Kit aren't available right now..."

I picked up the handset without censoring my excitement, "Hello, hello, I'm here."

The message finished over my words. "Leave a message and we'll call you back if we want."

"I'm here."

Whoever it was had already hung up.

I tried to plow through an intentional torts outline. My head was spinning and I couldn't focus. There was only one thing I could to do.

I dialed Atlas's new number.

"Yes." He answered on the first ring.

"Is this how you answer the phone now?" I heard the sound of boxes opening in the background.

"I'm answering your question. Yes."

"Yes, what?" My anticipation turned to aggravation.

"Yes, he'll call."

"Tonight?"

"If you want that kind of accuracy get a Magic 8 Ball."

"Atlas, I think Jim's The One."

"I know."

"You know what?"

"I know you think he's the one."

156

"Is he?"

"Haven't we already been through this?" Atlas said.

"Yes, but..."

When the phone rang again, I almost didn't look down to pick it up.

"Bill Pogue bragged that chicken soup and Kit Purdy were on the menu at his house tonight, so I thought I would take this opportunity to pursue our clandestine affair. Look out your window."

I peered through the curtains.

Jim's Porsche sat at the curb. He leaned against the fender with the cell phone to his ear, wearing jeans.

Harry Hayes

WHEN THE PHONE RANG, I AWOKE WHILE PLUMMETING TO earth in an out-of-control elevator, clutching a briefcase full of papers on *Mutual and Illusory Promises*.

"Hello?" I managed, lifting my head from page fifty-four of the Torts section.

"Rise and Sunshine. Just finished my morning meditation. I wanted to wish you light and blessings for your big day."

"Thanks, Esther." I looked at the drool-smudged outline next to me in bed. I'd fallen asleep to *Wanton and Willful Conduct*. "What time is it?"

"Time to greet the joy of a new day."

It was 6:00 AM and my wakeup call was for 7:00. On Abby's advice, I'd checked into the Century Plaza for some last minute studying in peace and quiet, but spent the evening soaking in the oversized tub worrying how long it would take to pay it off my Visa. "That won't be so easy today."

"Then, that'll be a wonderful challenge."

Her comment was too cloying for any kind of thoughtful response.

"Are you wearing your Aunt Gert's good luck pin?"

"Not on my nightgown." At Esther's insistence, I'd brought the giant cloisonné caterpillar to the hotel, but hadn't considered wearing it in public.

"It doesn't work unless it's pinned to your clothing."

"I know." I scanned through the Barbri and realized I'd forgotten contracts completely. "I've gotta go. I need to look at something before the test."

"Remember, deep cleansing breaths." She took a great inward suck of air and exhaled. "In through your mouth and out through your nose. And stay away from caffeine."

"Thanks, Esther." I made a pot of coffee and jumped in the shower. If only Jim was there to dry me off with a big, fluffy hotel towel and... There was no time to get distracted.

As I left the bathroom, I noticed a manila mailer tucked under my door. My heart skipped a little as I picked it up and ripped opened the flap. I recognized Abby's monogrammed Crane stationery immediately.

Sunny, I forgot to give this to you before you checked in and I didn't want to disturb you. Go get 'em.

Love you, Abby.

P.S. When you're finished reading the contents of the enclosed note, turn this over.

My name was written in someone else's careful print across the front of an envelope taped to the letter.

I opened it.

Dear Sunny, I am praying for success on your upcoming exam. Best of luck, Ted.

Was I doomed?

I turned Abby's note over.

Remember, Ted has the most direct connection of anyone we know to the Powers That Be. Aunt Ruth said he still has a spring in his step because of you! I couldn't think of a better good luck charm.

I opened my travel jewelry case, removed the giant multicolored caterpillar sitting on a cloisonné leaf and pinned it across my chest. Just in case, I tucked Ted's note into my pocket.

~*~

The head proctor cleared his throat into the microphone. "Good morning. I'm Harry Hayes and I'd like to welcome you to the California Bar Examination."

The nervous rumble that swept through the Grand Ballroom of the Century Plaza Hotel lodged in my stomach.

"In a few moments we will pass out the test booklets. You will have three hours to complete three essays, which comprise this morning's portion of the exam. We will break for lunch at noon and reconvene promptly at 1:30

P.M. for Performance Test Number One."

Seated in my immediate area I counted fourteen pencil twisters, twelve nail biters, six meditators and a nose-picker. A man, seated two rows in front of me began to cry.

I looked up at a chandelier as large as the sun and closed my eyes. *Please God, Earth Goddess, Buddha, Residents of Mount Olympus et al. I'm sorry for everything wrong I've ever done. Forgive me for being impatient with my family, running out on Alan, having sex with Ted, and judging Kit. From now on, I'll work hard to do the right thing. I'll try and be more understanding with Luna. I'll volunteer. I'll decode Atlas's cryptic comments and try to live by them. I won't ask for anything else. Please, just let me pass.*

I pictured God, doubled over, laughing.

The woman next to me inhaled and exhaled into a paper bag.

"It won't be so bad." I said to showcase my newly turned-over leaf. Nothing could be worse than the unknown terror of the next three days.

"It's my third try." She put the brown paper to her mouth again.

I resisted the urge to grab the bag from her.

Harry Hayes tapped on his microphone with a pointer. "I must ask for complete silence." He seemed to look pointedly in my direction, though I was ten rows back in the sea of test-takers. "If you have any issues or concerns, please direct them to a proctor. Speaking to those around you will be considered cheating. If you need to use the restroom, signal by raising your hand and someone will escort you."

I already needed to pee.

"And, do not open your testing materials until I say begin."

Droves of assistant proctors poured in from the side doorways, a retiree in pink polyester slacks and a matching floral top worked her way down my row. When she got to me, she stopped and stared at the caterpillar. She reached forward and clasped the pin between her fingers.

"It's my Aunt Gert's good luck charm." I was in no mood to chat about my costume jewelry with the only woman in the building who might find it attractive.

She held out her hand. "May I see it, dear?"

"Sure, but can I catch up with you at the break?"

"Please remove it."

160

Everyone within earshot turned.

Someone behind me muttered, "It's certainly creative. You gotta give her that."

How could I possibly stuff enough notes inside to help in the slightest? I unclasped the pin as fast as I could, pricking my finger in the process. "Here." I handed it to the proctor, who examined its black underbelly as I tried to stop the bleeding with my shirt. "It's a good luck pin for God's sake." I said loud enough for everyone nearby to hear. When I realized I'd shouted the Lord's name in vain, my stomach flopped.

"Can we please have quiet?" Harry Hayes asked into the microphone.

"You may have this back after we've examined it." She continued down the aisle.

The woman next to me handed over the paper bag.

I breathed in and out while I watched in horror as the proctor brought the pin to the front and handed it to Harry Hayes. Together, they examined it for crib sheets.

Everyone in my section stared at me as we awaited my fate.

Finally, Harry Hayes tapped the microphone with my caterpillar. "Good luck." He smiled at me. "You may begin."

I opened my test booklet and read the first question. Ted's note crinkled in my pocket. Sweat dripped down my back. The words appeared to be in Arabic or Japanese or maybe Hindi. I couldn't refocus my eyes. Beads of sweat broke out on my forehead. I rubbed at my eyebrows.

A guy two rows up and three people over fainted and fell to the floor. The nearest proctors ran to him and removed him from the test.

At least he wouldn't have to suffer through the whole exam, and then fail. I stared at my test booklet.

You can do it, Sunny.

My eyes began to register the symbols before me as real words.

On January 31, 2011 Sam prepares and signed a negotiable promissory note in the amount of one hundred thousand dollars payable to the order of Rick on January 31, 2012, intending to satisfy a debt owed to him by Rick.

I reread the first sentence.

That same day, during a visit to Sam's house, Al, a mutual friend of Sam and Rick, saw the note on Sam's desk and, having heard Sam promise for over a year to pay the debt to Rick, took the note while Sam was out of the room and gave it to Rick that evening.

Focus Sunny, focus.

Al told Rick that he took the note so Sam could not change his mind about paying the debt. Sam, assuming he had mislaid the note gave it no further thought.

Bernie didn't know I hadn't passed the bar in the first place.

The next day Rick, in need of immediate cash, indorsed the note in blank and sold it to Tim, at a slight discount.

Atlas and Luna thought I only became a lawyer to please Bernie.

Two weeks later Tim indorsed the note and sold it back to Rick for the face amount.

Would Kit snicker under her breath as I set off each morning for a firm in Long Beach or La Habra?

Rick drew a line in ink through Tim's indorsement on the note.

Would Jim ever wash the hair of a two-time bar flunkee?

On June 30, 2012, Rick gave the note to Harold as collateral security for a ten thousand dollar loan from Harold.

Where would I work?

Rick subsequently defaulted on his obligation to Harold and Harold kept the note in satisfaction of Peter's debt.

I squeezed my eyes shut, then reopened them.

On January 31, 2013, Harold presented the note to Sam with a demand for payment; Sam refused to pay the note. Harold gave prompt notice of Sam's dishonor of the note to Rick and Tim.

I reread the entire question.

What are the rights of all of the parties with respect to the promissory note?

It was a negotiable instrument question. I'd reviewed Uniform Commercial Code. The question dealt with the rights of an innocent holder in due course. I could do this.

I wrote a decent answer, moved on to a wills and trusts question and a toughie on constitutional law. I survived the morning.

After lunch, I returned to my spot and found Aunt Gert's caterpillar waiting for me. I pinned it to my chest and embarked on the first performance exam. It didn't go nearly as bad as I'd feared.

~*~

Neither did the evening.

I turned my room key in the lock and opened the door to Jim, spread across my bed on a sea of red rose petals. "I figured you could use a little stress release."

I dropped my bag of number two pencils and collapsed onto the bed next to him.

"You know, I aced the Multistate," he said as he pushed my hair back and kissed me. "I thought I'd show you a few more of my patented study break tricks."

And he did.

Afterwards Jim held me in his arms and whispered, "That was the most amazing hour of my life. I wish I had a video of it so I could relive it over and over."

Hopefully, I could manage not to replay it in my mind as I tried to concentrate on torts and criminal law. "Can you imagine, watching yourself, you know...?" I giggled. "My mother's friend and her husband made a video then accidentally taped over part of it. They sent out a Christmas CD of their daughter's first year that inadvertently included a re-creation of the conception."

Jim laughed. "We'll have to mark ours clearly." He pulled me on top of him and kissed my breasts, my lips, my everything.

We gazed into each other's eyes until Jim rolled me toward the end of the bed and pushed me gently with the ball of his foot. "Get in the shower and get studying." He pinched my bottom and winked. "For luck."

I padded off to the bathroom in a maelstrom of love, turned the spigots and slowly unwrapped the complimentary soap, expecting Jim to join me. "Jim?"

Maybe he'd dozed off.

As I lathered and rinsed, I missed the feeling of his hands all over me, of his soft lips, of his hair as it tickled my eyelashes. I resisted the urge to scream with joy as I wrapped myself in a towel and opened the bathroom door.

My room was empty.

In Jim's place was a silver tray set for one and a note. *Leaving for Dallas early in the morning. Wish I could stay all night. –J*

I gobbled down my dinner and tried unsuccessfully to banish Jim from my mind while I spent the night with the Barbri review.

~*~

"I'm half expecting that thing to turn into a butterfly in the middle of the test." The guy seated next to me wore a tweed jacket for the second day in a row. "How do you think you did yesterday?"

"Okay, I think." The caterpillar jabbed me in the chin as I looked away and smiled at Paper Bag Woman.

"How did you answer that second essay? It was obviously a contracts and criminal law crossover." He was committing the cardinal bar exam sin.

"I don't really remember." I said looking away.

"It was clearly a question of whether there was a mistake of fact or an intentional misrepresentation that induced the purchaser to buy the car." He snorted self-righteously. "There was at a minimum, a mistake, but the seller's mental state of being intentionally misleading or just careless determined whether it was also criminal."

"Oh." My stomach dropped. It hadn't occurred to me that the question had criminal law applications.

"Did you address the issue of the buyer's mental capacity since he had just left a tavern?"

"Yes," I lied. *Shut up, you supercilious jerk.* I rubbed the caterpillar. I'd forgotten to pack Ted's note in my pocket.

"Good morning, everyone." Harry Hayes appeared at the podium. "At this time, I must ask for complete silence as the proctors distribute your test materials. We will begin the multistate portion of the exam at exactly 9:00 A.M."

Mr. Tweed unwrapped a pack of Orbit and stuffed two pieces into his mouth.

Harry Hayes approached the microphone. "You may begin."

I read the first question

Pace sues Def Company for injuries suffered when Pace's car collided with Def Company's truck. Def's general manager prepared a report of the accident at the request of the company's attorney in preparation for the

164

trial, and delivered the report to the attorney. Pace demands that the report be produced.

Will production of the report be required?

A: Yes, because business reports are not generally privileged.

B: No, because it is a privileged communication from client to attorney.

C: No, because such reports contain hearsay.

D: No, because such reports are self-serving.

Would the driver escape with no injury and little fiscal penalty like Richard McKeen? *Focus, Sunny.* I reviewed the question and settled on B.

Tweed chewed like a cow working its cud.

The tangy, artificial fruit smell made my mouth water as I moved on to the next question.

Walker, a pedestrian, started north across the street in a clearly marked north-south... It rambled on for a quarter page. My strategy was to skip a few long questions and go back later since they were all worth only one point. I started on the next question.

The chomping grew louder.

I caught Tweed's eye and made the universal spit out your gum symbol.

The proctor gave me a stern look, but Tweed pulled a wrapper out of his pocket and obliged.

I cracked my knuckles and pressed on.

Sid was in the act of siphoning gasoline from Neighbor's car in Neighbor's garage and without his consent, when the gasoline exploded and a fire followed. Rescuer, seeing the fire, grabbed a fire extinguisher from his car and put out the fire, saving Sid's life and Neighbor's car and garage. In doing so, Rescuer was badly burned.

If rescuer asserts a claim against Neighbor for personal injuries, Rescuer will:

I thought of little Jesus Rodriguez and his badly burned mother. I blinked a few times and rolled my shoulders back.

A: Prevail because he saved Neighbor's property.

It couldn't be A so I scratched it off. B was a possibility and I had no idea whether it was C. *Shit.* I skipped and went on to the next problem.

The next problem filled the page. Skip.

Thankfully, the next three were easy and my confidence came back. I made my way through the short multiple choice questions and picked up the long ones with ten minutes to spare.

After an arduous day I turned off the phone, soaked in the tub and was asleep by 8:00.

~*~

Thursday, 1:30 P.M. I opened the booklet to the last performance exam question and the end of the bar exam.

A woman has come to your law office to meet with the senior partner concerning a serious matter. At the last minute, the partner is called away on a family emergency and asks you to handle the initial intake, note all relevant details and advise the client as best you can.

The client reports the following facts to you:

"As I was straightening out the contents of a drawer where my husband kept his business papers, I came across a sealed envelope marked "Private" in his handwriting. I was curious and slit the envelope open and found enclosed a torrid love letter to my husband from his secretary, plus some nude photographs of the secretary. I was incensed. I went to another drawer where I knew he kept his handgun and, I assumed it was loaded because my husband always told me 'You're safe around here because I've always got a loaded gun ready.' I headed off to my husband's office, which is just down the street, with the intent to do away with the secretary. I burst into the office, pulled the gun out of my purse, and pointed it at the secretary, saying, 'Here's your direct ticket to Hell, you home wrecker!' I pulled the trigger, but nothing happened because the handgun contained no ammunition. I ran from the office, but first I shouted, 'I wish I'd killed you.' The secretary called the police and I was arrested."

The jurisdiction's criminal code defines assault as (1) an attempt to commit battery; or (2) the intentional creation of a reasonable apprehension in the mind of the victim of imminent bodily harm. The code uses the common law definitions of homicide crimes.

The woman reports that the D.A. has filed Attempted Murder, Assault and Attempted Manslaughter charges against her. She is out on bail.

Prepare a memorandum to the partner advising him as to what charges will likely be upheld against her as well as the evidentiary issues that could arise and outline the factual issues that need to be investigated.

166

I giggled as I drafted my answer. *The client could be convicted of assault and either attempted murder or attempted manslaughter. She clearly intended to kill the secretary and did everything in her power to...*

While I didn't do criminal work at Walker, Gamble and Lutz, I had solid experience in memorandums and nudie photos.

Philip

UNLIKE THE FIRST-TIME EXAM TAKER'S TRADITION OF AN extended European vacation, or at least a weekend in Palm Springs, I was back at my desk playing catch up by Saturday morning. When Kit appeared in my office doorway on Monday, I was buried in new work and counting down the days until Jim returned from Dallas.

"I'm taking you out to dinner." The reflection of her green sweater cast a sickly pall on her fair skin.

"Tonight?" What bad thing had she done to me that I didn't know about? "What's the occasion?"

"We're celebrating the end of the bar." Kit smiled. "You'll die when you find out where I'm taking you."

Even though it would kill time until Jim came back, it didn't seem judicious to accept her invitation. "I have weeks worth of work to catch up on."

"You'll start catch up tomorrow." She walked around my desk and examined my black skirt, coordinating silk blouse and chunky low heels. "I'll bring you shoes. Meet me in front of the building at 6:00."

"But I..."

"I have an appointment out of the office this afternoon." Kit was gone before I managed to bow out of a too-expensive evening in her too-small footwear.

~*~

The headlights of Philip's Porsche reflected against the mirrored panels of my office building.

168

Kit was in the passenger seat.

Apparently, we were celebrating *à trois*, or whatever the French word was for third wheel.

"We're late." Kit passed a pair of black stilettos through the passenger window.

This celebration was either a ring-mistake-apology-dinner, or worse, Kit didn't want to be alone with Philip for reasons unknown. "Thanks for inviting me along, but why don't you two go on. I still have a few more hours of work."

"We won't hear of it. Will we, Philip?"

He twisted his pinkie around in his ear. "Nope."

Kit leaned forward, flipped the seat, and popped open the passenger door. "Get in."

I attempted a ladylike climb into the afterthought of a back seat without exposing myself to a passing male throng.

Philip readjusted the rearview mirror downward as I wrangled my skirt into position.

"Sunny, I invited a date for you, too." Kit wiped a mascara smear from below her eye. "But, I'm not sure if he'll make it."

Philip revved the engine and accelerated toward the 110 freeway on-ramp. "What?"

"Since you're not seeing anyone, I thought I'd fix you up."

Was this a test? Did she know about Jim? No way was I falling into her trap. I smiled and squeezed my size eight feet into her six-and-a-half shoes. "Great."

Philip smoothed his hair into the early makings of a comb-over and switched on the radio.

"Can you guess where we're going?" Kit yelled over the radio.

"No idea."

"I'll give you a hint. *Rien.*"

"Nothing?"

"Don't tell me you haven't heard of it?"

"It's a new restaurant with no name." Philip, not a stimulating conversationalist at his best, uttered his first real sentence of the evening. "Big deal."

"You could be a little more enthusiastic, Philip. After all, it's our anniversary."

"What?" Philip and I both said in unison.

"Technically. We met on February twenty-eighth. The day you started third grade at San Marino Elementary." Kit smiled and rubbed his arm. "I knew we were meant for each other the moment I saw you."

Philip patted the top of her hand as he sped north on La Brea. Moments later, he turned onto a side street and screeched to a halt in front of an abandoned building that looked like a crack house. A valet appeared out of nowhere.

Kit rechecked her makeup in the mirror. "Sunny, I can't believe you haven't heard about this place. The chef flies over from Paris every other week. They choose who gets a reservation and send them an email.

Philip set his sunglasses in their case, opened the driver's side door, and climbed out of the car.

The valet reached in and eased Kit from the low front seat.

In anticipation of my egress in obscenely high heels, I scooched my legs together and moved my knees sideways. As I extricated myself through the passenger side door, I banged my head on the top of the car.

"Sunny! Come on."

I was seeing stars even before Kit pushed me forward through the giant corrugated metal door and made a dramatic scan of the restaurant. "I guess your mystery date isn't here, yet."

I forced a smile and surveyed the stark interior of the converted warehouse for an unwelcome familiar face in the crowd.

Above the concrete floors and post-modern metal tables, thousands of tiny halogen bulbs hung suspended from wires in a breathtaking recreation of the night skies. Each dining space was lit by a recognizable constellation. The Big and Little Dippers illuminated the huge central bar to ensure crucial celebrity sightings.

A gorgeous Asian hostess swept a chunk of shimmery blue-black hair behind her ears and smirked at Philip. "Name?"

"One second," she whispered. "Philip, get me an Absolut Citron with a twist. Sunny, what are you having?"

My now-coherent plan was to have one drink and bolt. I reached into my purse. "A gin and tonic, please."

Kit rolled her eyes. "Bombay, Tanqueray, what?"

"Bombay." I pushed a ten at Philip. "Sapphire."

"Put your money away, Sunny." Kit shoved the bill back into my wallet.

"Reservation?" The hostess looked beyond us at her reflection in a vestibule mirror.

Kit sent Philip on with a push and leaned close to the hostess. "The reservation is under Pogue."

"No way."

I started for the door.

"Don't worry." Kit grabbed my hand. "He's not coming."

The hostess looked at the fax confirmation slip with lackluster interest. "The reservation is for two. Were you reconfirmed for three?" Light shimmered from her crystal-encrusted top.

"I just sent in the request this morning."

"For how many?" I asked.

Kit didn't answer.

"I'm not sure we can seat you," the hostess said.

"That's okay," I said. "I'm only staying for cocktails."

"Don't be ridiculous." Kit placed a few bills in the hostess's palm, took my hand and led me toward Philip.

I felt like a fly wrapped in just enough silk to prevent escape from the web I'd chanced into. "How could you do this to me?"

"Bill gave me his reservation, but he's not coming. I made up the date part so Philip doesn't get jealous."

"If Pogue shows up, I'm going to kill you, Kit."

"No worries."

Philip appeared beside us, the only man in a powder blue dress shirt in a sea of Versace and Hugo Boss. His pale skin looked translucent as he handed Kit and I our cocktails. "Go easy."

Kit scrunched her nose, guzzled, and handed the empty glass to Philip.

He polished off his martini in response.

"Kardashian alert!" Kit said, glancing across the bar.

I tried not to look. In the last year, Kit thought she saw Kim at the grocery store once and twice at the post office.

"She's fatter in person," Kit practically screamed.

"I think she looks great," I said. without looking.

The eyes of everyone within earshot shifted almost imperceptibly to assess Kit's claim.

The woman raised her drink in our direction and clandestinely gave Kit the finger from the side of her glass. I think she actually might have been one of them.

I polished off my Bombay and tonic.

Philip put a clammy hand on my shoulder. "Another, Sunny?"

"Me, too," Kit said.

Philip shook his head and set off to fetch another round.

As soon as he'd disappeared into the crowd, Kit whispered into my ear. "Philip said he *was* planning to give me a ring when he got back from Europe, but he wasn't happy with the quality of the stone. He told me the jeweler has a new shipment of diamonds to choose from. I wanted to warn you in advance because he'll probably want me to move in with him." Kit whisked her bangs sideways. "We'll have plenty of time to find someone to replace me. I heard Rhonda White may be splitting up with her husband."

Rhonda? Would she keep me working twenty-four hours a day? Kit was more than enough stress. Maybe I'd rent an efficiency. Unless Jim...

Philip returned and handed Kit her refill. "Please, take it slow."

"Don't say anything." Kit whispered into my ear. "He doesn't want to go public with this, yet—if you know what I mean."

"Any progress on our table?" Philip tapped the hostess as she sashayed by with a newly arrived party of four.

She pretended to ignore him.

"Do I have to deal with everything?" Kit huffed off toward the hostess desk.

I winced watching Kit try and talk her way into a table.

Philip shook his head. His thin lips were small for his wide face. "Sunny, I need to talk to you."

I took a deep breath and glanced at an alcohol-emboldened Kit, who'd taken up a heated discussion with the hostess.

The last thing I wanted to do was get in the middle.

"I love her, you know." Philip's eyes glistened. "As soon as she matures and shows she can behave properly, I'll ask her to marry me. Not before. No matter what the circumstances."

I'd promised myself not to say too much, but the gin I'd consumed had me feeling otherwise. "Philip, what if Kit just is who she is?"

"She's not ready for the responsibilities of marriage yet." He didn't seem to hear me. "When she proves to me that..."

"What if she doesn't change?"

"She will." He nodded. "If she wants the ring."

My stomach growled and my head was already starting to spin when Kit appeared with cocktail round number three. I didn't want to mention appetizers since I wasn't paying, but I couldn't go on much longer without some crackers or something to sop up the alcohol.

Philip reached for a handful of olives from the server station at the edge of the bar.

"Oh my God, Philip." Kit turned her back to him. "That's so embarrassing."

"I'm starved," he said through a mouthful of olives.

"Order us some appetizers."

"There's no menu."

"Ask the bartender."

"Why don't you? You're going to pick what we want anyway."

"It's obvious I have to." Kit polished off her drink and weaved from the bar area toward the bathroom instead of her stated destination.

A cocktail waitress slid past us with a plate of calamari.

"Do you want me to order something for us, Philip?" I would beg out after appetizers.

"Sunny, what I want is for you to help Kit understand that the ring is ready as soon as she is, not the other way around." He glanced toward the restroom door. "I'm not falling for any of her tricks."

Which of her tricks was he talking about?

"You seem like a *nice, normal* girl. Will you do that for me?"

Philip's nice, normal was clearly not the normal I aspired to.

"I'm starving, Philip." Kit reappeared having forgotten her original mission. "What did you order us?"

"What would you like?"

173

The hostess came out of nowhere and tapped Philip on the shoulder. "Pogue party. I have a table for two, not three."

"I guess the secret is out," she slurred. "Too bad he didn't make it, Sunny."

Philip downed his cocktail. "Why the hell is the reservation under his name?"

"I have other people waiting," the hostess said.

"Bill Pogue was supposed to be Sunny's date for tonight. He wanted me to set them up." She shrugged. "He must have gotten hung up in court."

"Table's all yours. I'm out of here." Philip started for the door.

"Wait!" Kit grabbed him by his monogrammed cuff.

"I've lost my appetite." He turned and glared at me. "Sunny, I'm surprised you'd be interested in Kit's sloppy seconds."

"I, I..." What could I say in my defense that wouldn't blow things for Kit?

He started for the door. "I'm not interested in making conversation with one of the other guys you're fucking."

"Shhh! Philip, people are staring."

A jaded-looking starlet in head-to-toe leather snickered and elbowed her friend.

"Like I care." He shook free of her grasp, weaving a little. "What do you think?" He turned to the women. "Should I break bread with the guy she's fucking?"

"I don't know," Leather said. "It's so hard to get a reservation at this place."

The other, in a black cocktail dress with a plunging back that stopped millimeters from her crack, added, "Besides, he's not even here."

"You wouldn't have minded so much if I'd brought Shelby Nelson instead of Sunny."

"All your freeloading friends are the same." He sprayed as he spoke.

My face heated up and I tucked into the gathering crowd. I would make my getaway as soon as possible.

"Speaking of which, how did it feel to be lost in the mounds of Shelby's big ass and fleshy gut?" Kit glared at him.

Someone stifled a giggle.

I froze.

"Funny you should mention that. Have you stopped seeing your good friend Abby's husband since he got married?"

174

The room started to spin.

"That's nonsense!" Kit said as she glanced sideways in my direction. She turned back and scowled at Philip. "Are you ever going to marry me? If you're not, it's over." She scanned the crowd. "Sunny?"

If she *had* slept with Charlie, wouldn't she have reacted more strongly? She'd have thrown a fit or walked out or...

Or what?

Philip pulled Kit across the restaurant to a quiet corner. For a moment, their voices were inaudible above the din of the restaurant, but facial expressions belied their drunken negotiations. They had all but forgotten I was invited to keep them from this moment.

With three cocktails for courage, I snuck behind a human shield of people who had given up the guise of being too cool to stare and gaped like spectators at a prizefight. The enrapt hostess didn't even notice me until I tapped her on the shoulder. "Listen, would you please give them the table? There will only be two."

"I really don't think so."

"Please, I'm sure it's generally your policy only to seat famous people, but they'll need food to sober up."

The hostess didn't acknowledge me.

A man placed a hand on her shoulder. "Serena, please give them my table."

Serena flashed a spectacular smile. "Are you sure, Adam? I'd hate to have you and Jordana wait any longer."

"Ms. St. Clair is right. They shouldn't be on the road and we're in no hurry." He turned to me. "How are you, Sunny?"

I wanted to die on the spot.

His hair was shorter, and his ensemble upgraded to Armani from a Phish T-shirt and carpenter jeans, but I recognized him in an instant. Adam Dey. Alan Fine's friend, Adam Dey.

"St. Clair as in Atlas St. Clair?" Serena was suddenly standing so close I could smell the scent of her shampoo.

I nodded while I tried to regain some composure.

"Atlas is the best." Serena smiled. "I'm going to check on a couple tables. Be right back."

"Thank you for offering your table, Adam." I glanced at my too small, too

175

high heels.

"We all have our difficult friends," Adam said.

I glanced across the restaurant at Philip and Kit who were well into round three of their world-class bout. "You can see how Kit's doing. How is Alan?"

"Good." Adam eyes sparkled. "He's been promoted to president of the under-apparel division."

"Great news, two tables are coming up soon." Serena, animated and sugary sweet, reappeared at my side. "You'll be staying for dinner, won't you, Sunny?"

"I need to get back to the office." I glanced again across the room. Kit was stroking Philip's arm. "Soon."

"I'd offer you a ride," Adam said. "But, I'm afraid I'm in the midst of a business dinner." He turned to the bar where a stunning brunette newscaster I'd seen on the local NBC affiliate smiled at him.

"I wouldn't dream of it, but thank you."

"My pleasure." He touched my shoulder lightly. "Would you please call Sunny a cab?"

"Of course." Serena's silver toggle bracelet made a tinkling sound as she reached below the stand, picked up the phone that supposedly didn't exist, and dialed Yellow Taxi.

"Good to see you, Sunny." Adam took off toward the bar.

"Isn't he a doll?" my new best friend Serena asked.

"What does he do?" If he was in construction, he was definitely the boss.

"He's a bigwig at the LA Times."

Before I could ask her anything else I spotted Kit and Philip starting for the front of the restaurant. "Gotta run, thanks for everything."

"Say hi to Atlas for me!"

I ran outside and took a deep breath of chilled smoggy air. At least Bill Pogue hadn't shown up.

176

Minerva Steele

FOR THE NEXT COUPLE OF WEEKS, KIT ACTED MORE LIKE A trail horse than a wild mare. She was either embarrassed, she'd decided to take Philip's ultimatum seriously, or both. I needed to talk to her about Charlie and confirm the rumor was just that, but didn't want to rock the boat until the right moment. Besides, I had my clandestine affair to conduct.

Or, so I thought...

"That Jim Wolfe reminds me of my Herbie when he was young." Old Delores met me with her mail cart just as I reached my office door.

"How's that?" The word was out.

"In my day, I liked the bucking broncos, too." Delores winked and lifted the bifocals nestled in her sagging bosom. "I got the best of Herbie. His poor wife had to deal with everything else."

Herbie as in Herbert Lutz?

I shook my head and watched her shuffle down the hallway to red-X the next associate who hadn't made the early-bird list. Mr. Lutz had been dead for twenty years, but the gossip mill was very much alive. How could I ever believe my romance would remain a secret in a place like Walker, Gamble and Lutz?

Before I ran upstairs to warn Jim, I stepped into my office to drop off my mail and briefcase. A fresh phone message slip rustled in the air conditioning breeze on the middle of my desk. *Abby Crawford called.*

My stomach turned.

Since *Rien* with Philip and Kit, I'd avoided Abby by only texting and returning her calls when I knew she wouldn't answer. Kit's boat needed to

177

be rocked soon so I could look Abby in the eye again.

As I reached for the note, a letter slipped from my mail stack and fell to the floor. The seal of the California State Bar Association practically singed my fingers. Beneath the insignia, the return address read *Minerva Steele. Investigations.*

The bar results weren't due until the end of May. Had I reached a phase of the process I'd never reached last time or...?

I tore open the envelope.

Dear Ms. St. Clair:

A request for investigation was made by Richard McKeen regarding Rodriguez vs. McKeen. Enclosed is his statement. I have been assigned to investigate this case. Please review this information and contact me at your earliest convenience to set up an interview. You can reach me at 213–555– 1000 X 110.

Sincerely, Minerva Steele. Investigator.

It took almost half an hour before I could hold my face expressionless and navigate the hallways to Jim's office. I collapsed into one of his client chairs.

"What's up?" He asked as though he didn't want to know. His hair flopped into his eyes as he glanced at his computer screen. "I'm swamped."

I put my face in my hands to keep from sobbing.

He came over and gave me a stiff hug. "I don't mean to sound callous, but I'm expecting an important conference call in less than five minutes. Can we talk about personal stuff later?"

I nodded. Someone must have already tipped him off.

"Listen, I'm leaving for a meeting as soon as I get off the phone. I'll stop by your place on my way home. Okay?"

"Sure." My voice shook. "But, this isn't about personal stuff."

He looked slightly bewildered, or maybe annoyed. "I've only got a couple minutes, so talk fast."

I gulped some air then erupted into a fast stream of words. "The thing is, Helene mailed the unrevised copy of a sworn statement to a client I was working with. I checked the file and the revisions were stamped and the settlement had been approved by the court and all the moneys were disbursed and everything seemed right but..."

"But what?"

"I think Conrad Slater may have filed the wrong statement with the court."
I swallowed a floodgate of tears.

"Conrad Slater? He's too pickled to do anything on purpose."

"I'm in huge trouble."

"Babe, you're overreacting." He kissed my hand. "I think you've got the
legal version of med-schoolitis. You're exhausted from studying too hard."

His phone rang before I had a chance to tell him about the letter.

"Talk to you later." Jim picked up the receiver and blew me a kiss.

What was I supposed to do until then? For the next half-hour, I circled the
nineteenth floor aimlessly.

"I've been looking all over for you." Jillian grabbed my arm as I started
down the stairs to my floor. "Your lunch date is in reception."

"I don't have a lunch date."

"Well, a young woman who doesn't appear to be an attorney is waiting for
you." Jillian pointed to my face. "Her name is Abigail Crawford."

It took everything I had not to burst into tears.

She dropped me off in front of the ladies' room. "Perhaps you should run
some water on your face before you greet your guest."

My fingers trembled as I dabbed mascara smears from under my eyes. I
ran cool water over my hands. What was I going to say? What could I say?
I tried to swallow my suspicions and fears, and started down the hallway to
reception. I took a deep cleansing breath and opened the door.

Abby greeted me with her beautiful, trusting smile.

Charlie

SORRY, I COULDN'T GET AWAY FOR A PROPER LUNCH." I PULLED the pickle-soaked crust from my bread and bit into the dry roast beef. "I've been so busy lately."

"I'm just glad you could join me at the last minute." Abby took a dainty bite of a prepackaged Chinese chicken salad consisting of a few crispy wontons atop a bed of iceberg lettuce and processed chicken chunks. "I was sure Charlie said lunch on Friday."

Her honeymoon tan had long since faded.

"I'm sure there's a logical explanation." *There had to be—for everything.* I set down my diet root beer on the wobbly metal table in the lobby deli-convenience store. "What did Charlie's secretary say when you got to his office?"

"She wasn't in, either." She smiled and looked down at her engagement ring, which looked even more enormous on her now bony hand. In fact, Abby looked as if she'd dropped ten pounds she didn't have to lose. "I must have gotten confused."

"Is everything okay?" I asked almost reflexively. How could she be okay if there was any truth to the Charlie and Kit rumor?

"I'm fine." She smiled. "Just a little run down from all the house renovations.

"Why don't you call Charlie again? Maybe he wants to meet us?" If I could see him in person, with Abby, I could look in his eyes and know there was no truth to the rumor. Then, I could move on to wondering if Minerva

Steele would be a hawk-faced old lady with cold hands or a nervous young woman with a severe hair-do and a chip on her shoulder.

"I'm sure I switched the days with all the appointments I've been setting with contractors." Abby picked the wontons off her salad and lined them up on the side of her paper plate. "Getting the house put together has turned out to be a way bigger job than I expected."

"I can't wait to see what you've done." Abby's dorm room was photographed for a back-to-school issue of Better Homes and Gardens.

"I just hope Charlie likes it. He's been so busy he hasn't given much input."

"Oh, Abby. How could he possibly improve on your taste?" Charlie was lucky to have a woman like her. He had to know that.

"I suppose it's just as well that he hasn't been involved, because I've exceeded my budget." Abby wrinkled her brow. "By quite a lot."

"He knows you're making him a wonderful home." Would Jim help make decorating decisions or would he just set me up with a budget? Would Jim even stay with me once I earned the distinction of becoming the first attorney in the history of Walker, Gamble and Lutz to be dismissed for ethics violations before passing the bar?

"I hope so." Abby's diamond studs shimmered in the florescent lights. "Listen to me going on and on about myself. I haven't asked you about the bar or anything else."

I think I was framed and will probably end up in women's prison. "The exam went okay." *And I'm praying Kit didn't sleep with your husband.* "And, there's nothing much else to tell."

"That's not what I heard."

"What exactly did you hear?" Had Kit picked up the other extension at home? Put a tape recorder in my office? How far had she stooped this time?

"Just that he's the office hunk." Abby smiled. "Kit was otherwise uncharacteristically mum."

I shook my head. What was next? "It's been killing me not to tell you, but I swore to Jim I wouldn't say anything to anyone, even you, until we knew it was for real."

"I understand."

"Please forgive me for keeping secrets, Abby." She had to be furious with me, and she didn't even know the worst of it. "I didn't tell you about Alan because I didn't want to bother you with my problems in the midst of your wedding. The Ted thing was..."

"I'm not upset with you." Her smile seemed genuine. "Really."

"Oh, Abby. I swear you would have been the first one, but somehow Kit..."

"It's hard to keep anything from her." Abby's hand trembled as she sipped her Evian. She looked down. "I've never been able to."

Don't project, Sunny. "What exactly did she tell you?"

"I haven't actually spoken with her. It seems like I'm out every time she calls. She always catches Charlie."

It took the rest of my diet root beer to dissolve the hunk of roast beef that lodged in my throat. I had to say something to make her feel better. I had to talk to Kit ASAP. "I really think Philip is going to come up with a ring soon."

"I hope so." Abby nibbled on a piece of lettuce.

"Abby, I..." I had no proof and even if I did...

"Let's not talk about Kit." Abby tucked a honey blonde strand of hair behind her ear. "Other than to make a toast to her and Philip." She lifted her water. "Then, I want to hear all about this Jim."

As I reached for my paper cup, Mr. Wakeman strolled by with Conrad Slater.

My forced smile transformed into a grimace.

Wakeman gave Abby a lingering once-over, but didn't acknowledge that he even knew me as they made their way toward a waiting limo.

I forgot the toast.

"What's wrong, Sunny?"

"Let's talk about Jim." Sheer dread settled into my bones as I watched Wakeman and Slater exit the building and disappear into the limo. "The work stuff is long and boring."

"I've got all afternoon. Give me the boring news first, and then I want every last detail about your love life."

As much as I tried to hold them back, tears filled my eyes and flowed down my cheeks. "Oh God, Abby, I'm so glad you here," I whispered. "I'm in such trouble."

She didn't glance at her Piaget, re-cross her legs or even blink as I recounted every detail of the McKeen fiasco. We never even got to Jim. When I finished, Abby looked straight into my eyes. "You need to cover your ass."

I began to sob. I'd never before heard her use a bad word.

Abby grasped my hand. "How does Helene prepare documents? She uses Word, right?"

"Yeah, of course."

"I have an idea."

~*~

I spent the rest of the day building up my courage.

At 7:00 P.M., I crept upstairs, searched the corridor for signs of Slater, Helene or late night workers. Once satisfied everyone was long gone, I wiped the crumbs from Helene's seat, logged on to her computer, and scrolled down the list of Word files until I found McKeen. The document was drafted at 2:30 P.M. on Thursday, January 20. The next document, McKeen revised, was dated 7:30 A.M. Wednesday, January 26.

I swung Helene's chair around and pulled open the *closed file* drawer and located the hard copies. As before, the *filed* stamp on the motion for approval of the settlement read Friday January 21, but it was attached to the revised affidavit which wasn't created until almost a week later.

That bastard.

Slater filed the original sworn statement without McKeen's changes, took the first page and attached it to the revised document so it would look as though the revised version was approved by the court.

And I had given McKeen my word that the changes were made.

How could that sleezeball Slater do such a thing to the Rodriguez family?

How could I work in an office with such a man?

Before I lost my nerve, I went to the copy room and made duplicates of the McKeen paperwork. I tucked the originals back into the *closed file* drawer and hurried toward my office to lock the copies in my desk drawer. My ass was covered.

But the path to my office was blocked.

Rhonda

ALL FOUR FEET AND ELEVEN INCHES OF RHONDA STOOD IN my doorway. "Have you finished the Thompson memo?"

"Almost." My voice squeaked as I tucked the McKeen copies under my arm.

Rhonda narrowed her eyes. "Bring it to my office before you go."

"Would first thing in the morning be okay?"

"I need it within the hour." She turned and disappeared around the corner.

I managed to shut the door to my office and dial Atlas's number before I started sobbing.

His voice mail clicked on right away. "Hi, you've reached Atlas. Leave a message and I'll catch you soon. Hang in there, Sunny."

~*~

"Just put it on my credenza." Rhonda pointed a nicotine-stained finger across her office.

I released my pile of work on the cluttered table with stiff, robotic arms.

"Sit." Rhonda motioned me to sit in one of her client chairs.

As I did as instructed, Rhonda perched on the edge of her desk and crossed a surprisingly sleek leg. "You're a brave woman, Sunny."

"What?" My voice sounded husky, like a middle-aged man. My face felt frozen from holding my mouth in an expressionless line.

"Jim Wolfe." She grabbed her e-cigarette and took a deep pull. "He's a real ride."

I made a vague nodding motion. *I can't handle your take on my love life right now, but if you have any opinions on the least painful method of suicide...*

"Did you know he was a year ahead of me at law school?"

I felt like I was melting.

"Has he said anything about me?" She looked out her window at a view only partially blocked by another high-rise.

"He thinks you're a great lawyer." I managed. Maybe I was having a nightmare. I pinched my arm. My reality remained unchanged. Why were we having this conversation?

Rhonda sort of blushed.

Was Rhonda in love with him? How much worse could this get? How would I word my resignation letter?

"Listen," she said. "I've known him a long time. It isn't easy going out with him, but he seems to really like you."

I forced myself to half-nod.

"Well, that's my little Jim Wolfe sermon." She smiled. "Would you hand me the things you worked on? I should probably look things over before you go."

"Thanks, Rhonda." I was too distressed to analyze why I felt so befuddled. My head throbbed. My body ached. My arms and legs were numb. I tried to stand and walk to the credenza, but my façade began to crack.

"Hang in there." Rhonda said. "It'll blow over."

What was she talking about? She couldn't possibly know about the McKeen case. No one had seen the letter but me.

She patted my shoulder as she grasped the papers from my hand.

Although I wasn't exactly surprised by the psychic surge, somehow Rhonda's touch sent a rush of thoughts into my brain that made my knees crumple beneath me. Rhonda thought I had potential. She thought Kit was a worthless bitch. She lusted for Mr. Wakeman because he was so powerful. Her favorite foods were Jell-O and shrimp. She liked me.

I collapsed into her arms.

But there was more...

Rhonda slept with Jim a couple times in law school and once on Mr. Wakeman's desk in her first year. She wasn't in love with him but was turned on by his wild side.

His wild side?

"Put your head between your legs." Rhonda eased me into the chair. "Don't worry about Jim and me. It was just sex."

When the spinning stopped, I lifted my head slowly and grasped her wrist, hoping to answer the one question I had to know. As soon as my fingers touched her skin, I knew the answer. *Rhonda can be trusted.*

I took a deep breath. "Rhonda, I need to ask you something. It isn't about Jim."

She knitted her brow. "Then what is it?"

My deep breath sounded like a gasp. "I got a letter today from a state bar investigator."

"Oh?"

As I detailed the McKeen case, Rhonda crossed her arms and leaned against her desk. When I finished, she nodded and handed me a tissue. Then she sighed. "Sunny. This is completely off the record," she said. "I'll deny this conversation to my grave. Understood?"

I nodded.

"Slater was afraid the judge would toss out his settlement agreement with the client's increased income figures, so he filed the original statement, then took the first page and attached it to the revisions. It's called top-sheeting."

It even had a name. "Why?"

"To keep himself out of the million dollar club."

"The what?"

"Conrad Slater is a washed-up drunk who brings in a ton of business because of his family connections. The rest of us handle the work while he naps in his office. For appearances, he takes the low-dollar, worthless crap while the other partners cross their fingers he won't fuck up." Rhonda shook her head. "Getting a million dollar verdict against your client is highly frowned upon. Even for him." She whistled. "I'd wager that dumb shit either forgot to tell Helene or was too drunk to care."

"What should I do?"

She furrowed her brow while she examined her desk calendar. "Today is March fifteenth. Wakeman will be in a good mood tomorrow. He and Slater went to sign up a big client this afternoon. First thing in the morning, you have a heart-to-heart with Wakeman and do what he tells you."

"And everything will be okay?"

"Think of it as the first flaming hoop in a trial by fire."

I thought of the trial by fire the Rodriguez family endured. "I haven't even passed the bar yet. Can they deny me admittance even if I passed the test?"

"Wakeman will figure it out." Rhonda's grim face sent a wave of nausea and fear through me. "But you'd better play dumb and put that evidence you photocopied somewhere safe. And don't tell another soul about this. *No one*."

I got up and started toward the door on numb legs. "Thanks, Rhonda."

"You're not the lightweight I might have thought." She patted my shoulder. "I guess the whole contest thing pales in comparison."

"The what?"

"That *Guess the Naked Attorney* wager Kit had going on. That mole on Jim's leg in the photo was a dead giveaway." Rhonda took a drag off her e-cigarette. "Don't you think?"

The blood froze in my veins.

Atlas's voice boomed in my head: *Beware the Ides of March.*

Wolfe

ET TU BRUTE?

Jim sat waiting for me on my front steps with a bouquet of grocery store flowers.

I left the McKeen file locked in the trunk of my car and met him at the top of my landing.

"Hey." He tried to kiss me as he handed off the flowers.

I offered a tear-stained cheek. I'd cried so hard in the car, my eyes ached.

He threw his arms around me, smashing the arrangement of mums, daisies and babies' breath against my chest. "Sunny, I'm so embarrassed."

I pulled loose from his grasp and tried to straighten the twisted petals. "Me, too."

"I'll try and explain." Jim's eyes glistened in the moonlight. "If you'll let me."

"Jim, I..." *Please let there be an explanation.* My fingers shook so hard I couldn't get the key into the lock. What could he possibly say that would make it all right?

"Sunny, that photo was taken at Bill Pogue's bachelor party three years ago." He ran his hand back and forth over the rough stucco facade. "I didn't know the picture even existed until..."

"Until?"

Jim's face flushed. "Rhonda told me this morning."

"Rhonda." My headache was degenerating into a migraine.

"Honey, I didn't tell you about her, because it was never serious and it's been over for years." He grasped my hands. "Listen, it's best to lay this all out."

How many revelations could I bear in one day?

"I don't remember the evening because I was stinking drunk. I have no idea who the women are." Jim shook his head. "And I don't have a drinking problem. You know I rarely have more than a single beer."

It was true that I'd never seen him drink more than two cocktails. "Then why?"

"It was one of those nights. I'm not proud of it, but that's the truth. If Bill Pogue hadn't been snapping pictures, I would have woken up with a terrible hangover and a bad feeling, but that would have been the end of it."

"He took the photo?"

"It's the only possible explanation. He's been hanging on to it, waiting for an opportune moment to use it against me." He put his arms around me and gazed into my eyes. "Sunny, I'm so sorry you saw it. I'm so sorry about the whole thing. I hope you can eventually forgive me for being so stupid."

I wanted to be mad. I wanted to push him away. I meant to, but I just couldn't. As I watched tears well up in the corners of his eyes and roll down his face, my heart emerged as the victor in its battle with my brain. Jim hadn't gotten drunk and caused a fatal traffic accident. He'd simply been foolish enough to drink himself into a stupor in the company of Bill Pogue. "Why couldn't it have been Pogue in the picture?"

"He was too busy gathering dirt on me." Jim held my face in his hands. "I'm so sorry, Sunny." He kissed me. "Let me come in. I need to have you next to me tonight."

I let him take the keys from my hand and open the door.

Although she'd certainly fled hours before, Kit's new favorite fragrance, lingered in the living room.

As soon as I flipped on the lights, I spotted her handwriting on a sheet of birth control pill shaped paper. I shook with rage as I walked toward the coffee table, put down my purse and the bouquet, then picked up the note.

Sunny, we need to talk soon. Kit.

"Is that bitch here?" Jim looked down the hallway toward Kit's empty room.

"No way."

"She'd better have left town, because I'll kill her when I see her." He took the paper from my hands and crumpled it. "You know Pogue put her up to this, don't you?"

"Why? Why would they do this?"

"Pogue's pissed because I had a little *talk* with Wakeman about him. I have no idea what Kit's deal is."

Nor did I. *Oh, Abby. What about Abby?* For the first time, I didn't try to explain Kit off or protect her. "I'm so sorry, Jim."

"You have nothing to apologize for. This is all my fault, remember?" Jim pulled me close. "*You* are wonderful." He kissed me with a passion I'd never felt before. "I love you."

He loved me?

"Forgive me." His eyes were damp with tears. "I'm so sorry."

Wasn't this whole situation much more embarrassing for him than for me? If we were SunnyandJim, then I had to stand by him. "We'll get through this." It came out kind of squeaky, but I managed to smile. "Together."

Jim nibbled on my ear and rubbed his hands lightly across my breasts and belly. "I'd like to make love with you tonight, but I'd rather just hold you."

Jim loved me!

"Let's go to bed. I'm beat and I have a court appearance at 9:00 in San Diego." He swept me into his arms and carried me toward my bedroom.

He loved me!

We undressed and fell into my bed in an exhausted stupor.

Jim kissed me softly, and wrapped his arms around me. "I love you, babe."

"I love you, too." I settled into the overstuffed pillows and fluffy down comforter and snuggled next to him. With his warm breath against my neck and his strong arms around me, everything was perfect.

Perfect, if only Conrad Slater and Minerva Steele weren't in bed with us, too.

Jim twitched.

I couldn't sleep.

Would Jim also advise me to meet with Wakeman in the morning? Jim knew Slater and he knew the game. But what of Rhonda's warning? *Don't tell another soul about it. No one.* Did the man I love count as *no one*? Did she mean don't tell anyone about the letter, or just the files I'd copied? Jim already knew I had suspicions about Slater. If I could accept Jim's photo, certainly he would support me through my office trials. The letter could only give me credibility. "Jim?"

He rolled over and snored.

As I lay staring at Jim's strong back, wondering if I should really wake him, I thought of the McKeen file sitting in the trunk of my car. What if someone stole the Audi with the evidence inside? Would Jim wake if I tiptoed down to my parking space and grabbed the papers? Where would I hide them in the house? How long would it take for Kit to get wind of a scandal and begin to snoop?

Silently, I slipped out of bed, closed my bedroom door, crept into the living room, and reached into my purse for the keys. I stood by the window and rechecked the alarm. It made a satisfying *WHEEEP.*

I climbed back into bed and spooned against Jim. We were SunnyandJim now. Jim would tell me what to do in the morning. *Everything is going to be okay. Everything is going to be okay. Everything is...*

Eventually, I dozed off.

When I woke up at 6:00, Jim, his support, and his good counsel were already on the way to San Diego.

I tried his cell phone, but each time I dialed, it rang directly into his voice mail.

I was left to face Wakeman on my own.

Mr. Wakeman

FOR ALMOST TWO HOURS I SAT AT MY DESK WITH A KNOT IN
my stomach and hands so sweaty I couldn't even hold a pen. As I finally
stood and steadied myself for a too-short walk down the hall, the phone
rang.

I picked it up as though it was a last-minute stay of execution.

"Hey, I found *the* spring." Luna didn't announce herself or bother to ask if
it was a good time. "I need to send you the paperwork to look over."

My sister was a far cry from the governor. "Luna, can I get right back to
you? I'm about to go into an important meeting."

"Every time you say that, three days go by. I need you to look this stuff
over."

"Fine." She'd never understand the demands of a real job. "Listen, I've
really gotta..."

"This old farmer started a small bottling plant near Arrowhead. The locals
swear it has healing powers. His widow can't handle the business on her
own and she loved my plan to combine her naturally sparkling water with
organic juices. It's an ideal situation."

Did Wakeman really have the power to heal my status with the state bar?
What if I failed again, anyway? I'd only ever been into Wakeman's office
for a welcome-on-board handshake. I tasted bitter terror in the back of my
throat.

"We made a verbal agreement, but I told her my sister is a lawyer and we
should sign a contract and..." Luna took a shallow breath. "Sorry, the babies
are taking all my oxygen. What do you think?"

I think suffocation sounds like a viable suicide option for me. "Sounds great."

"I'll email the paperwork over now."

"Fine."

"This is so exciting, I can hardly stand it!" Luna squealed.

"Good for you, Luna." I looked at my watch. It was 9:02. I hung up and didn't give another thought to my sister's spring.

I walked down to Mr. Wakeman's, took a seat on the sofa in his outer office, and waited for his secretary, Elizabeth, to acknowledge me. I pretended to scan a document I'd brought along, knowing she wouldn't look up for fifteen minutes, the requisite time for a first year to gain an audience with the secretary of the managing partner.

As I tried to gather my faltering courage, I spotted Bill Pogue's greasy carrot-top through Wakeman's slightly open door.

Wakeman's muffled voice echoed into the waiting area. "It's come to my attention that you decided not to sit for the February bar."

"Sir, I wasn't quite ready."

"Mr. Pogue, despite your unique stature in this firm, you know you must take and pass the bar."

How was it possible that he hadn't taken the exam yet? Pogue was a third year attorney. This had to be what Jim had reported to Wakeman.

Wakeman glanced past Pogue, spotted me and pushed a button on his desk. His door slammed shut.

Shit, shit, shit.

A second later Elizabeth's buzzer sounded. "Yes, sir," she answered in a clipped tone. "Right now." She hung up the phone and smiled at me as though I'd just arrived. "How may I help you, Ms. St. Clair?"

"I'd like to see Mr. Wakeman, please."

"As you know, he is in a meeting." She readjusted the barrette holding back her long hair and flashed her you-may-be-a-lawyer-but-I'm-in-charge-smile. "He's set aside some time for associate issues next Friday. At 2:00."

I felt like I was choking. "I need to speak with him today."

"Regarding which file?"

"It's personal." I looked down at my designer pumps. Would my next job require a polyester uniform and a name tag?

"I'll check." Elizabeth exhaled and shook her head as she picked up her phone and buzzed Wakeman. "Terribly sorry to bother you, but Ms. St. Clair, a first year, insists she must meet with you ASAP."

Was it possible that he didn't even know who I was? My office was only five doors down the hall.

"Exactly. I've gone ahead and scheduled her for next Friday at 2:00. Again, sorry about the interruption, sir." She hung up and motioned for the doorway. "Well, then..."

I mustered all my strength and managed to smile. "Would you please tell him I received a letter from a bar investigator regarding one of the partners?"

Her smirk faded.

"Thanks for your help." I detoured for the bathroom and unloaded the contents of my stomach.

When I returned to my office, a note sat on my desk. *Mr. Wakeman will see you in fifteen minutes.*

It took that long for my legs to stop shaking and walk back down the hall.

Upon my return, Elizabeth nodded, but didn't get up and escort me through Wakeman's heavy double doors.

I clutched the letter from the state bar in one hand, pressed the latch on the brass handle with the other, and let myself into his cavernous office.

Mr. Wakeman sat behind his enormous mahogany desk. Behind him, underscoring my fate, hung a Thomas Hart Benton oil painting of the shooting death of Jesse James.

I felt like I might need to rush back to the restroom.

"Ms. St. Clair. Have a seat." Wakeman offered his hand. I'd never been close enough to see the blackheads embedded deeply into his craggy cheeks or his pronounced piranha-like under-bite.

Would I be eaten alive?

"I understand you have a matter of some importance to discuss with me this morning." He took the damp letter from my hand and read the contents without waiting for my answer.

"Yes, sir."

"When did you get this?"

"Yesterday."

"With whom have you shared its contents?"

Play dumb and scared. Rhonda's words echoed in my ears. "Only Elizabeth knows of its existence."

"Good." Wakeman motioned me to a brown buckskin sofa as he sat in a matching club chair next to an eight by ten of his black Ferrari. His far too pretty wife and half-grown children smiled from portraits on a faraway credenza.

Wakeman gazed out the window at his unobstructed westward view. "What did you do?"

What did *I* do? I tried to swallow my outrage. "Sir, Mr. Slater asked me to prepare a sworn statement, have him okay it, and fax it to the client, which I did. When I faxed the sworn statement, the client signed off on the last page, but insisted that some revisions be made, the most notable being a substantial increase in his net worth. I brought the signed fax to Mr. Slater who assured me he would make all the changes and released me from the case."

"Then why are we hearing from a bar investigator?"

I took a silent deep breath. "After the settlement was approved by the court, the client called me because he received a copy of the document that was stamped by the court. None of the revisions were made."

Despite the law against smoking inside public buildings, Wakeman opened a gold box, grabbed a cigarette, and lit up with a matching gold lighter. "What did Slater say?"

"He said Helene mailed the wrong document in error to the client, but Helene..."

"How did you handle the client?"

"I assured Mr. McKeen it was a mix-up."

"I see." Wakeman exhaled a plume of blue-gray smoke into the custom-filtered air in his office. "Ms. St. Clair, I thank you for coming in and bringing this to my attention. Feel free to call the bar investigator and tell her exactly what you've told me."

"But, sir." It slipped out before I had a chance to stop myself. "I don't believe that's what happened."

Wakeman raised an eyebrow. "What *do* you think happened?"

"Sir, with all due respect, I believe Conrad Slater may have top-sheeted the file when he discovered that his client's net worth was double what he'd originally reported. Don't I have an ethical obligation to report that to the bar?"

Wakeman's smile vanished into a grimace. "Where did you hear of top-sheeting?"

Play dumb and scared. Think Sunny, think. "I saw it on a legal drama." *Shit, shit, shit.*

"That's a serious allegation, Ms. St. Clair. I'm sure you don't plan to tarnish the spotless reputation of one of our most senior attorneys with a plot from a television show."

"Sir, I..."

Wakeman smiled. "Aren't you a first year, who if I'm not mistaken, has not yet passed the bar?"

I felt my cheeks flush. At least I'd taken the bar.

"I assume you value your job and long term career?"

"Very much." Somehow, I managed to look straight into Wakeman's watery eyes. "That's why I came straight to you."

"Unlike a television law firm, we are team players here at Walker, Gamble and Lutz. One of the standards by which we judge partnership is your dedication to our office family." He patted my shoulder. "It's hard for me to imagine that Conrad would make such an egregious mistake, but a first year attorney, anxious to save her job? Now that's an interesting plot."

"Sir, I..." My blood was boiling. How could I have been so stupid?

"Did you know that Helene is a single mother? With so many responsibilities, it's understandable that she might get flustered by our pace around here sometimes, don't you think?"

I nodded like a sheep.

"You make a call to the state bar investigator, stating the sorrow you feel over Helene's unfortunate mistake. Conrad will speak to the client and opposing counsel on behalf of the firm. It's my experience that an apology which includes financial reparations is a welcome solution in the case of an honest mistake."

"Yes, sir."

"There's no harm in a win-win situation, is there?" He smiled broadly, flashing unusually small teeth. "If the stress over this situation affected your

196

recent bar exam, perhaps the partners will make an exception to our two strikes rule."

I nodded again, too stunned to speak. At least the Rodriguez family would get their money.

As he stood up to see me out, I put my hands in my jacket pockets to avoid a handshake.

"Ms. St. Clair." He pushed the door open button on his desk. "Take the rest of the day off. Contact the bar on Monday morning."

"Thank you, sir."

I slinked from his grand suite to my closet office and packed my briefcase. Would a three-day weekend be long enough?

Purdy

THE ENTIRE WALKER, GAMBLE AND LUTZ FAMILY FILLED the Biltmore Hotel grand ballroom. The cleaning crew giggled and pointed at me as they sipped Luna's murky bottled water from champagne flutes. Even before I looked down, I knew I was naked.

Jim stopped nibbling on Delores' sagging ear, pulled a video camera from his suit coat and zoomed in on my private parts.

Slater gave me a dirty look and resumed his intimate dance with Wakeman. They gently ran their hands through each other's hair.

I spotted Kit and chased her down a long hallway filled with rooms. In each doorway, a different rumple-haired partner lay on the bed, cigarette in hand, with Kit's lipstick prints over his face. Kit was long gone.

As I ran toward an exit, Bill Pogue materialized and blocked my path. He hoisted me onto his shoulders and carried me back into the sepia-toned ballroom singing, "You and Me Against the World."

Wakeman tapped the podium. "Ladies and gentlemen, may I be the first to introduce you to Mr. and Mrs. Bill Gamble Pogue."

I looked up toward the balcony and watched in horror as confetti shot from the breasts of two topless marble sculptures of my mother and Luna.

As the crowd roared and clapped, Bill let go of my feet and raised his fists in triumph.

I toppled off his shoulders and landed onto a pile of files in the arms of Rhonda White.

"Help me, Rhonda." I began to cry.

"Sunny, wake up." She shook me. "Sunny, please wake up."

I opened my eyes, not to Rhonda, but to Kit hunched over me. Dark circles underscored her puffy eyes.

"Go away." I rolled over and tried to re-enter my nightmare.

Kit slouched on the edge of my bed. "It's important."

"Is anything truly important to you?" I turned to her and grabbed her wrists. "Do you care about anyone?"

I realized I was shaking her and let go of her arms.

"I'm sorry." Kit massaged the red imprint my fingers left on her skin. "I want you to know I sent an email to everyone in the contest and told them the mystery lawyer turned out to be a friend of someone in the firm. I even returned the five dollar contributions."

"It's not enough."

"I know." Kit bowed her head. "Sunny, you weren't dating him when I found the photo."

"You mean, when Bill Pogue gave you a blackmail picture of Jim which you happily circulated all over the office?"

"It wasn't like that."

"Then how did you get the picture?" My voice was thick with rage.

"I picked the lock on Bill's desk drawer."

Either she thought I was unbelievably gullible or Pogue was an idiot savant. Could he possibly be clever enough to put the photo into his desk drawer, drop Kit a hint, and run down the hall for coffee knowing she'd have a bobby pin out in no time? "You expect me to believe your bullshit?"

Kit didn't say anything.

"Then how do you explain why the lawyer's identity remained a mystery until my relationship with Jim went public?"

"I didn't even know it was him." Tears streamed down Kit's face. "I didn't know who the lawyer was until Rhonda recognized Jim in the photo."

"You knew I was seeing him. Abby told me so."

She seemed to flinch at the mention of Abby's name. "But, I didn't know who the mystery lawyer was." She glanced at the floor. "If you remember, I guessed Nick Beebe."

"You don't need to keep lying. Jim told me all about Bill's bachelor party, the booze, the women, everything. Jim had no idea the photo even existed until you and your little fuck toy spread the picture all over the firm to get him back for blowing the whistle on Bill's bar status."

Kit grimaced. "But, Sunny..."

"How could you do that to him? Or me?"

"Sunny," Kit fiddled with the tie on her sweats. "There's something more you should know about Jim."

"I don't want to hear any more lame lies. Pogue's despicable." My skin tingled. "You're worse."

The corners of her mouth trembled.

"It's too late. The damage is done."

Anguish grayed Kit's face.

"Kit, unlike you and that scumbag Bill Pogue, or poor desperate Philip, Jim and I will get through this." I forced a smile. "We have a relationship built on honesty and we're in love."

"I'm so sorry." Kit threw her arms around me and burrowed her head into my shoulder. "For everything that's happened."

Instead of the familiar electric feeling and an unhappy flood of Kit's miserable rationalizations, her tears felt hot, like acid burning through my T-shirt and skin.

The truth hit me all at once: her sickness, her greenish pallor, and her tears. *Oh my God, she's pregnant.*

"Kit, tell me you're not pregnant." I pushed Kit away in horror. "Tell me, it's not true."

Kit slid to the floor. "You're all I have, Sunny. I need you. Please, help me!"

~*~

"Where's Philip today?" I asked as I spun the Audi through Beverly Hills feeling like a getaway car driver unable back out on a gang hit.

"Golfing."

"Is it his?"

As soon as she matures and shows she can behave properly, we'll marry. Not before. No matter the circumstances.

"He told me not to call him until the situation was dealt with."

Which meant what? "What about Bill?"

"Bill paid." Kit pulled her third consecutive Marlboro Light from her weekend smoking cache and blew hazy O's out the passenger window.

200

"Which means he's the father?"

"Doesn't matter." Sunlight accentuated a sprinkling of acne along her jaw line.

"Doesn't it?" I couldn't get myself to utter the name Charlie.

We continued down Wilshire in silence.

"Make a right on Beverly Drive."

I followed Wilshire past Rodeo, turned south and headed toward Pico at the low rent edge of Beverly Hills.

Kit pointed to an office building.

She didn't say anything about Doris Day as I eased into the space directly in front of the tidy brick building. Did the parking spot even qualify if Doris would never, ever, come to such a place? "What time do you think you'll be done?"

"Please, stay." Kit's voice trembled as she clutched the door handle.

"You expect me to sit through this?" I shook my head.

"Don't leave me."

I wanted to shake her, strangle her, and then disappear. Instead, I followed behind and watched in horror as Kit disappeared into the inner office.

She didn't glance back as I sat in the waiting room.

The woman next to me dabbed her eyes, blew her nose softly into a tissue, and eyed my progress on an outdated Vogue. When our eyes met accidentally, we didn't smile or exchange pleasantries.

I waited.

A football game lent a frenetic green cast to the dimly lit room. Three men stared at the flashing screen, none daring to hoot over a great play or holler about an unfair call.

And I waited.

Each time the head nurse opened the door and examined her clipboard, we all looked without looking up.

"Who's with Sue S.?"

A boy, no more than seventeen, closed a school text covered in brown butcher paper with "Scott plus Sue" scribbled on the back in a feminine cursive. His shaggy blond hair hung in his face as he shuffled toward the nurse.

The woman next to me placed her copy of Glamour on the coffee table and gazed intently at a Tide commercial.

I waited thirty seconds, dropped the Vogue within her reach and pretended to dig through my purse for a mint.

When the football game returned, she stood up, stretched, and grasped the Vogue.

I tugged the edge of her abandoned magazine, pulled it toward me, and lifted it into my lap. It fell open to an article entitled *Dirty Little Secrets*. I turned the page to banish Jim and his drunken *ménage à trois* from my consciousness, but I couldn't stop thinking of Kit in the back of Charlie Crawford's car; the tulle of her bridesmaid's dress filling the back seat.

The door opened and Ellen T's nervous significant other attempted a nonchalant walk toward the nurse. He twisted a wedding band that likely bound him to somebody else.

An older woman, cowering in the corner, tucked her knitting into a bag then shook her head as she was called to retrieve Sharon L.

Finally, the door swung open. The nurse appeared and examined her clipboard. "Who's here with Kit P.?"

I grabbed my purse and stared forward as the nurse led me into the clinic. The heavy, disinfected air couldn't mask the stench of blood, fear, and fateful decisions.

I stepped over a red set of footprints taped to the linoleum and a matching piece of tape pointed to a sign that read: *ADMITTING*. I looked up and gazed into the eyes of a plump, grandmotherly nurse I'd have expected to see cradling babies in a nursery. "Is she okay?"

"Physically she's fine, maybe a bit groggy and unsteady." Her dark wig shifted as she shook her head. "But she came out of the anesthesia screaming."

I attempted a weak smile. "Then she's probably okay."

"There's still a risk of hemorrhage and we can't seem to settle her down." The nurse motioned me to follow her down the one-way hall. "If you can't help, we'll need to sedate her."

How would I even look at Kit? "I can try."

I dodged the various color-coded footsteps like sidewalk cracks, and followed the nurse from the admitting area down the assembly line corridor— Step Two: *COUNSELING*, Step Three: *EXAMINATION*. A dull mechanical whir and muffled groans of pain lingered in the air around step four: *PROCEDURE*. Despite the air conditioning, sweat rolled from the nape of my neck, down my spine and soaked the band of my micro-fiber underwear.

The nurse stopped before the double doors marked Step Five: *RECOVERY*. "Your friend is scaring our other patients."

Was she ever really my friend?

The nurse pushed open the door and led me into a room filled with women covered in white linens on rolling gurneys.

"I hate these goddamn cookies!" Kit's voice echoed through the large ward. "Sign my paperwork. I need to go, now!"

A nurse in surgical scrubs ministered to a row of sleeping patients at the front of the room. She gave the head nurse an exasperated look.

"The friend is here." The head nurse patted my shoulder.

I nodded as the duty nurse shoved a pink kidney-shaped bowl under a patient's chin just as she vomited toward her lap.

Kit banged the wall. "I need service."

A woman in a nearby bed opened then closed her eyes. Kit's demands went otherwise unheeded.

The head nurse hurried me to a semi-walled section in the back of the room. As I passed by, an almond-sized bloodstain spread across the stark white sheets of an unconscious young woman. It grew into a crimson baseball.

"We've got a bleeder on bed two!" The nurse shouted. She shoved me toward the storage area. "Your friend's back there."

As I rounded the corner, a team of nurses rushed to the bleeding woman's bedside.

Kit's semi-private room consisted of a cot angled into a supply cubicle. A pile of cookies and a cup of apple juice lay untouched on a small file cabinet next to her. She looked pasty and flushed at the same time. "I hate Windmills. They make me sick," she screamed over the gathering flurry of voices and medical equipment.

"Kit, stop shouting and eat the cookies."

A nurse rushed in and grabbed a handful of gauze from the cabinet.

"Tell them I want chocolate chip." Kit glared at the nurse who was already on her way out the door.

"Quiet." I pushed the juice at her. "That other woman is hemorrhaging."

"Aren't we all?" Her eyes filled with tears as she grasped the juice cup.

I had no intention of hugging or comforting her.

Kit took a small sip and sunk into the white of her pillow. "That stupid Bill Pogue and his cocktail-weenie dick. The condom was big on him. Couldn't even feel it inside." She pulled her legs in and clutched her uterus. "Illegitimate loser couldn't keep a wife. And Philip... I thought at least one of them would want a baby."

"Did you do this on purpose?"

"Damn cramps." Kit tried to get out of bed but fell back grimacing. "I have a stack of stuff on my desk that needs to be done by Monday."

"You didn't answer my question."

She guzzled the remainder of her juice. "Philip was supposed to bring home the ring or..."

"Bill or Guy or God knows who else, was supposed to make a better offer? Did you kill a baby because you didn't get a suitable bid?"

Kit clutched her knees to her chest. "It wasn't like that."

How could I have shared my home with this person? How could I have ever called her a friend? "That's what you keep saying."

"The condom broke," she shouted.

The main room was nearly silent. Kit had made such a spectacle that she'd apparently piqued the interest of everyone in the recovery room. At least the bleeding woman was stabilized.

"Whose condom?" My heartbeat throbbed in my temples. *Please deny it. Please, Kit. Say it isn't true.*

Kit's face went blank. "It was an accident."

I leaned forward. "Charlie or the pregnancy?"

"The pregnancy."

"Was that baby Charlie's?"

Kit turned to face the wall.

"Kit, how could you?"

Tears rolled down her face and dropped onto her pillow. "I don't know."

"What have you said to Abby?"

"Only Charlie knows," she whispered

"And, I know." I opened my purse, pulled out two twenties from my wallet and dropped them on the bed. I glanced at the crumbs on her cookie plate. "I'm sure they'll sign your walking papers. I certainly have."

As I tried to escape, Kit grabbed my arm. The fire that blazed in her murky eyes sent a shiver to my soul. "Before you take off, there's one more thing you should know."

What other unspeakable atrocity had she committed? A wave of clammy cold rushed through me. "What is it?"

"About your precious, humiliated, Jim."

My heart broke before she uttered a word. "Tell me you didn't."

"I wish." Kit's laugh echoed against the cubicle walls. "But, I hear he has quite a photo collection of everyone that has."

The coldness rushed to my head. "Liar."

"There are videos, too."

I pictured Jim looking deeply into my eyes in my bed at the Century Plaza Hotel. *That was the most amazing hour of my life. I wish I had a tape of it so I could relive it over and over.* "It's not true."

"Don't you think it's quite a coincidence that the bachelor party carpeting was exactly the same plaid pattern as the offices of Walker, Gamble and Lutz?"

The pain sliced through me like hundreds of sharp knives. Jim wasn't at a bachelor party at all...

I stumbled out into the miserable sea of empty wombs and ran the wrong way down corridor to Doris Day's nightmare parking spot. It was all I could do to fall into the car and drive home to my Mom.

Esther

ESTHER KNOCKED ON THE DOOR AND LUMBERED IN WITH another steaming mug of tea. "You'd feel better if you had a few sips."

"This is way too serious for chamomile." I placed it next to the other four untouched cold mugs.

Esther's fingers felt like sausages as she felt my forehead with the back of her hand. "Is it the Bar?"

"The results don't come out until Memorial Day weekend, but it may not even matter if I pass."

I'd spent the better part of two days lying in Luna's canopy bed, staring blankly out beyond her balcony into the wilds of Thousand Oaks. When the sunlight flooded the spacious room filled with Sears "Little Princess" furniture, I felt a certain peace. I understood now why Luna came home for mental health weekends. Nevertheless, I kept one foot on the floor to stop the spinning visions of Jim, Wakeman, Slater, Kit, Abby, and Minerva Steele. "I don't even think I want to be me anymore."

"You?" Esther stroked my hair. "Or the path you've chosen?" She nodded meaningfully and eased herself onto the foot of Luna's canopy bed. The mattress virtually crumpled beneath the broad expanse of her maternity shift.

"I don't know." I came rolling toward her and threw my arms around as much waist as I could grasp. The baby was lucky to be inside where it was safe and warm. "I just don't know."

"Sunshine, take a sip of tea." She grabbed the cup from the table and handed it to me. "Tell Mommy what hurts."

My sobs sounded like a cat with a hairball. "Everything."

Esther massaged my leg. "Deep cleansing breaths. Let it all out." She grabbed a Sleeping Beauty throw pillow and reclined against the footboard. "Deep breaths. In through your nose, fill your diaphragm, and release."

If only Kit had used a diaphragm.

"You're not focusing, Sunny. Open your chakras. Let it all out. Breathe, hold, release."

I took a deep breath.

"Good girl." Esther's voice grew loud and confident. "Out poison thoughts! Out mental toxins! Let it out!"

Was my mother becoming a New Age evangelist?

"Let it out," She screamed.

I just stared at her.

"Do I look like I'm joking?" Her red face rivaled any preacher. "Let it out!"

I began to let it out.

"The managing partner at my firm ordered me to lie to the state bar to protect a partner who cared more about his win-loss record than a badly burned family who needed money for medical care. If I don't do it, I'll lose my job."

Esther closed her eyes and rocked back and forth as though in a trance.

"I'm not sure I even want to be a lawyer, and I may be the first person in the history of my firm to commit an ethics violation before ever being admitted to the bar."

Esther lifted her palms to the sky. "Life is filled with decisions and crossroads."

I pulled my knees to my chest.

"And apparently, Jim keeps photos and a video library of all his conquests. There may be explicit pictures of me floating around the office or I may even be starring in some sort of home movie. I just don't know."

"For goddess sake." Esther shook her head. "I can't say I didn't expect this."

"What?"

"Every time I did a reading the Devil came up in his cards."

"Does the Devil card mean he'll love me in sickness and in health, or just while I look good in front of a 35mm lens?"

"It means..."

I was in no mood for Tarot 101. "Did the cards tell you about Kit, too?"

Esther shook her head. "I didn't ask about her."

"I took her for an abortion yesterday morning."

Esther clasped her belly and rocked back and forth.

"Kit's had safe sex with half of Los Angeles, but somehow managed to get pregnant from a few stolen minutes with Charlie Crawford." I stuffed my head under the pillows to stifle the sounds of my anguish. "On the wedding day."

"Oh, dear." Esther rubbed my back.

"I don't know what I'm going to do to help Abby."

"Be the very best friend you can be." Esther lifted the pillow from my head and kissed my cheek. "Sunny, I've been waiting for this moment."

She was looking forward to my nervous breakdown?

"You're finally willing to admit how you really feel." A warm, purplish glow surrounded my mother. "You have some hard issues to face, but now you have the divine opportunity to decide what you really want and who you want to be."

"I wish I knew."

"Sunny." Esther rubbed my cheek. "Your job as a friend is to support Abby, and I know you will. Your job as a mate is to provide respect, trust, and friendship, then receive it in return. You have to ask yourself if you can do that with Jim."

I'd do anything for Abby, but could I ever trust Jim enough to do the same?

"As for your job, I often wonder whether you really wanted to be a lawyer, or if you did it to appease your father."

For the first time, I had no inclination to defend my career choice or, for that matter, any of my other choices.

Esther heaved herself off the bed and reached her hand out to me. "Stand up."

With rubbery legs and a strangely emptied sensation, I followed my mountain of a mother to the sliding glass door.

"Open it all the way."

I followed her command.

"Now, come to the other side of the room." She took my hand, led me to the opposite wall and spun me back around. "Sweep all your worries out. Like this." She spread her fingers wide and made a circular motion with her hands. "Banish the toxins from your life. Push them out." She put her hand on my back. "Push."

It might not help, but it couldn't hurt.

Together, we flapped our arms like palsied birds until all my bitter words had been swept from the room and scattered into the eucalyptus surrounding Luna's balcony.

Esther took a deep breath, slid the door closed, and brushed her hands against each other. "There's nothing like a good cleansing."

"Is that all?" My words were headed toward Simi Valley, but my problems still awaited me at work in the morning.

She reached into Luna's top drawer and pulled out an incense stick, lit it, and set it on the dresser. "Now, you ask The Universe for guidance."

"The Universe?"

Esther's gray curls bobbed as she nodded.

"Formulate the questions you need answered, send them out and let go." Esther flashed her Earth mother, princess-of-peace smile. "Believe me, The Universe will answer."

"And, what should I do in the meantime?"

"Eat. Hugh's adding chicken to the vegetarian stew. We thought it might make you feel better."

A ray of setting sun bathed my mother in golden light.

"Thank you, Mom. Thank you."

Esther blushed scarlet. "Actually, I can't stop eating meat. I had bacon for breakfast and I went to a drive through yesterday. I'd forgotten how delicious it is."

"Baby Hughie picked a good mom."

Esther kissed me and patted her belly. "I've been blessed with the best children."

My stomach did an unexpected tumble. What about Baby Hughie's biological dad? Was it possible she'd already told Bernie and I'd somehow managed to avoid the fallout? "Mom?"

"What, sweetie?"

"Did you tell Dad about the baby, yet?"

"I'm waiting for *my* sign from The Universe."

The Universe

I PULLED THE PRICE TAGS FROM A BLACK BUSINESS SUIT and matching blouse I'd uncovered in the back of Luna's closet. As I tucked the black shirt into the skirt and prepared for my black day, I felt strangely jealous of my sister. Apparently, she'd been smart enough to consider a real job, but even smarter to think better of it.

Esther put her arm around me as she walked me out to the car. "Trust The Universe."

The words rung in my head as I traversed the valley and looped into the center of the L.A. business universe.

As I made my way off the elevator and into reception, Jillian placed her telephone back into the cradle. "Good morning, Ms. St. Clair." For the first time, her pinched smile looked authentic. "How are you?"

"I really don't know." I didn't try to force a smile as I started toward my office. By now, Jillian had likely seen nude snaps of me caught in what I thought was the most passionate act of love I'd ever felt. Was there any point in pretending that she didn't know about Jim, or that Elizabeth hadn't reported my predicament with the state bar? I turned back before I opened the door to my corridor. "Would you do me a favor, Jillian?"

"What is it, dear?"

"Would you wait an hour and sign me in late on the secret time sheet?" I hadn't been home or checked my phone. Jim had to be wondering what was going on.

"You know we don't keep track of the comings and goings of..." Jillian stopped mid-sentence and simply nodded.

Somehow, I made it to my office, closed the door, and collapsed into my chair without being pecked by any of the other vultures. What in the world was I going to do?

Perhaps divine guidance *was* the only answer.

How did one speak to The Universe? Was I supposed to beseech in silence or speak out loud in a reverent but urgent tone?

"Hello, Universe?" I asked, gazing upward. It felt as manufactured as the acoustic ceiling tiles above me.

"Universe, it's Sunny St. Clair." I tried a silent query facing my window and a view of the next building. I felt like a Judy Blume character praying that my first period wouldn't soak through my white shorts during gym. "Universe, as you know, I've never done this before, but surely you're familiar with my family. Esther suggested that you might consider my request." I put my hands together. "I need to know what to do about my job, my boyfriend, and my friends. And by the way, I wouldn't presume to suggest how you should handle anything, but Esther should probably mention the baby to my father because..."

The phone rang.

The Universe must have considered me an emergency case.

"Hello?" I answered before it could ring again.

"Grace agreed to sell me the rights to the spring." Luna was beside herself. "It's all mine!"

"Grace?" Excuse me for the interruption, Universe. My sister didn't mean to disrupt the most important spiritual moment of my life. Please try to ignore the fact that she interrupted our conversation to tell me she'd fleeced a sad old lady. This couldn't be good for my karma.

"Did you make any changes to the contract? I need to get up to Arrowhead and finalize the deal this afternoon."

I'd forgotten all about her contract. On top of everything, my sister was going to get herself into a financial disaster because of my neglect. "Luna, I need to review it again. It may take me days to make sure everything is water tight. Ha-ha."

"Sunny, you haven't looked at it yet, have you?"

"I have. It's just that I'd like to have another attorney in the firm look it over before I send it and..." I stopped myself mid-sentence. I'd just lied in front of The Universe. "I think you'd better reschedule the meeting."

"Sunny, I'm going today. This is the opportunity I've been waiting for. Don't let me down."

"Luna." I felt horrible. "It was a terrible day on Friday. I admit, I totally forgot. I..."

"I heard."

"I'm so sorry." I paused to collect myself for the well-deserved lecture I was about to receive. "Tell me what you need and I'll get it done, but promise me you won't do anything without my okay."

"I know what I'm doing. Just look it over and get it to me by lunch. Please?"

I owed her that. "I promise."

"Everything will work out, Sunny."

Depending on your definition.

~*~

I dashed to the stairwell, made my way up to the nineteenth floor, and peered around the corner toward Jim's office. Luckily, his door was closed, and I was able to make it to the copy room unseen.

Never taking my eyes off Jim's office, I scanned the wall filled with mail slots, grabbed Luna's contract from the cubby below my name and rushed down the hallway.

I was halfway to the stairwell when I hear a door creak open. Without turning to see who it was, I barreled into the ladies room. My heart thumped so loud it seemed to echo off the bathroom walls.

"Mrs. Sunny Wolfe." Vera Johnson, a partner from the business department, dabbed gloss on her pale lips. "It has a nice ring."

She'd obviously missed the latest inter-office email.

Luna's paperwork slipped from my shaking hands and dropped at Vera's feet.

Vera leaned over, picked it up and scanned the contract. "Giving up litigation?"

It sure looks that way. "I told a client I would take an unofficial glance."

"Hmm." She didn't look up.

"Actually, I planned to let someone from your department look it over."

Was I committing malpractice on top of everything else? I attempted a nonchalant hair toss. Vera was rumored to be nice, but... "What a coincidence to run into you at this moment." Had The Universe confused my request with Luna's?

Vera glanced at me over the top of her glasses and went back to the contract.

"I really appreciate this, I'm going to..." I pointed to the toilet. "Real quick."

I bolted into a stall and attempted to go, but couldn't force even a trickle. After thirty seconds, I flushed anyway.

"This doesn't look half-bad," Vera said over the swirling water.

"Great!" I tugged up my underpants and readjusted my skirt. How could that be possible?

"Looks self-prepared, but..."

"My client isn't the most sophisticated." Oh God, I hadn't looked to see if *Luna St. Clair* was scribbled everywhere. I could be accused of both malpractice and giving free legal advice without consulting the pro-bono coordinator.

"Your sister definitely did her homework." Vera's voice echoed through the bathroom.

Hopefully, Vera's kind heart wasn't just another vicious rumor. My jaw clenched. Luna might as well have written *no charge* on the fax transmission sheet. I pulled a length of toilet paper from the roll and dabbed at the beads of sweat bursting on my forehead.

"It looks to me like she researched contracts extensively, then cut and pasted together a decent mineral extraction rights deal."

Luna's homespun water agreement passed Vera Johnson's scrutiny? "Really?"

"There's a lot of competition in the bottled drink market but she seems to have a handle on it."

"One can only pray." The lilt in my voice had to sound as forced as it felt. "I know I should have cleared it through pro-bono, but she plans to sign the deal at noon. I was afraid she'd do something stupid."

"I understand." Vera nodded. "You know I can't officially sign off on it. But, I'll be glad to take it down to my office and look it over more closely."

I dared to venture out of the stall. "Thanks, Vera."

Vera smiled and headed for the door. "Your sister would make a great contracts lawyer."

Maybe she could take over my job. I shook my head and doused my face with cold water. I'd jumped over one hurdle, but I still had to make the frantic dash back to my office.

~*~

"Sunny?" Jim's sexy drawl reverberated down the hallway.

Shit.

Could I pretend I hadn't heard him?

"Ms. St. Clair." Wakeman's fearful baritone.

I froze and turned toward Wakeman's gaping doorway where they stood together like Father Time and the Grim Reaper.

The Universe hated me.

My heartbeat thumped in my ears. "Good morning."

Mr. Wakeman jangled the spare change in his pocket. "I trust you had a refreshing weekend?"

"Where have you been?" Jim moved toward me but stopped short of hugging me. "Why haven't you returned my messages?"

I gazed down. "Family emergency."

Wakeman and Jim traded a dog-ate-my-homework look.

Any reasonable medical condition would be considered a lame excuse. "My mom is having complications with her pregnancy. I had to run home unexpectedly and take care of her."

"Your mother is pregnant?" Wakeman furrowed his brow. "How old is she?"

Jim's eyes grew huge. "Don't you mean your sister?"

"Forty-eight and no. They're both expecting." For the first time, I was eager to recount my family saga.

"You never mentioned that."

You never mentioned your X-rated photo collection.

There was a snicker from a nearby secretarial cubicle followed by rapid keyboard strokes. A secret email was undoubtedly on its way to Jillian.

Jim shook his beautiful head.

Could he really be that deceptive?

215

Stars filled the thick air between us.

"Ms. St. Clair?" Wakeman broke the silence. "I assume all went well this morning?" He smiled meaningfully.

It's kind of you to inquire about me for the first time ever. If you're referring to the state bar, however, I haven't called yet. I nodded back meaningfully.

"Very well, then," he said. "I appreciate your contribution to the Walker, Gamble and Lutz team."

"Thank you, sir."

Wakeman disappeared into his suite. I was left with Jim and my fake smile.

"Sunny, what the hell is going on?" Jim's highlights shimmered in the office light.

Maybe Kit lied or maybe there's a legitimate excuse. Maybe...I fought a longing to kiss him, to feel the soft pressure of his beautiful full lips, the roughness of his whiskers brushing against my face.

Universe, what do I do?

We stood staring at each other.

For a second, I thought my legs were giving way. My feet seemed to wiggle without direction from my brain.

Then the rumbling started.

"Earthquake!" someone shouted. "Head for the stairwells!"

Screaming secretaries and paralegals darted for the stairs. Bill Pogue dashed toward Jillian in the reception area. Rhonda sauntered by, never lifting her head from a brief.

As the building rocked and swayed, Jim and I dropped to the floor and covered our heads with our hands.

From my vantage point on the ground, I saw chairs roll away from desks, pictures slide off the walls and paperwork scatter. A box of candy teetered on a cubicle ledge.

Why was I swinging nineteen stories above the earth at this place? Would I die and spend eternity with Wakeman, Jillian, and Bill Pogue? And Jim, who huddled next to me with his hands over his head?

I still didn't know what I wanted, but suddenly, I knew for sure what I didn't want. *Please God, spare my life so I can get out of here.*

Wasn't God the ruler of The Universe?

At that moment, the box of assorted chocolates tumbled into my lap.

I had my answer.

"Thank you," I said out loud.

What a fool I'd been. The Universe had given me a family who had already told me everything I needed to know, but I was so thick it took an earthquake to shake me into listening.

As I bit into a chocolate filled with sweet coconut, the earth stopped rumbling.

I began to giggle.

"You okay?" Jim asked, helping me to my feet.

I stuffed a Rocky Road into my mouth. "I'm great."

"That was quite a ride."

"Yes, it was."

"Can I get you something? Some water?"

I looked into his breathtaking brown eyes. "How about any videos or pictures you've taken of me."

"Sunny, I don't know what...?"

"Why did you lie to me about the bachelor party photo?"

"I..." Jim grabbed my hands, but didn't meet my gaze.

As an aftershock vibrated up the base of the building, my voice held firm. "How about the truth?"

Jim gazed down the litter-strewn hallway. "I didn't want to hurt you."

"Are there photos of me? If so, I want them."

"I never took any of you."

"Were you planning to start?"

"I love you."

"That doesn't mean you don't want to add me to your collection."

A group of hysterical secretaries fell silent as they passed.

Jim picked up chocolates from the plaid carpeting backdrop of his love-fest, and tossed them in the trash. "I wouldn't do that to you."

"Why not?"

"You're different."

"How's that?"

"I respect you." Jim ran his fingers through my hair then looked deeply into my eyes. "They were just..."

217

"Flings?" I offered coolly.

He nodded.

He's not The One. My brain filled with static. *He's not The One.*

"Please, Sunny. Forgive me. We can get through this. I love you."

I looked into his eyes and smiled. "Jim, I won't put my wedding book on a shelf next to the album of all your prior conquests."

"There's no actual album."

"You get my point."

"I don't want to lose you."

He loves you. He's the most handsome, sexiest man you've ever known. You may never feel this way about anyone again. Don't be an idiot! I took a deep breath. *Be strong, Sunny.* Esther's voice blared in my head. *There are men you date and men you marry.* Before I lost my nerve, the words fell from my mouth. "I'm sorry, Jim."

Wakeman's assistant secretary looked up from a scattered pile of papers and gave me the thumbs-up.

Maybe, there was no such thing as *The One.*

I walked over the debris down to my office, locked the door, pulled all my cases from the inbox and sat down to dictate final memos.

~*~

Mr. Wakeman's secretary sat staring at the computer screen. Wisps of long brown hair hung loose around her face. The barrette at the base of her neck hung lopsided.

"Are you okay, Elizabeth?"

"Fine." She swiveled away from the monitor and stared out the window.

"I heard it was a 6.0."

She nodded.

Most of the staff had been sent home to regain their composure. Elizabeth's salary and stature was considered fair compensation for the stress of natural disasters and other such inconveniences.

"I just want to go home," she said.

"Me too." I handed her my resignation in a sealed envelope. "Give this to Mr. Wakeman, please." I'd written personal and confidential across the front, but Elizabeth would open it as soon as I stepped out the doorway. "It says thanks, but no thanks."

I said goodbye to my little office and packed my belongings in the empty laundry basket that lay hidden under my desk for over three months. I was no longer embarrassed to carry it through the building.

On my final walk down the hallway, I stopped at Rhonda's office.

"Doing laundry?" Rhonda barely raised an eyebrow.

"I'm spring cleaning my life."

She looked over the top of a file. "So, this is it?"

I nodded.

"You had potential."

"Thanks." I tried to smile. "I guess I'm not as strong as you thought."

"You're stronger."

"Thanks, Rhonda."

She blew a puff of e-smoke, set down her cigarette and offered her hand.

I walked across her office and hugged her instead.

On my way home, I met with Minerva Steele, a handsome black woman with a warm smile. I gave her an affidavit that outlined all the details of the McKeen case, complete with attached exhibits.

In return, she shook my hand.

For the first time, I felt like a real lawyer.

SunnyLuna

AND THEN REALITY HIT.

When I got home, a lamp was all that was left of the living room furniture. Kit's bedroom was empty save for stray cellophane wrappers and yellowing Neiman-Marcus price tags. The slow drip of the leaky sink echoed through the empty apartment.

I searched for a goodbye note filled with words like embarrassed, humiliated, ashamed, or even sorry. All I found was our shared answering machine blinking in a nest of dust where Kit's end table used to be. I pressed the button expecting a garbled forwarding address.

You have one message.

Monday 5:00 P.M.

Congratulations. You survived The Big One.

Atlas's timely pronouncement echoed through the room.

"I may have made it through The Big One, but the aftershocks will surely do me in," I said aloud to my apartment and The Universe.

I stumbled to my bedroom and collapsed into bed.

~*~

In the blinding light of a new day, I sat Indian style on the floor, alone with my morning coffee. I skimmed the online want ads, carefully skipping the legal services section.

Looking for your dream job? If happiness, prosperity and career satisfaction rank one, two and three on your list, call 213–555–0000 extension 101.

Maybe my job search wouldn't be so hard. I reached for the phone and dialed the number.

"Thanks for calling Human Resources. The store manager position has been filled, as have the sales positions. We're taking applications for assistant managers in linens and electronics."

My dream job. As I hung up, I pictured Atlas giggling with The Universe as they awaited my next pratfall.

I glanced at my watch then dialed Atlas's hotline number.

"The Universe doesn't giggle." Atlas answered on the first ring. "But sometimes it laughs."

"I'm not laughing."

"You should be."

"As of this morning, I have no job, no boyfriend, no roommate, and no job prospects. I *do* have a huge stack of bills. That's sort of funny, I guess."

"Ladies and gentlemen if you're just joining us, I'm on the line with Jane from La Mirada, a second time caller. Jane, I sense that you've called to find out what to do next," Atlas said in his silkiest radio voice.

"Aren't you a little high on your psychic horse?"

"Giddyup." Atlas chuckled. "To your sister's house. And don't call her. Get over there. She's waiting for you."

The line went dead.

As annoyed as I felt, I knew better than to ignore Atlas anymore, especially when he was being so direct. I threw on jeans, ran a brush through my hair and flew out the door. I was cruising west on Venice Beach Boulevard in record time.

My tires screeched as I pulled up and stopped inches behind the parked Probe. I rushed up Luna's steps.

"You're finally here." Luna patted her enormous squirming belly and hoisted herself out of a double-wide beach chair. Even her ankles looked pregnant.

"What is it?"

She smiled. "Atlas warned me that you probably wouldn't get by until today, but I made steaks last night just in case."

"Steaks?"

"I already ate them both. We'll have lunch, instead."

221

"So I rushed over here for lunch?"

"A thank you lunch. Because of you, everything went great with Grace." Luna grasped my hand and led me across her tiny cottage. She pulled the heavy handle of her ancient refrigerator and poured two glasses of greenish ice tea. "It smells like cow shit, but Esther says it's great for the babies, so..." She pinched her nostrils together and took a sip. "With all the junk I'm eating, I'm afraid the babies will come out looking like corn dogs."

The doorbell rang.

"Or pizza." Luna waddled over and opened the front door to a delivery boy. She handed him cash and accepted two large boxes which she put on the center of the dining table next to a large salad and a tray of assorted cookies. "Let's eat." Luna sat and placed three napkins across her lap.

I wedged myself between the table edge and her kitchen window. "Thanks, Luna." I lifted my jelly jar glass and clinked it against hers. "To your new business." At least one of us had a job, sort of.

"Everything fell right into place." She smiled.

"Grace wanted to see her husband's dream live on, and I wanted to live out my dream."

"Did she sign the deal with our corrections?" Despite the earthquake, Vera Johnson dropped it off on time at 11:55 A.M. with a few handwritten corrections. I faxed it by noon.

Luna nodded. "The water report came out perfect, so Grace stuck to her guns on the purchase price. But she relented a little on the royalties." She bit into a slice of pizza. "Twenty percent is plenty fair, considering I'll have to revamp some of the machinery."

"That's great, Luna." I knew the contract was sound. All Luna could lose was the meager capital she managed to scrape up. But, how was I going to support both of us and the babies when Luna's futile venture to take on big corporate bottled water sunk. I surveyed her cluttered house for a newspaper. I needed a job ASAP.

"I'm going to need your legal services from now on." She bit off another hunk.

"Luna, I can't sign off on anything until I get my license in May." I stabbed a fork into my salad. "Besides, I quit my job."

"That's what I heard." Luna nodded. "We'll have to make do until you're legal." She laughed at her dumb pun.

I glanced out the window at my Audi, which didn't seem to glow in the sunlight as it once had. I fanned myself. It was only March and the temperature was fast approaching ninety. Would my trade-in car even have air conditioning? For the first time, I eyed the Probe jealously.

"Can you afford the car and the apartment without that big job?"

Maybe assistant managers in the linens department made more than I expected. "Don't know."

"I'm running out of space here."

"I don't think Kit's room is big enough for the three of you."

"For my business, dummy."

"Luna, you can use the space until I get a roommate, but I can't cover the rent, even if I give up the car." As long as I wasn't working for her, perhaps Rhonda White would make a decent roomie.

Luna smiled. "It's funny how the tables turn in the blink of an eye."

I couldn't tackle a pregnant lady, so I sat on my hands while I tried to come up with something to say.

"What was Kit's half?" Luna asked.

"A thousand." Saying it made me choke.

"I'll pay eleven hundred."

"This is no joke, Luna."

"I'm not laughing. Look around."

Her tiny apartment *was* stuffed full. The table and couch overflowed with paperwork. Two cribs would completely fill the second bedroom.

"How are you going to pay me eleven hundred a month Luna? You just started a business. Even if..." I stopped and rephrased my question so I wouldn't offend her. "I can't expect you to support yourself, and pay me until you turn a profit."

"Why not?"

"Actually, I already have another job."

"Really?"

"I'm going into management at the May Company."

"Cut the bullshit, Sunny."

She sounded so much like Bernie we both stared at each other.

"People in glass houses..."

"I have a rock. Production starts tomorrow. I have suppliers for the fruit juices, and I hired a bottling manager to work with Grace up in Arrowhead. I need an office in town that's up and running ASAP."

If she didn't look so earnest, I'd have started to laugh again. Instead, I fought back tears. My poor deluded sister. Poor me.

"What do you need a month to keep the car and make rent, and your monthly expenses, Sunny?"

"Bare minimum? Four thousand dollars per month." Why was I telling her this? "Maybe forty-five hundred."

"What were you doing with that big salary from Walker, Gamble and Lutz?"

I felt my face redden. "At least I make my own money, Luna. What have you been living on?"

"You know how we all accuse *you* of being just like Bernie?" Luna waddled over to the kitchen and opened a carefully organized pantry filled with papers. She handed me a bank portfolio. "Look at this."

"How...?" I scanned her records. How was this possible? Her savings account topped one hundred fifty-thousand. There was even more spread amongst the checking account and two or three CDs.

She ambled over to the computer perched on her kitchen table, and pulled up spreadsheets detailing all her investors and their investments down to the penny. She'd calculated interest projections over the next five years. Every dime was accounted for.

"After it's all said and done, I guess I inherited Bernie's cheap gene. I have to say, it was a surprise blessing."

"Does Bernie know about this?" Maybe I'd finally get to tell him some good news.

Luna smiled. "He's one of the biggest investors."

What would Bernie say when he had to bail *me* out in a few months? "I can't take your money, I..."

I started to cry.

"Have your emotional breakdown later. I'm not just giving it to you. The babies are coming soon and I'm going to need some help."

So that's what she needed. I suppose it made sense. Who better to watch her kids, than a family member? I'd gone from lawyer to daycare provider

224

in one day. "I'll love them and everything, but I don't think I'd make the best nanny."

"Dumb shit, you're going to be my business partner."

"What?"

"I wrote you into my business plan from day one. My only problem was getting you out of that Godforsaken job." Luna smiled. "But, I asked The Universe, and, like magic, here you are just in time."

"I don't believe this." My mouth hung open.

"Believe it." She pushed me into the bedroom. "Go into the nursery."

Lined up against the back wall were cases of water. I stepped into the room and picked up a bottle. The label featured two women, one dark-haired and the other fair, wearing flowing gowns. They sat smiling from the crook of a crescent moon back lit by a giant sunburst. *SUNNYLUNA Organic Sparkling Asian Pear* ran across the bottom.

"We're starting with three flavors, Asian Pear, Star Fruit and Mandarin Magic." Luna smiled. "I'm thinking something pineapple next."

I stared at the bottle. "How did you get this together so quickly? You just signed a deal yesterday."

"It was a chicken-egg thing. Grace and I both wanted this to work, so we ran some samples to test the market. Now, everything's official so it's full speed ahead."

"I, I..." I couldn't believe she had such amazing business acumen.

"We'll need to draft a partnership agreement pretty quick. The business can't pay what you'll be worth right away, but your salary will cover your monthly expenses until we turn a profit." She grinned broadly and looked out toward the street. "Oh, and keep the car. Image is crucial."

Had Luna really said that?

"We're going after upscale restaurants, high-end gourmet and natural food stores." She handed me a stack of distribution leads. "I've lined up a few potential outlets, but I'm obviously in no shape to call on them, so set up the appointments as soon as you can."

Had I just been given an offer I couldn't refuse by my ne'er-do-well sister? "Luna, I should really think about this before I commit..."

She opened the bureau next to her, pulled out a box of business cards and handed it to me. Beneath the *SUNNYLUNA* logo it read:

225

Sunny St. Clair
Director of Marketing

"But, Luna..."

She smiled. "I'll be by with the movers first thing in the morning."

Abigail

LUNA WAS ON MY DOORSTEP BY 8:30 IN THE MORNING WITH another stack of leads. A moving van was out front. "Start making calls, Sunny. I'll deal with the movers." She wolf-whistled and two of her beefy tattooed Venice Beach pals hopped out of the U-Haul.

Would I ever get used to calling Luna boss?

I went into my bedroom, closed the door and organized the leads on my desk. I sat carefully, put my shoulders back, and stared at the phone. Exactly what was I supposed to say?

I reorganized the leads again.

Hello, this is Sunny St. Clair.

Sir, Sunny St. Clair with SunnyLuna Sparkling Beverages.

Sunny St. Clair here. I've called to speak with you about a new and exciting product in the upscale, organic, vitamin-enriched, sparkling beverage arena.

My fingers wouldn't move toward the keypad. I sat up straighter and took deep breaths. How hard could this be after my year at Walker, Gamble and Lutz?

May I have a word with the purchasing manager? This is Sunny St. Clair, director of marketing at SunnyLuna Sparkling Beverages.

Luna was too pregnant to do any lifting, and knowing her, she wouldn't pay any attention to doctor's orders. I got up and opened the door to check on her and the moving progress. "Luna, by the way, if I'm the director of marketing, what are you?"

"You're also the president. I happen to be the CEO and Human Resources director." Luna pointed the movers down the hall with a file cabinet. "Don't be afraid, Sunny. Just dial a number, tell them about us and ask if you can talk to them about carrying SunnyLuna in their store."

She disappeared down the hallway.

I went back to my desk and flipped through the pile of three- by five-inch cards. What was I scared of? After all, I was a lawyer less than a week earlier. I settled on Young's Gourmet Market and dialed the number.

"Young's Market." Foreign music blared in the background

"Mr. Young, please." What if I couldn't do this? Would my own sister fire me?

"This Mr. Young." His accent sounded Korean.

"Sir-this-is-Sunny-St,-Clair-with-SunnyLuna-Water." I enunciated each word slowly.

"We no need." The line went dead.

I tore up the card, picked up the next, and tried again.

"Lucky's."

Let's hope. "Hello, Sir, this is Sunny St. Clair with the SunnyLuna Corporation. We are a forward-thinking corporation on the leading edge of the upscale organic health-water industry. After extensive marketing surveys and the highest quality standards, we have developed an exciting product certain to be in huge demand at your establishment. At your convenience, I'd like to give you the opportunity to stock our product before anyone else in your area..."

"You probably want to talk to my Dad."

"Uh, yeah. Please?" I felt like banging my head on the desk.

"He's not in."

"I'll call back." I hung up the phone and began to hyperventilate.

"Relax, Sunny. You don't have to convince a jury, just a store owner who wants to carry the items his customers want." Luna was standing in the doorway. "Remember, no one wants to hear from a lawyer."

"Shouldn't I at least tell them who you are, and what you're offering?"

"You're not working for me, you're working for us." She smiled. "Have a good time with it. We've got a great product. Just introduce yourself and ask for an appointment."

The next card read, *Fountain of Health Foods, John Russell, Buyer*. "It's a chain, maybe I should wait until I get better at this."

"Call them! Call everyone!" Luna bounded out of the room like a dancing hippo.

I sighed and dialed the number. "Hi, this is Sunny," I said, trying to sound casual. "Can I speak to John?"

"This is John."

"Hi, John," I said, and he didn't hang up. "You're in charge of new products, correct?"

"Correct."

"I would love to come by and introduce you to SunnyLuna sparkling beverages." I paused for the no. He didn't say anything, so I kept going. "We're a new, locally-owned company offering a great organic alternative to soda and I think your customers..."

"Today's sample day. How fast can you get out here?"

I glanced at the card. "The Pasadena store?"

"Yep."

"An hour?"

"See you then."

"Luna!" I shot down the hall to our emerging office.

"Do you think our desks should go on opposite walls, or sort of next to each other?" Luna's back was to the door.

"Whatever. Luna, I did it! They want me to hand out samples at Fountain of Health Foods."

She turned to face me. "When?"

"Right now!"

"Oh my God!" Luna tried to jump but could only bob. "If it goes well, they'll order for all six stores. Get changed. I'll have the movers load the samples into your car. I've gotta call Grace and put her on alert."

The phone rang.

"I'll get it. You get ready, Sunny."

I ran back to my bedroom, threw on a pair of pants and a sleeveless sweater then touched up my makeup. Working from home had definite advantages.

"Good luck, partner." Luna closed my sample-filled trunk.

"I'm really excited." I climbed into my car. "By the way, who called?"

229

"It was for Kit. She said she'd try her at the office."

"Did she leave a name?" I turned the ignition.

"Sylvie something."

"Parker?"

Luna nodded.

As the engine turned over, so did my stomach.

~*~

As I set a stack of business cards next to the tray of Dixie cups filled with SunnyLuna Sparkling Asian Pear, all I could think of was Abby.

When customers said they liked the refreshing flavor and loved seeing my face on the label, I thanked them and smiled, but my mind was on Abby. *What did Sylvie Parker know? Why did she call Kit?*

My entire supply of Mandarin Magic sold out at Fountain of Health Foods before I finished handing out samples. I left the store with an introductory order of ten cases per week, per store, and an overwhelming sense of dread.

Instead of rushing back to the office, I looped through Pasadena, past the Huntington Gardens, onto a tree-lined side street and up the long cobblestone driveway of Abby's Country French "starter house." What kind of awful friend was I?

My heart thumped as I pushed the brass knocker against the freshly painted faded blue door.

Charlie answered.

"Hi, Sunny." Dark circles underscored his blue eyes. His blond hair was the color of dishwater from yesterday's hair gel and an untaken shower or two.

"What are you doing home?"

"Took the day off."

"I was in the neighborhood and I thought I'd let Abby give me a long overdue tour." How could I have not stopped by sooner?

He didn't meet my gaze, not that I could look him in the eye. "She's not here."

I glanced at the garage, renovated to look like a barn *en Provence*. Abby's SUV was parked in one of the stalls. "Where is she?"

"I sent her to a spa for a few days." He adjusted a screw on the antique mailbox. "She was worn out from the wedding and all the work on the

230

house."

You're lying, you bastard. Was she in the house? "Would you mind if I use the phone before I head home? My cell phone is dead."

"No problem." He opened the door and I stepped into the entrance hall. Newspapers and pizza boxes lay scattered around the living room amidst Abby's collection of authentic French Country antiques and toile upholstery.

"When did she leave?"

"Yesterday."

I followed him down the hallway into a kitchen painted the color of golden wheat. Carefully placed dishes lined the open cabinets and shelves. The sink was overflowing with dirty plates.

"It's hard to imagine Abby leaving the house like this." I whisked crumbs into my hand from the butcher-block center island. I couldn't contain my rage any longer. "Did you have a party last night, or was it just you and Kit?"

Charlie put his face in his hands. "I haven't spoken to Kit since before..."

The thought of Kit doubled over with cramps made me ache anew for Abby.

Sunlight reflected off the bougainvillea surrounding the bay window. Pink-tinged light filled the room. The careful beauty of Abby's home filled me with an overwhelming sadness. "Could an afternoon romp with Kit Purdy have been worth it?"

I waited for an answer.

He slumped onto a kitchen bar stool.

"Did Abby leave you?" My voice echoed down the hall.

"I want to be a good husband."

"Where is she?"

"I'll take care of her from now on. I promise."

Abby's prized heirloom, a turn-of-the-century grandfather clock, chimed in the front entry.

His apologies meant nothing to me. "Where the hell is she?"

"She's going to be fine. She'll be back in a few days."

~*~

I sat on a slippery vinyl chair until a white-uniformed nurse verified my paperwork and buzzed me in.

A decorative iron grill covered Abby's only window in a room noticeably absent of sharp objects and dangerous materials. A shatterproof mirror doubled as a viewing window from the nurse's station.

Other than a dozen mixed bouquets, which filled the stark surroundings with color and a floral designer's engineered scent of spring, there was no confusing this place with a spa.

"Does my Mom know you're here?" Abby was as white as the starched sheet carefully affixed to her bed. Broken capillaries lent a slight flush to her hollow cheeks. She untangled her IV tubes and tucked a stringy clump of hair behind her ear.

Had I not missed lunch, I would have been sick.

"No one is supposed to know I'm..." She managed a weak smile. "not well."

"Charlie tried to tell me you were at a spa." I sat on the edge of her bed. "Abby, what happened?"

Abby tugged at her hospital ID bracelet. "I didn't try to kill myself. I didn't. I was just so tired and I couldn't get any sleep and..." Tears rolled down her face. "I woke up here."

"I'm so sorry, Abby." How could I have let her down?

"Don't worry, Sunny. Everything's okay now." Abby plucked a rose from the huge bouquet by her bed. "Charlie brought all of these."

"Oh, Abby." I sat beside her on the edge of the bed and hugged her. Of course, she knew everything. She had all along. "I should have said something as soon as I heard the rumor, but I didn't know what to say. Or how." I choked on a sob. "I've been a horrible friend."

"You are my best friend." Abby clutched my hand in her bony fingers. A look of intense sadness swept across her face. "There was nothing you could do. Kit has always tried to take away everything I care about. I should have been watching."

"Abby, I'm so sorry."

"It was my own fault." Abby shook her head. "I was too distracted with the wedding and the house. I wasn't thinking of Charlie."

"How can you possibly blame yourself for his behavior?" I couldn't utter either of their names. "Or hers?"

"Short of running off to the circus, Charlie and Philip and Kit and I have always known our destinies. Kit fought it and see what happened?" Abby pulled the petals from a rose. "I don't blame Charlie for sowing his oats. He's known he'd be stuck with me since we were kids."

I grasped her free hand. "Oh, Abby."

"I just wish it hadn't been Kit."

"I hate her," I said. "She's moved out. For all I care, she's homeless."

"She's with Philip, where she belongs."

"You've spoken with her?"

"I don't have to. It's the only place she can go." Abby shook her head. "I feel sorry for her."

"For Kit?"

Abby smiled placidly. "This time, I think she's finally learned her lesson."

"Abby, how can you sit back and..." I glanced at the restraints tucked discreetly by the sides of her bed. She was probably medicated, and I didn't need to aggravate her condition. "I'll never, ever speak to her again."

"I won't either, for a year or two. Then she and Philip will get married and I'll dance at her wedding like it never happened."

"Abby, why?"

"Because, it's the right thing to do for everyone."

"It's right for you?"

"Charlie was at my bedside for two straight days and my mother canceled all her obligations until I'm rested and better." Abby sighed. "I just need to be more thankful for all my blessings and not dwell on life's negatives. I know that, now."

"Abby, you don't have to accept this." I felt like jumping up and down. "You're smart. You're beautiful. Your family has the means to allow you to be anything you want to be. You can have anything."

"What I have is a trust fund I have to pay back with interest." Abby grazed my arm with her bony fingers. "Sunny, you're the lucky one. You're the beauty with the wonderful family and the unlimited resources."

At that moment, a buzzer sounded and Sylvie Parker burst into the room. She looked at me with horror. "Sunny?"

I wanted to strangle Sylvie Parker until her pinched smile was bright blue. Abby squeezed me as a warning, but I already knew what she wanted me to do.

"Your daughter was just telling me that she was going to start eating more and not let herself get run down to the point of exhaustion." I kissed Abby's cheek and hugged her tight. "As soon as you get home we're going out for pasta and banana splits."

"Thanks, Sunny." Abby smiled and turned to her mother.

~*~

I came home to a desk wedged sideways in my front door. A note was taped to the side. "Went to get some WD-40. Back in a minute."

Luna might as well have written, "Small, nimble, thieves: climb in and take what you like."

It was good to see that my business tycoon sister was still Luna.

I sat down on my front steps and cried my eyes out for Abby. Then, I thanked The Universe for my crazy family.

Hughie

"FUCK, THIS HURTS. I FORGOT HOW THIS FUCKING HURTS."
A lounge full of cross-country truckers on a Saturday night had nothing on
Esther after ten hours of labor.

"This is cruel and unusual punishment." Luna appeared on the landing
outside the master bedroom. Her black maternity sweat suit accentuated her
pallid skin. "Atlas, it's your turn again."

"Get back in here." My mother moaned. "You need to see this, you
ungrateful little..."

"Esther, Esther, focus your love energy. Save the anger for pushing." The
comforting voice of Tess, the midwife, was having little effect on Esther's
hormone-deranged psyche.

Luna tiptoed down the stairs and collapsed on the couch. "I can't take
much more."

I looked to Atlas for reassurance. "She should be in a hospital with an
epidural. She's too old for a home delivery and it's been almost twelve
hours. How much longer are we going to let this go on?"

Atlas glanced up the stairs with a pious gaze, like a priest trying to gauge
the severity of the possession. "It's going to get way worse before it gets
better."

"I'm starved." Luna pulled out a beef-jerky package, handed me a chunk,
and bit off a thick slab. "Can't we do something?"

Atlas winced. "We could call Dad and get a second opinion."

I coughed meat across the room as Atlas had certainly planned. "That's

235

not even funny."

Atlas shrugged.

"She's ready to push. Get up here." Hugh appeared on the landing. His gray hair hung in a ratty mass. He looked as though he'd been beaten.

We abandoned our snack and ran to the master suite.

"Can we tone down the incense?" Luna pinched her nose as she positioned herself in the one armchair that didn't have a direct view. "It's making me nauseous."

"Shh." Tess smiled. Flickering light from hundreds of birthing candles sparkled in her eyes. "It's almost time."

"I said not to touch me, Hugh." Esther broke the reverent silence. "This is all your fault."

"Technically, honey... " Hugh wrung out a cool cloth and dabbed Esther's forehead.

"Bastard."

Hugh squeezed Esther's hand.

"Don't touch me." She gasped short staccato breaths.

Fearing a head spin-pea soup maneuver, I stepped back from the demon that had inhabited my mother.

"The miracle of our body is that we forget the intense physical trauma of childbirth and remember the pleasure of new life." Tess gave a patronizing alternative-health-provider smile.

Hugh nodded reassuringly.

"How... would... you... know?"

Esther fell back into her pillows.

"Esther, honey, when you feel the next contraction coming on, start pushing."

"Come on out, little Hughie." Hugh, with one of Esther's legs in hand, craned forward and peered inside.

Esther pushed.

She pushed again.

And again.

"How long should this take?" The last time I'd been so focused on my mother's vagina, I was on my way through it.

Atlas smiled. "You were apprehensive then, too."

I flashed my best dirty look.

"Esther, as you push through this contraction, I'm going to check on the baby's position," Tess said.

Despite her cherubic face, I could see concern in her eyes.

"Everyone, send your love energy on to Esther and Baby Hughie." Tess placed one hand low on Esther's abdomen and another inside the birth canal.

Esther howled.

Luna clutched her own belly and winced. "I can't do this. I can't."

"No negative energy." Tess took in a deep cleansing breath. "Atlas. Could you help your mother push through the next contraction? Hugh, I need you to prepare some towels and supplies. I'll show you what needs to be done."

"I'll help, too." I followed them into the bathroom. "What's going on?"

"Shh." Tess put a finger to her mouth and flipped on the fan. "What I need you to do, Hugh..."

"My mother needs to be in a hospital."

Hugh's eyes grew wide. "Is Esther in danger?"

Tess grasped our hands. "Not at this point, but the baby seems to be stuck in the birth canal."

"Stuck?" I let go of her chubby fingers. "This natural thing has gone too far. I'm going to call an ambulance right now. My father is Bernie..."

"Let's not jump the gun."

"I agree. The last thing Esther wants is to end up delivering in the hospital. She'll see it as a failure." Hugh crossed his arms across his chest. "If she's not in danger and the baby is safe, I say we give it some more time."

"She's exhausted."

"Your mother is strong. There's nothing to worry about. I'll call for back up if we need it. We all want Esther to experience the sheer joy of home birth, now don't we?" Tess patted my shoulder.

Esther expressed her joy in pitiful whimpers and groans.

"Hugh, I'll need you to help her push with her legs while I try and nudge the baby out as she contracts."

Hugh nodded. "Let's do it."

I wanted to barricade Tess and Hugh in the bathroom, and load my mother into my car. Instead, I watched impotently as Tess and Hugh returned to my mother's side.

"Ready, Esther?" Tess chirped and gave the thumbs-up.

My mother barely responded.

"Let's try this one more time, honey." Hugh grabbed a leg. Atlas followed suit while the midwife practically stood on Esther's belly.

"Ahhhh!" Esther gave a startling shriek and wilted into her pillows.

"We're making progress." Tess wiped sweat from her dripping brow. "Once more."

"I can't." Esther was ghostly white. Her body was almost motionless save for her trembling legs.

She couldn't go on like this much longer. I couldn't take another New Age birthing moment, nor could my mother. Something had to be done. "I'll go get some ice chips." I waltzed out the door as though I hadn't a care in the world. Once out of sight, I scrambled down the stairs and made the call. "Dad, it's Sunny. Get over here, now!"

~*~

Bernie stood in the front hall for the first time in ten years. His voice boomed up the stairs.

"No Goddamn midwife is going to deliver my baby."

The color drained from Tess' face. "Who is that?"

Atlas giggled. *I'm not, I repeat not, telling him about Esther.*

I put my hand over my Third Eye as a symbolic gesture. It was too late to worry about whether or not I'd made the greatest mistake of my life.

"Dad?" Luna yelled. "We're up here. Come quick!"

Hugh sighed, but looked relieved as my father burst into the room.

The midwife quickly paled to the shade of Esther. "Bernie St. Clair?"

He gave her a dismissive nod. "Tess."

"*How is this your baby?*" Tess clenched her pudgy fists. "She's my patient."

"It's my sperm." Bernie glared at Esther. "Or, so I'm told."

"That's a very unique arrangement, I... I... imagine it could make some sense in certain circumstances, it's just that..."

Esther began another contraction, but was too tired to swear or even whimper.

"What's the status of the delivery?"

238

"The baby is stuck in the pelvis." The midwife struggled to regain her professional composure. "Her vitals are steady but weakening. I was on the verge of taking her in when you got here." Her look of confusion returned. "To deliver *your* baby?"

"How long has she been pushing?"

"Almost two hours."

Bernie grabbed a pair of gloves, and plunged a hand inside my mother.

Atlas, Luna and I averted our eyes in unison.

"Hugh, call an ambulance." Bernie said.

"I don't want to leave her."

Luna gagged.

"Atlas, call the ambulance and get Luna the hell out of here." Bernie shook his head. "She shouldn't have been watching this Goddamn New Age hocus-pocus."

"I take exception to that, Dr. St. Clair," Tess said.

"Call me Bernie." He flashed a bonded, bleached smile. "Massage her perineum while I give this baby a push and we'll discuss my aversion to midwifery later. I have to deliver my baby."

Tess shook her head but she followed his command.

Hugh and I held Esther's legs.

"One, two, three. Push!" Bernie pressed her belly.

Hugh shrieked.

Esther went slack as though she was losing consciousness.

"Watch this." Bernie winked at the midwife. "Esther, baby, who was better, Hugh, the turkey baster, or Morty Feinberg?"

Esther opened one eye. She barely uttered, "The baster."

Hugh looked hurt. "Who is Morty Feinberg?"

"He's the lawyer that's going to represent me in my lawsuit against you. He's an old friend of ours, huh, babe?"

"The swapping was your idea, not mine," she moaned.

"You didn't seem to mind it too much."

Hugh edged closer to Bernie. "I'm not going to stand for this in my house, Bernie."

"Who bought the house? Seems to me it was the same guy who donated the seed for this project."

Hugh's face broke out in angry blotches. "Bernie, this is wrong."

Tess whispered into Hugh's ear. "He's trying to make her angry so she'll push."

"Oh!" Hugh nodded and winked at Bernie.

Bernie ignored him, and reached into his bag for a pair of forceps. "I want the dining room table back."

Esther grunted in anger.

"And while I'm here, where is Grandma St. Clair's china?"

"I can't stand you." Esther grunted. "Ahhhhh."

"Force it inward." Tess urged. "Force it inward."

"One more push," Bernie said.

"Come on Hughie, come to Daddy."

"Hughie?" Bernie let go of the forceps grips and took a step back. "I'm not delivering this baby if you're naming him Hughie."

"Work this out later. Deliver the fucking baby already!" Tess screamed. "Do it!"

Everyone stopped and stared at her for a second.

"Come on little Bernie," Bernie whispered as he resumed the delivery.

"His name is not Bernie." Hugh, looking surprised by his own show of bravado, stared down my father.

"Well you damn well won't name him Hughie, either."

With perfect timing, Luna and Atlas burst through the doors flanked by emergency technicians as Baby Hughie-Bernie's head emerged.

We all stared in stunned awe as the baby took a first breath.

"Well lookie, lookie," he said. "I'm going to have to agree that Bernie isn't my first choice, either."

"My baby." Esther sighed and collapsed into the pillows.

"Hughie." Tears rolled down Hugh's cheek.

The baby began to shriek.

"Esther, I let you give the older ones the weirdest names on earth. I'm not going to let you name a girl Hughie."

Atlas moved in closer. "A girl?"

Hughie was indeed a girl.

Atlas shook his head. "Can't be."

"I've only been doing this for twenty-five years. This would be my first mistake." Bernie handed the baby to Tess.

Atlas followed her over to the washtub to reconfirm the pronouncement. "Mine too."

"Finally, I get to name one of my offspring," Bernie said.

"You can't name my baby," Hugh said.

"Your baby? You stole my seed from the sperm bank. Sunny, you're a lawyer. What might a judge say?"

"Bernie, what do you want to name her?" My mother said softly as she gazed at her newest daughter. "We owe him some consideration, Hugh. Just look at her."

We all stopped to gaze at the baby. She had Atlas's ice blue eyes, my curls and Luna's coloring.

"Esther, you know what her name will be," Bernie said.

Esther cooed at the baby. "It's such a boring name."

Bernie turned to me. "Sunny, it would have been your name if I hadn't been called out on a delivery as she was signing the birth certificates."

"Could we at least spell it with a Y?"

Spell what with a Y?

"I don't care how you spell it. Just say it normal or there'll be litigation."

"Wait just a minute." Hugh's mouth curled into a pout. "We already agreed on a girl's name. Philomene, after my grandmother."

"Is she alive?"

"No."

"Then we can use the name." Bernie's insistence on the Jewish tradition of naming children in honor of deceased loved ones seemed ridiculous given the circumstances. He nodded then cleared his throat. "Her name will be Jayne Philomene or I'll see you in court."

Jayne?

I could have been named Jane?

Alex and Sophia

"BIG NEWS." LUNA LUMBERED INTO THE OFFICE ON THE Tuesday before Memorial Day and handed me a stack of mail.

My bar exam results sat atop the pile.

We'd been in business for less than three months and SunnyLuna products already graced the coolers of twenty local restaurants, some mom-and-pop gourmet shops, and a medium-sized health food chain. Other than a now-inconsequential pass or fail on official stationery, my legal career was a fading memory.

I hesitated for a second, but tossed the unopened letter into the trash.

"You don't want to know?"

"Docsn't matter."

"I certainly hope you're more interested in my next bit of news."

I glanced up from a paid invoice. "What's that?"

"My water broke while I was getting the mail."

~*~

Luna made me promise not to call anyone until after the babies were born, so we packed the car and went to the hospital without the usual St. Clair fanfare. Her contractions were two minutes apart by the time she checked in.

I gave her neck massages and ice chips. I put a cool cloth to her forehead as she contracted. I held her hand as the anesthesiologist slipped an impossibly long epidural needle into her back. As I watched the monitor and listened to the soulful music of two tiny heartbeats, I gave no thought to the

242

letter at the bottom of the wastebasket, or not much, anyway.

"My prediction is a boy and a girl, but if I'm wrong again, I may need a job, too." Atlas appeared in the delivery room just as the nurse pronounced Luna fully dilated.

"We can always use a delivery boy." Luna grimaced. "I'm glad you're here. What did you tell Esther and Bernie?"

"That you'd be going into labor in about an hour."

Luna's face and hair glistened with sweat. "I couldn't take another birthing circus after the Esther escapade."

The lines on the contraction monitor grew dense and formed a thick upward spike. They peaked and fell off.

"No need to explain." Atlas said.

Luna moaned. "I feel like I need to push."

Old hands at birthing babies, Atlas rang the call button and I adjusted the video camera. We took our places on either side of my sister, as a team of medical professionals materialized before our eyes.

"We love your show around here," the doctor shook hands with Atlas before he washed his hands in preparation for the delivery.

"Will you autograph this for me?" A neonatal nurse grabbed a fresh latex glove from the box and handed it to Atlas.

He smiled and pulled a pen from his shirt pocket.

"Only in L.A." Luna shook her head and began to push.

Unlike Esther's harrowing birth experience, Luna delivered a son in less than a half-hour. Five minutes later, she also had a beautiful, healthy daughter.

Tears poured down my face as the nurses handed my sister her pink and blue bundles.

"Keep your day job, Atlas," I said.

"Official time of births, 4:16 P.M. and 4:21 P.M." The doctor smiled.

~*~

Exactly an hour later, Bernie's voice boomed down the maternity ward. "My daughter, Luna St. Clair, is about to deliver. Where's her room?"

"We're in a big hurry. My son, Atlas St. Clair, said the babies are coming right away," Esther proclaimed.

Atlas consulted his watch. "The onslaught is right on time."

243

Seconds later, Esther, Hugh and Bernie, with baby Jayne in his arms, crowded the doorway in a tangled grandparental mass.

"We missed it?" Esther pushed her various husbands aside and rushed to Luna.

Hugh stared at the twins in their side-by-side isolettes. "She already had the babies?"

"No fucking kidding, Hugh." Bernie handed Jayne off to Hugh and instinctively rushed to Luna's side, punched on her uterus, then checked her vitals.

"I, I, just don't know what's happening to me." Atlas glanced at the wall clock. "I was sure the babies would be born at 5:30, but they came just before 4:30."

"Atlas, maybe The Universe is telling you to take a vacation." Esther ran her hands though his spiky hair. "Maybe you're on Hawaii time."

I looked away so I wouldn't laugh. "This is my fault. Luna's water broke and she went right into heavy labor. There wasn't time to call anyone."

"What a shame." Esther shook her head. "I wish Luna could have had the babies in a more gentle environment. I highly recommend the experience of the home birth."

"You're fucking kidding, right?"

Esther waved a finger. "Don't swear in front of the babies, Bernie."

Luna shook her head. "You could have *died,* Mom."

"Nonsense. Of course, I was glad that Bernie stopped by, but the miracle of the family birth experience shouldn't be underestimated."

Perhaps nature helped my mother forget the pain, but the rest of us would never recover from the *miracle* birth.

"I suppose it doesn't matter. Look at my grandbabies. They're beautiful." Esther gazed adoringly at the twins in Luna's arms. "I'm a grandmother!"

Baby Jayne lodged a protest scream.

Esther plucked Jayne from Hugh. She settled into an armchair and unleashed a torpedo breast.

Jayne made happy slurping noises as she latched on greedily.

Luna glanced at her sleeping babies. "How am I going to nurse two at once?"

"Nursing twins is one of nature's beautiful blessings." Esther smiled at

Atlas and me. "Do you two remember?"

Atlas nodded while I rolled my eyes. I was starting to miss the possessed Esther.

"What's your name, little angel?" Hugh cooed at Luna's daughter and scooped her into his arms.

"She's Sophia Ariel and he's Alexander Simon."

A look of horror crossed Bernie's face. "You named them in honor of Sunny and Atlas?"

"I hadn't even thought of that." Luna chuckled. "That's even cooler."

"Have you signed the birth certificates?" Bernie scooped Alexander into his arms. "You have to think of new names, and quickly, or it's bad luck. God won't recognize their souls." He started for the nurse's station.

"Stop, Dad." Luna smiled. "They *are* named after dead people."

"Who? We already used Great Uncle Abner for Atlas and Sunny is named for Aunt Sadie." Bernie looked at Sophia in Hugh's arms and then at Hugh. "You didn't name them after *his* family did you?"

"Hey," Hugh said. "She's my stepdaughter."

He and Bernie circled each other.

"Stop it, you two." Esther swatted at them with her free hand. "This is a day of joy and happiness."

"Then who *did* you name them after?" Bernie kept an eye on Hugh.

"They're named after people on the father's side." Luna reached for Sophia and Alexander. "That's all I'm going to say."

"Who is he?" Esther asked.

"You're getting married?" Bernie asked.

"No, and don't ask me any more questions."

"Is he paying child support?" Hugh chimed in.

"No, and none of your business."

Atlas winked at me.

What's going on?

Let it go. Trust me.

Bernie interrupted our psychic conversation before I could get any real info. "How in the hell are you going to take care of two little babies with no husband?"

"I'll manage."

A toilet flushed in the next room.

"Oy." Bernie shook his head. "That sounds like my investment going down the drain."

"Don't worry. I've got a business partner."

Bernie massaged his temples. "Partnerships never work."

"This one will."

I looked down and took a deep breath. More shocking news for Bernie, delivered by, of course, me. "Dad...?"

"That reminds me of something," Luna said. "Dad, grab my overnight bag. It's behind you."

Bernie looked from me to Luna and back again, shook his head, then reached for the bag propped against the wall.

"There's an important letter in the side pocket. Can you hand it to me?" Luna winked.

"Oh, no." This couldn't be happening. "Luna!"

"What the hell is this?" My father held the letter from the state bar.

"Sunny's bar results."

"What do you mean, Sunny's bar results?"

"Open the letter."

It was one thing to tell him I'd quit my job and gone into Luna's business. It was quite another for him to find out I failed the bar, twice. I rushed toward the hallway and my safe escape.

"Freeze, Sunny!"

I stopped in the doorway, staring at freedom, mere inches away.

"Sunny, you took the exam a long time ago. You..." I could almost hear him shake his head. "I don't even want to know."

"I...I..." What was I so afraid of? I turned back to face him.

"So, she didn't pass the first time." Luna shrugged. "But this time..."

"What if I was wrong?" Atlas sounded genuinely concerned.

"Dad doesn't want to know, and I don't care. I turned, rushed toward my father and tried to snatch the letter from his hands. "Besides, it doesn't matter if I passed or not."

"It certainly does matter. Think of the money we'll save on legal services." Luna smiled. "Besides, you worked so hard to become a lawyer, I couldn't bear to see you throw the letter away without at least knowing what you decided not to be."

My father kept his iron grip on the letter. "What the hell are you talking about?"

"Dad, Sunny is my new business partner."

My father stared at us, open-mouthed.

"I think it's great." Esther smiled.

Bernie glared at Esther.

"We didn't want to tell you until everything was up and running, but your investment is safe. Sunny and I signed up almost thirty stores already. Of course, I'll be taking some maternity leave." Luna turned to me. "I assume you're okay with the standard eight weeks, and then maybe we figure out some flex time."

"If you weren't a mother, I'd kill you." I reached for the envelope and attempted again to tug it from Bernie's hand.

"Oh, no you don't!" Bernie's face was beet red. Steam practically poured from his nostrils. "I paid for law school. You better have passed or you'll be paying me back for..." Bernie muttered as he tore open the letter. "Failed the goddamn bar and didn't even tell me..."

My arms began to itch.

"Dear Ms. St. Clair..." He cleared his throat.

Even the babies were silent.

It doesn't matter. It doesn't matter. It doesn't...

"We are pleased to inform you that you received a passing grade on the February California Bar Exam..."

"I knew it." Luna shook my hand. "I think this calls for a raise."

Atlas, Esther and Hugh all hugged me.

I couldn't help but smile.

"Oy," Bernie said, then shook his head. "You two better make a fortune. Sunny spends money for a living and Luna..." He looked at the babies. "This harebrained scheme better work."

Moe, Larry, and Curly

OVER THE NEXT TWO YEARS, SOPHIA, ALEX, AND JAYNE GREW almost as fast as SunnyLuna Corporation. With Esther as vice-president in charge of daycare, Luna and I added store after store to our roster of clients. In six months, we had a delivery person and a small staff at the plant. In a year, we had the money to do some upgrades to the bottling equipment, a truck with our logo across the side, and two new flavors.

As a card-carrying member of the California Bar who specialized in *not* practicing law, I was the happiest attorney in the state.

My love life however, was a very different story.

~*~

There was triathlete Craig...

I tugged down my oversized T-shirt, lightened the weight stack by one and tried to look nonchalant as I lifted the bar to an unrealistic location above my head.

"It doesn't do any good if you don't use any weight." The guy next to me on the seated bench press chuckled. The weight pin on his machine was almost at the bottom of the stack.

"Oops, didn't realize." I sucked in my stomach, rechecked my posture, and set the pin into the third rung.

He glanced over my shoulder at the fitness schedule developed by the first-visit trainer. "You might think about adding a couple sets to the abs and backs portion. It'll build core strength and your overall endurance will increase way faster." His muscles rippled as he did a chest press.

"Thanks." I smiled. "My job has kept me so busy lately. I've let the workouts slack off."

"It's a challenge." He punched out twelve more reps. "Most days, I'm here by 5:30 A.M."

"Do you work here?"

"I'm a professional triathlete."

"Wow!" I tried not to stare at his taut, lanky body. "I'm Sunny, by the way."

"I'm Craig."

"We still have to weigh you and get a body fat assessment." The gym trainer, every girl's nightmare in extra-small workout shorts and matching sports bra, pointed toward the scale.

Shoo! Shoo!

Craig smiled at me.

"Have a nice workout, Sunny." He started for the cardio room. "I hope to see you in the morning."

Yes!

My alarm buzzed the next morning at 5:00 A.M. I pulled on my black yoga pants and tank top, gathered my hair into a rubber band, washed my face, and applied a hint of makeup. I dutifully sleepwalked to the car with a cup of coffee, a low-fat bran muffin, and a bag packed with work clothes.

By the end of the week we were riding stationary bikes alongside each other, jogging on the treadmill, even taking aerobics class. After a few weeks and an inch off my waist, I agreed to a morning swim.

"Hey!" Craig smiled from the edge, set his goggles, and took off across the pool. His round ass bobbed in the water with each strong kick of his legs.

I shuddered at the thought of his wide chest and washboard stomach. A proper date had to be in the near future. Didn't it? I was so sore.

Before he returned, I dropped the towel from around my waist and hopped in at lightning speed, eager for the slimming optical illusion afforded by partial submersion.

"Swim across the pool so I can watch your stroke."

I smiled and pushed off, trying to remember my best third grade swim team moves.

"Not bad," Craig said upon my winded return. "Not bad at all." He stood behind me and guided my arms through a series of proper strokes. "Try this."

His wet chest pressed lightly against my back. His hairless body felt sleek and soft against my skin. I turned so our faces were close enough for what was sure to be a fateful water kiss.

"Sunny?" he asked.

"Yes, Craig."

"I find you attractive but I don't allow myself physical diversions during racing season."

The next morning, I set my alarm for a reasonable 7:30 and started going to the gym after work.

~*~

Then there was Dave...

I didn't think it was odd of Dave to drive all the way to Cerritos for "authentic Indian" until I spotted his wedding ring tan line as he handed the waiter cash.

~*~

And Christmas with Christopher...

"I haven't seen Mother Wilson in almost two years," Christopher said as we headed toward Hancock Park in his Pathfinder. "She couldn't make the trip last Christmas."

"Mother Wilson?"

"My grandmother. She made this for me." He patted the needlepoint Nissan logo stretched across his center console.

I smiled a Christmas smile.

Santa had come down the chimney of Christopher's family home and we were on our way to partake in the revelry and merrymaking of my first real Yuletide. I couldn't wait to meet Mother Wilson or watch his darling, shiny-haired nieces and nephews open mountains of gifts and pose for photos in front of Christmas stockings that matched their holiday loungewear.

We would spend the morning helping the kiddies piece together toys that would never suffer the indignity of a missing part. We would chase the new puppy or kitten that wouldn't dare poo on the carpet or hack up a hairball in front of his mom's slippered-foot. We would watch Christopher's dad

250

throw another log on the fireplace with his pipe hanging from the corner of his mouth. To top it all off, I'd be asked to place the figgy pudding on the sideboard while the other women hustled a proper holiday dinner onto the festive table laden with holly and greenery.

In reality...

I snagged my new red and green holiday cardigan on a plastic branch of the fake tree. A hamster got loose in the living room. Christopher's father reeked of eggnog and he wasn't wearing anything beneath his robe. Worse, Mother Wilson, the battle-ax, tsk'd when I passed the mashed potatoes counter-clockwise.

"What time do you open presents at your house, Sunny?" she asked while the red-faced Santa embroidered on her Christmas sweater stared me down.

Christopher squeezed my hand, hard.

"Uh, we celebrate Christmas Eve."

"Hmm." Mother Wilson's steel-blue curls bobbed as she nodded her head. "At least she's not a Jew like the last one."

~*~

Ryan the chest man slipped his tongue in my mouth and cupped a breast in his hand. "Have you ever thought about having your boobies done?"

~*~

Stan from match.com was fifty pounds heavier than his picture and one hundred times more boring.

~*~

Delicious Dario...

When I met Dario in line at Jamba Juice, I was trying to decide if I cared whether a Berry Lime Sublime had more calories than a Razzamatazz.

"What smoothie you drink?" He pronounced the word *smuthee*.

I turned and gazed into a pair of intense hazel eyes, framed by mink-thick lashes. He was built like Arnold Schwarzenegger, but Italian and much more handsome.

"The Berry Lime Sublime, I guess."

He ordered a peanut-butter-banana-protein something or other. He paid for both and ushered me to a table.

"When did you come to the U.S.?" I tried to dislodge a chunk of fruit wedged in my straw without making an offensive sucking noise.

"I'm leeft weights professional." He put down his smoothie and hoisted an imaginary barbell. "I train two months, then go home."

"Do you like Los Angeles so far?"

"Beyouteeful." He smiled at me. "Beyouteeful weemen." He kissed my hand.

I blushed.

"You know this restaurant Charthoosie?"

"Charthoosie?" It was probably some happening Italian place I hadn't yet heard of.

"Chart-hoos-ee," he said. "On beach Santa Monica."

"Oh, the Charthouse?"

He smiled broadly. "I take you there, you want."

I smiled back and nodded. A Greek statue would feel intimidated by his rippling muscles.

He made the motion of paper and pencil.

I pulled a deposit slip and a pen from my purse and jotted my number.

"I no car." He smiled. "You pick me up?"

Why not? He was already more interesting than my last few dates.

The next night, Dario greeted me at the door with a bottle of Chianti, a disarming smile, and a splash of European cologne.

After one glass of wine, some meaningful stares, and a kiss, we both realized it was pointless to try and exchange histories in sign language over pricey steaks.

It was a blissful two months. Nothing he could say, in English anyway, could ruin the magic.

~*~

Lovey-dovey Tim...

"I love you so much." Tim looked deeply into my eyes and polished off his fourth or fifth beer.

I hadn't expected the "L" word. We'd only been together a month, and that counted the week from the night we met at a bar, until we went on our first date.

"I...I..." I hardly knew him.

Tim wrapped his arms around me. "Are you my little baby?" He showered me with wet, boozy kisses. "I love you so much." Tim released me from his too-firm grasp, rested his head on the back of the couch and closed his eyes. "Will you marry me, Karen?" He passed out.

I left a note before I took off. *I don't want to be your little baby. Sincerely, Karen.*

~*~

Pasta Paul...

"The promotion was mine. It was mine." A piece of pasta dangled on Paul's trembling lip. "It's not fair."

I kind of pointed, then dabbed at my own mouth so he might take the hint.

"Why does this always happen to me?" He spun another glob of spaghetti onto his fork and shoved it into his face. Red sauce sprayed on his chin.

"Have you tried to talk to your boss?" What was I thinking when I accepted a second date? I'd already lost a perfectly good Saturday night consoling him about his childhood while he splattered Mexican food all over himself.

"It won't help." He blew his nose.

The remainder of the evening was a blur of employment woes and crumbs.

At my insistence, we were back at my doorstep by 10:00.

"Aren't you going to invite me in?" Paul smiled, flashing a green thing I hadn't bothered to tell him was stuck in his tooth.

"I feel a cold coming on." I swallowed for effect. I don't think it's a good idea."

"Me too, so it doesn't matter."

"I've got an early meeting."

"Want to get together tomorrow night? I know a great Thai place."

"I can't tomorrow. Sorry."

"Then how about a goodnight kiss." Paul leaned in close.

"We probably shouldn't cross contaminate." I wiped a stray bit of sauce from his chin, kissed him on the forehead and bounded into my apartment.

~*~

And finally Mr. Right...

Howard seemed nice enough until he picked me up in a black Lamborghini. His license plate read *Mr. Rite.*

Every time we passed another car, the driver looked in my window to catch a glimpse of the idiot who fancied herself Ms. Rite.

253

That was the night I swore off dating, forever.

Seth

I HANDED LUNA THE LATEST PRINTOUT. "HAVE YOU LOOKED over the projected production increases?"

Work was my life. Though I still felt it best to avoid the Humane Society or any outlet for adoptable stray cats, I'd come to think of myself fondly as a hard-driving single career-gal.

"Do you think my hair is too severe?" Luan glanced at a framed poster of the SunnyLuna logo and tried to twist her chin-length locks into an up-do. "Would it look more feminine if I grew it out?"

SunnyLuna Water was widely available all over California and I had upcoming meetings in Chicago with our first national distributor. Strangely, Luna, at least of late, had become more MIA than CEO.

"Why are we talking about your hair again? Can we please focus on important things, like doubling our output in time to meet demand?"

"Just asking." Luna glanced into a hand mirror. "I checked the reports. Everything's cool."

"I don't care about cool. I care about perfect."

"Everything *is* perfect." Luna put the mirror down and made a half-hearted pass through a pile of invoices. "What are you doing next Saturday?"

"Are you thinking a last minute strategy meeting?" Perhaps Luna's spacy-cool routine was just a strange way of coping with the unusual stress of our impending success. I glanced at the calendar on my phone. "What time?"

"Saturday evening."

"How about afternoon? I need to pack for Chicago that night."

"Pack Sunday morning before you leave." Luna sashayed toward the file cabinet.

"My flight's at 9:30. I'd have to get up before 5:00 to pack, get to the airport and through security." My patience was wearing thin. "What's going on with you?"

"I'm getting married."

"Very funny."

"I *am* getting married."

Her coy smile unnerved me like fingernails on a chalkboard.

"You can't be. You haven't had a date since..." I took a deep breath to avoid saying something that might exacerbate her mental state. "Since the babies." But, maybe some guy had finally asked her out. "If you have a date or something, I'll be glad to watch the twins."

"They're in the wedding." Luna smirked. "And you're the maid of honor."

Poor Luna. She couldn't even admit she was interested in someone. "You don't need to be embarrassed. I realize you haven't been in the dating world for a while, and it probably won't be easy, but there's nothing wrong with companionship." I started over to her. "The right man won't be intimidated by your success or the fact that you're brave enough to raise two children on your own."

She barely looked up from a water quality report. "Are you done, now?"

"I'm not trying to lecture. I'm really happy for you." I gave her a big squeeze before releasing her from my supportive bear hug. "If you need me, you know I'll watch the kids anytime."

"You didn't believe I could start a bottled water business, either." Luna plucked a piece of my red sweater fuzz from her black sleeveless top. Then, she held up her left hand.

Sparkles of sunlight bounced off a large diamond on her ring finger and shimmered throughout the office.

"Oh, my God!"

"Told you."

"How can you be getting married?" *Luna's getting married?* "You're not seeing anyone."

"You're not seeing anyone, Sunny. I never said *I* wasn't."

I waited in disbelief for her blasé description of the organic farmer who supplied our strawberry juice, or the owner of a tattoo parlor and his multiple piercings.

"His name is Seth." Luna gazed at her big round diamond set in platinum and flanked on either side by deep blue sapphires.

Apparently, it was a successful tattoo parlor.

"His name is Seth? That's it? Who is he? How long have you known him?" I picked up a photo of Sophia and Alex peering out of their stroller in matching black sunglasses. "What about the kids? How do you know that he'll be...?"

"They already love him." Luna smiled. "He's their father."

"What?" A rush of hurt and anger washed over me like a tidal wave. "Why haven't you said anything?"

"I did. I told everyone the babies were named after his side of the family."

"That was supposed to be enough information?"

"It had to be."

"Because?"

Luna sniffed and tucked a stray hair behind her ear. "I wasn't about to give in to societal expectations."

I felt strangely reassured. At least the old Luna hadn't totally disappeared.

"Like marrying the father of your children? Historically, it ranks amongst the top three reasons for a quick wedding."

"Sunny, I met Seth at a Labor Day party, of all things. We had too many margaritas and woke up next to each other in my friend's guest bedroom. The next thing I knew, I'd missed my period and this guy I didn't know was asking me to marry him." Luna blushed. "That's why I didn't tell anyone."

"I'm not anyone." I felt the prickle of impending tears and grabbed a wad of tissues. "I'm your business partner." I swiveled my chair toward the desk. "I'm your sister."

"Don't be hurt." Luna scooted her chair close. "I couldn't tell anyone until I was sure."

"Sure he was the father?"

"Sure he was *The One*." Luna looked down, but I could still see her grin.

"Have you been secretly engaged this whole time?" I shredded the Kleenex in my hands as I choked back tears.

"Of course not. The last thing I wanted was some sperm donor lurking around, trying to turn me into a housewife when I'd worked so hard to realize this dream. I had no intention of settling."

She had a point. When Alan Fine tossed the ring into my lap all he said was, "So what do you think?"

"Then why are you getting married now?"

Luna's moony smile said it all.

"Let me guess, despite your feminist protestations, this Seth person forced his way into your house, got down on one knee, and pulled the giant rock from his pocket. When you declined, he wrestled you to the ground and forced the ring onto your finger. What choice did you have but fall in love?"

"Hardly." Luna laughed. "I did such a good job of convincing him that we didn't need to get married, it took over a year until he accepted *my* proposal."

"You asked him?"

"I fell madly in love." She picked up the photo of the twins and smiled. "One morning the three of them were rolling around on the floor laughing and something just snapped. I knew we all belonged together, as a family."

Luna was in love. I was overwhelmed with jealousy, but could I really be angry? I swallowed hard. "I'm happy for you, Luna."

"You know what Esther says—if he's right, go after him with all your might."

"Esther always told me not to chase boys."

"I'd have told you the same thing."

I rubbed my temples. "I can't believe this. Luna men-are-only-necessary-for-procreation St. Clair is madly in love and getting married to the actual father of her children and I am betrothed to the business." I felt dizzy. "You've become me and I've become you."

"Whatever." Luna shrugged. "We've both struggled our way to happiness, and the truth is, *you've* become *you* and *I've* become *me*."

Could my sister the philosopher-CEO-housewife actually be right? "As long as you're living what I thought was my dream, *is he a doctor, a lawyer, or engineer*?" My Bernie imitation was perfect.

She smiled. "He's a dentist."

"A what?"

"You heard me."

Somehow, I couldn't envision *my* Mr. Right surrounded by giant inflatable toothbrushes and posters of smiling molars. "Are you sure you're not just doing this to make Dad happy?" I grabbed a handful of mints from the candy jar on my desk and stuffed them in my mouth so I wouldn't laugh. "Bernie's gonna love this."

"I know." Luna shook her head. "It's the only down side."

I choked on a peppermint.

"Enough of this messing around. We have important business to attend to." Luna whisked a catering menu from her drawer and tossed it over to me. "I have to confirm my menu today. Pick the appetizers, would you?"

I looked over the array of vegetarian specialties and marked the most edible sounding choices. At least restaurants could prepare palatable meat-free delicacies. And, there was fish. "So, where's the wedding?"

"You know that one house near the strand?"

"Your dream house?"

Luna nodded.

"They rent it out for parties?"

"We bought it."

I'd had my eye on a condo in Santa Monica, but a house by the beach? I broke out in a sweat thinking of her mortgage payment. "The business is going well, but don't you think you should wait before you take on a house like that?"

"Seth's a very successful dentist."

"I don't believe this." I put my head in my hands. "What's his last name anyway?"

Luna's voice dropped to a whisper. "Lipschitz."

"Luna Lipschitz?"

I thought I'd heard everything.

~*~

Esther pinned the veil into Luna's hair. "Seth will make a great husband."

"And you know this because?" I brushed a smattering of blush on Luna's already glowing cheeks.

"Because he loves his mother, of course." Esther smiled knowingly. "Did you see the diamond broach she's wearing? Seth gave it to her for no reason at all."

"Maybe it's cubic zirconia." I wasn't ready to nominate him for sainthood quite yet. In the week since we'd been formally introduced to the mythical Seth Lipschitz, Esther had extolled his virtues as though she'd known him since birth.

Esther swept a gray curl from her eyes and straightened a spaghetti strap on my black bridesmaid dress. "Sunny, sweetie, don't be jealous. It's just not your time yet."

"I'm not jealous." I smiled and hugged *The Bride* to underscore my feelings. Until I met Seth, I have to admit that I did envision Luna heading down the aisle toward a younger version of red-nosed, hundred and twenty-five-pound, foul-breathed Morris Greenblatt, our family dentist. As it turned out, Seth was fairly cool and looked more like a musician than an oral practitioner, but not my type at all—whatever that was. "I don't need a man to complete me."

Luna bestowed the coveted bridal smile upon me. "Certainly not the wrong man."

I only wanted to die for a second or so.

Bernie peered through the door. "Ready?"

Esther shook her head. "Believe me, The Universe works in mysterious ways." She glanced at her watch. "Oh Goddess, I better get downstairs. Give Grandma a kiss you beautiful kiddos." She bent down and gathered Sophia and Alex into her arms for a last-minute squeeze, then bounced down the steps to join the guests gathered for a sunset wedding in the fabulous Lipschitz great room.

Bernie stood in the bedroom doorway staring at Luna as if hypnotized. "You do look pretty. You really do."

Luna beamed. "I guess marriage is for a moron like me."

"It makes some sense, I suppose." Bernie stepped toward Alex and straightened his tiny bow tie, then handed Sophia her greenery and ribbon-laced flower girl basket. "Given the circumstances and all." He glanced at me. "At least I have one daughter left with a head on her shoulders."

"I love you, Daddy," Luna said.

Bernie glanced at his reflection in the tips of his rented tux shoes. "I'm proud of you both."

Luna and I stood speechless, staring at Bernie.

"Enough of this love fest." He glanced out the door toward the stairs. "Let's not keep my son-in-law-the-dentist waiting."

"God forbid." I shook my head and smiled. Then I stepped out into the hallway, peered down the stairs, and gave the signal.

A quartet of Venice Beach musicians, scrubbed clean save for a few loose dreadlocks and a stray pair of scuffed Converse high tops, began a spirited rendition of The Wedding March for guitar, accordion, flute and, it seemed, a zither.

Seth waited next to Atlas under a rose-covered huppa set in front of the floor-to-ceiling windows. A sunset of pink, red, and orange sprawled across the sky as though God and the florist had collaborated on the color scheme.

"It's time," I said, then led Sophia and Alex toward the steps. "Sophia, spread your rose petals as you go. Alex, hold on tight to your pillow." I gave them each a kiss and scooted them around the landing to the top of the staircase.

A sigh filled the room.

Sophia, in black taffeta, and Alex, in matching tux and custom-made black shirt, started down the steps holding hands. They made it halfway before Alex dropped the pillow. He stopped to watch it bounce to the bottom of the staircase. Sophia clutched her basket to her chest and refused to drop a single petal in her path.

As the guests giggled, Seth gazed adoringly at his children, whose dark curls and fair skin were clearly as much Lipschitz as St. Clair. As the twins reached their father and their unexpected fate as a normal, nuclear family, Seth scooped them into his arms and kissed them. Rose petals traveled in the evening breeze and scattered on the intimate crowd.

I smiled at Bernie and Luna. "I'm next."

Luna kissed my cheek. "Yes, you are."

Bernie pulled me toward him and embraced me in an awkward hug. "Get a move on."

"I love you too, Dad."

As tears poured down my face, I took a deep breath and stepped onto the smooth blond wood stairs. *Don't trip. Don't trip.*

Your tripping days are over. Atlas smiled. His spiky white hair shimmered with the vivid color of the waning sun.

261

I took another step and looked out into the small crowd. Though music filled the room, I was suddenly, and without warning, bombarded with the sound of everyone's thoughts.

Or, at least, what I assumed everyone was thinking.

She's crying. Oh, Sunshine, you'll find someone, someday. Esther dabbed her eyes. *I hope.*

Drake, stunning in a tan suit and French blue shirt the shade of his eyes, gave me a surreptitious thumbs-up. *This has to be hard on her.*

She's a pretty one. Why is she still single? Horatio, the contortionist, shifted in his seat. *These chairs are so uncomfortable.*

Seth's high school girlfriend flashed a pinched smile. *Black is just not their color.*

I winked at her.

As I reached the bottom of the stairs, Aunt Gert caught my eye. *Oy Vey. She'll never find a man now.* She's too successful. She rubbed at her penciled-in eyebrow.

Too picky. She's just way too picky's all. Tiny Uncle Herb licked his finger and fixed Gert's smudge, then gave her ample bottom a firm pinch.

Hugh tucked his hair behind his ears. *I could really go for a burger right now.*

Was this what Atlas dealt with every day?

Atlas nodded.

The cacophony of inner voices grew deafening as I neared the chuppa.

Does the sister date? I could fix her up with Seth's cousin the urologist.

Other than his paunch, the rabbi seems a good catch for Sunny. He's single and you can hardly see his bald spot when he's wearing the yarmulke.

She's not old yet, but they say it gets harder and harder every year.

This was ridiculous. I couldn't take anymore. I grabbed a huppa pole and thought as hard as I could—*I'm happy, damn it. I really am. I'm successful. I'm a happy spinster. I could use a little sex, but I don't need a man. I'm enjoying my sister's wedding.*

The band paused and the crowd turned to the top of the stairs.

Luna appeared on Bernie's arm wearing a simple white silk Vera Wang gown.

Everyone gasped.

"She looks just like an angel." Seth's mother covered her mouth.

"She's breathtaking," Joe from Hot Dog on a Stick said aloud.

Having spent the afternoon helping her prepare, I assumed I was well over the shock of seeing her for the first time in twenty years sans noir, but even I was overwhelmed. Luna radiated pure joy. She was the most beautiful bride I'd ever seen.

Tears ran down Seth's cheeks as the band burst into an accordion-filled, Reggae rendition of "Here Comes the Bride."

Luna floated to the huppa. She joined Seth and their children before God, Buddha, Apollo, The Earth Priestess, Jesus and all the rest. As they shared their first kiss as husband and wife, the sun met the horizon and a bright burst of light flashed through the room.

It was mushy, sickening and wildly romantic.

Adam Dey

WHILE THE NEW MRS. LUNA LIPSCHITZ HONEYMOONED ON a remote tropical island, I inked our first national distribution contract. SunnyLuna products would soon be available at specialty grocers, health food markets, coffee houses, and upscale restaurants all over America.

My trip to Chicago would have been perfect, had I only chosen the vegetarian plate at my fateful business lunch. I'd barely ever used an airplane bathroom, but somewhere west of Utah, my triumphant return to Los Angeles took an inglorious turn; I found myself in the plane's lavatory.

Despite my inner turbulence, I eventually finished my business. In deference to the next occupant, I flushed twice hoping that the pressurized toilet would suck any noxious fumes from the tiny cabin. I washed my hands and squirted an extra pump of scented soap into the metal basin to give the air an added burst of vanilla-hyacinth. As a final precaution, I counted to sixty before I flipped the lock to vacant-libre and unfolded the doors. I'd never see the next passenger in line again, but...

"Sunny!"

I froze in the doorway. *Oh, no!* It was none other than Alan's buddy, Adam Dey. Had I wiped around the sink? "Adam!" How could I stall him? "How are you?" I asked rather slowly.

"I'm good." He smiled and shook his head. "What a coincidence."

My favorite journalist, always on the beat for my most humiliating moments. Is it a coincidence?

"I'm on my way home from Alan's wedding."

Alan Fine got married? "In Chicago?" I said, for lack of a cogent re-

264

sponse. Butterflies started their migration pattern in my gut again.

"Florida. Connecting flight."

"Oh." I nodded. *Alan Fine is married. Luna is married. I'm never getting married*. Stop it, Sunny.

"You okay? You look pale?" Adam touched my shoulder lightly. The feel of his hand lingered on my skin.

"I just don't like to fly."

The man behind us glanced at his watch.

"Sorry, go ahead." Adam stepped aside and led me over to the galley area.

"So Alan got married in Florida!" I didn't want Adam to even consider that my paleness was the result of his news or that I was jealous. "Good for him." I willed away an itch on my leg like I hadn't felt for two years.

"He moved back six months ago. Irma made him an offer he couldn't refuse."

"Good for him." *You said that twice, Sunny.*

"Angelique was part of the executive relocation package."

"Angelique. What a pretty name."

"Angelique Finkel Fine. She's Alan's perfect woman."

"Really?" Did I sound jealous?

Adam burst into a dimply smile. "Because Irma recruited her for the job."

I couldn't help but notice his eyes were the same deep green as his V-neck sweater.

"It's the classic win-win. Alan got a wife. Irma got a hand-picked daughter-in-law. And Angelique got a Caddie."

I looked down so he wouldn't see me blush.

"Somehow, I didn't see you cruising Palm Beach in a Cadillac." He leaned against the emergency escape hatch. "Besides, you aren't his type."

I glanced at my velour sweat jacket. Who was this fabulous Angelique? For a moment, I wished I hadn't changed out of the suit I'd worn to the luncheon. Did he think I wasn't attractive enough or smart enough or good enough for Alan Fine? I took a breath. What was I thinking? I was a successful businesswoman. Who was Adam Dey, anyway? "If you'll recall, he did ask me to..."

"You aren't his type..." Adam looked into my eyes. "Because you're nothing like Irma."

"What?" It took a second before I realized what he'd said.

We laughed.

"Irma." I shook my head. "I felt badly about how it all ended with Alan. I shouldn't have run out the back of the restaurant. I should have..."

"It was the only way." Adam ran his fingers through his sandy hair. "Irma wouldn't have let someone like *you* get away."

Not that it exactly mattered, but he wasn't wearing a ring. Was he still seeing Jordana the newscaster?

"Adam, I think I may owe you an apology, too."

"For what?"

"I'm sorry if I was at all rude that day when you returned my clothing. I assumed that since you and Alan were good friends, he'd sent you to humiliate me and..."

"We're not good friends, we're old friends."

I nodded. It had been two and a half years since I'd spoken to Kit. Abby, true to her word, had already forgiven her.

"Alan was so pissed that I rescued the last of your clothes from the bonfire, he wouldn't speak to me until he met Angelique. I'm sorry. I didn't mean to embarrass you by bringing your things into the office."

"I wasn't embarrassed. It's just that..." What was the point of trying to explain away the hellish world of Walker, Gamble and Lutz? "It's not my office, anymore."

"Congratulations." Adam smiled. "Especially on the success of SunnyLuna."

I felt myself blush. "You know about SunnyLuna?"

"I was delighted to see your face on the bottle at Fountain of Health Foods."

He was into health food. A bad sign.

"But, it's better to see you in person." He smiled. Those amazing dimples creased the center of his cheeks.

Why didn't I notice how really cute you are? "You, too." My ears felt hot and a tingly sensation ran down my spine. "By the way, it was very kind of you to give up your table that night. I hope your date wasn't too upset." I glanced at my Pumas.

"That was a business dinner."

266

We stood staring at each other.

A nasal voice came over the airplane speaker system and interrupted the possibility-filled silence. "Ladies and gentlemen, the captain is about to turn on the fasten seat belt sign in preparation for our landing in Los Angeles. Please return to your seats as soon as possible."

Adam glanced toward the bathroom. "I kind of lost my place in line."

Thankfully. I turned for the aisle to avoid an awkward moment. "It was nice talking to you."

"You, too." He stepped toward the lavatory, then stopped and turned toward me. "Sunny, do you have someone picking you up from the airport?"

"I was going to grab a shuttle."

"Can I give you a lift?"

Yes, yes, yes. "Are you sure it wouldn't be any trouble?"

"None at all."

"Then, see you when we land." As I started for my seat, I realized that I still didn't officially know what he did for a living, but I knew for sure he passed the jeans test.

~*~

"I'm the foreign affairs editor at the L.A. Times." Adam guided his classic Alfa Romeo out of the parking structure.

"You must travel all the time."

"I used to." We headed out of LAX toward Westchester. "Now I kind of have a desk job. For a journalist, anyway."

I stole a glance at his strong-looking thighs as he shifted gears.

"Weren't you on your way somewhere the day you came to my office?"

"I was with the Associated Press. I was on my way to an extended assignment in Europe." He smiled. "I probably forgot to tell you that."

"You may have mentioned it." But I was such a dummy, I didn't hear. I pretended to look for something in my purse so he wouldn't see me swoon, or worse, know I was admiring the cute blond hairs on his arms.

When I looked up, I found myself gazing into the smiling face of Rapunzel, the buxom billboard maiden from her perch atop the site of my ill-fated engagement dinner with Alan Fine. A rivulet of silty grease ran down the length of her chin as though she'd actually dined on their infamous prime rib.

"I hope you don't mind if we stop for a second." Adam veered into the right lane mere feet from the entrance to the parking lot.

At Rapunzel's? My stomach, compliant for the last hour, tumbled in protest. This couldn't be a joke, could it? Be cool. Don't overreact. "No problem." This time I would remember to grab my bags if I had to make a quick run for it.

"I'm driving on fumes." Adam glanced at the gas gauge. "My tank was on empty when I rushed to catch my plane." He drove past the restaurant's driveway.

I uncurled my fingers from the door handle.

"Sunny, don't worry." Adam chuckled. "I'd never take you to Rapunzel's."

"I'm sorry. For a second I thought that maybe..."

"I think once with Irma is more than enough for anyone." He shook his head. "Besides, I'm a semi-vegetarian."

"Semi?"

"Every so often, I have to have a burger. Or a steak."

Could he be the first guy I'd ever met that might be able to weather a meal at Esther's?

He glanced sideways and leaned his head in my direction. "Sunny, I want you to know that the Alan thing isn't weird for me if it isn't for you."

I resisted the urge to rub my eyebrow. "It's only weird because I can't believe I was ever that girl."

"That girl wasn't half-bad either."

"Then it won't be weird at all."

"I was hoping you might say that." Adam pulled up to a gas pump—at the 7-Eleven on Manchester.

I took a silent deep breath. I wasn't the desperate girl who had fled from across the street, anymore.

"Do you want anything from inside?"

"I'm okay, thanks."

"Be right back." He hopped out of the car and started for the convenience store.

I tucked my hair behind my ear and acted nonchalant until Adam was safely inside and had disappeared behind the frozen cappuccino machine. Then, I flipped down the vanity mirror for an emergency makeup deficit

268

assessment.

As soon as I glanced into the mirror, I forgot all about my smudged eyeliner or stray blemishes. A bum had appeared from behind a dumpster. He was pushing a grocery cart.

I turned to look at him.

Despite the glare of the afternoon sun against the metal buggy and empty aluminum cans, I spotted a dozen copies of my own face peering out from bottles lined upright around the inside perimeter of the basket.

But, it wasn't my face that interested me.

"Sam!" I yelled.

Sam didn't hear me over the rattling of the cart and the crunching of his worn wheels on the rough parking lot. He pulled up to the spot where we'd sat together and perched on the sidewalk below the small brick ledge. He wore the same filthy army jacket and boots as he had on the first time we'd met.

I dug through my purse for the money I'd wanted to give him so long ago. I stuffed a wad of ones and some spare change into my pocket, and opened the car door.

Sam put the harmonica to his lips.

I came over, sat with him on the brick ledge and listened.

A moment later, Adam came out of the 7-Eleven. He glanced at the bottles in Sam's cart.

"I'll explain later." I whispered.

Adam didn't flee to his car and peel out of the parking lot. He simply nodded, sat next to me, and listened.

Sam finished his song, wiped off his harmonica, and replaced it in the tattered pocket of his jacket.

Adam handed Sam a twenty before I had a chance to fish the bills and change from my pocket.

He winked at Adam. "Life's good when you make everyday a sunny day."

"Couldn't agree with you more." Adam looked into my eyes.

Sunny day?

Couldn't be.

Sam grasped the worn metal handle of his cart and pulled himself upright. He grabbed an empty SunnyLuna bottle from his cart and held it up. "Here's to figuring out where you want to go." He pushed off and started across the parking lot.

I shook my head.

Sunny Dey.

It just figured.

About the Author

Linda Joffe Hull is a native of St. Louis, Missouri and a graduate of UCLA. She lives in Denver with her husband, daughter, and the pets her sons left behind when they went off to college. Linda is a former board member of Rocky Mountain Fiction Writers, a current director-at-large on the national board of Mystery Writers of America, and was proud to be named the 2013 RMFW Writer of the Year.

Frog Kisses is Linda's fourth book.